Saving Seven
Book 1

Flint Ory

For Brennen. The world isn't black and white, nor is it meant to be.

CONTENTS

1   Death, Taxes, and Confession   Pg 1

2   Joss   Pg 19

3   Fat Saturday   Pg 31

4   Jailhouse Blues   Pg 47

5   Breadcrumbs   Pg 58

6   Wicked   Pg 78

7   Three Steps   Pg 99

8   Crossing the Line   Pg 112

9   Animals   Pg 131

10   Lessons   Pg 147

11   Arches   Pg 161

12   Best Laid Plans   Pg 173

13   Vigilante   Pg 194

14   Unison   Pg 202

i   Acknowledgments   Pg 209

ii   Credits   Pg 210

iii   About the Author   Pg 211

Chapter 1
DEATH, TAXES, AND CONFESSION

My first life's last vision was feet: one pair of blue flats, and one pair of scuffed pink tennis shoes.

I'd been following Christine Dru and her daughter, ducking behind trees, slinking away from the streetlights. I had to know why she was in St. Louis. I had to know why she was still looking for my father after all this time. Did she know where he was? Did she know what he did with the book?

I was forming a plan in my head when I first heard the SUV. The eight cylinder engine roared to life, filling my lungs with exhaust. My head swam in the fumes, dizzying my senses. I stumbled forward. Crouching behind a covered bus stop, I tried to get a look at the driver. Blinded by headlights, I swiveled back to Christine. She was oblivious to the danger, calmly ushering her daughter to the crosswalk.

The vehicle jolted from the curb, picked up speed, and bee-lined for the girls. I had to do something. I had to find out what she knew. My mind went blank, adrenaline took over, and my body obeyed. I broke into a sprint, hurdling benches and dodging parking meters. All I could feel was the strain of my muscles, fighting against the strength of my instincts, to live.

That's when I heard the voices. The little red figure on my right shoulder asked me what I was doing. The little white figure on my left asked me the same. Both were, for this unique and solitary moment, in unison.

I yelled at Christine, but I couldn't look away from her daughter. Her little face stretched into a terrified gasp beneath short, brown locks. She clung to her mother's petrified arms.

I had to save her. I didn't know why, but I had to. I wished I could tell her not to worry, not to cry. I wished I could tell her it would be all right, but there wasn't time. My actions would have to convey that message for me. I threw my body at Christine, knocking them both out of the way.

My first life's last thought was a question: Was this SUV really going to kill me?

* * *

I was born and, let's not call it raised, in Vegas; son of an Irish druggie and her dealer. To state the obvious, my childhood wasn't typical. On top of dad's profession, he was also a compulsive gambler. So naturally, school consisted of counting cards, and learning to avoid my mother's lows. I didn't know her for all that long, but I knew the happiest times of my life were when she was high. We rode that roller coaster together. My addiction for her attention mimicked her addiction for coke. Both of us were continually in search of the next high, anything to avoid the pain. I used to get excited when she said she was quitting. After a few failed attempts though, I figured out the truth-coming down, and watching her come down, was more painful than watching her kill herself.

Despite all of her faults, Mom did one smart thing. She kept track of dad's deals, his customers, his partners, anything that could incriminate him. She wrote them down in a journal. I know because she read it to me my whole life. It was the one place he'd never look-my baby book. Mom said a lot of crazy things, but she swore that book was going to keep us safe.

She OD'd when I was thirteen. Dad kept paying rent for the rat hole apartment, but he stopped sleeping there. He'd show up to make sure I was still breathing and drop off some food, but that only lasted for a few months. After a few days without food, the neighbors called the cops and before I knew what happened, my failure parents were replaced by two failing systems, the police department and foster care.

I was nearly fourteen when they put me with family number one, the Schellers. It didn't last long. They weren't ready for a child, let alone one that'd been self-trained in the art of survival. They didn't have any clue what to do when I stole his baseball cards to hock on eBay, or when I hoarded my food like a squirrel, never knowing when I'd get my next meal. I'm sure it was a relief when I ran.

Family number two, the Hiltons (not of the hotel chain variety), weren't any better. They were transplants, like everyone else in Vegas, but they hadn't gotten acclimated to their surroundings yet. They were used to small town life in North Dakota. When times got rough, or a little crazy, or when I ran an underground sports book for the junior high, they flipped out. Needless to say, I took off.

There were whispers of juvee after that stunt, but the system was designed for kids like me. How could they give up and admit it didn't work? No, the system wasn't the problem. The problem was that they underestimated my needs. Yes, of course. Family number three, the Livingston's, were nut jobs. They were religious freaks, but not like the Sunday school, upstanding members of the community variety. They, meaning them and their six children, were the you're-so-out-there-I'm-uncomfortable, cult-member crazy. I didn't do anything to them, but only because they scared me. I lasted a week before pre-dinner hug time sent me over the edge. I didn't even pack. I just left. Thinking about them made me question the theory of natural selection.

After that debacle, they sent me to the Nazi's. That wasn't an exaggeration. One hundred percent of German origin, the Bergmann's weren't going to put up with my bullshit. They had more rules than I cared to remember, but that was opportunity. I did things to that family that weren't right. The swastika in the front yard was a little much. I wasn't proud of that. The messed up part was that I wasn't even sure they disliked me. Creating rules just seemed to be in their nature. Either way, he chased me, rightfully so, from his house with a shovel. I wouldn't call that running away, but the end result was the same.

Through all of that, I learned a few things. First, I came to grips with the fact that I needed to leave Vegas. Everywhere I ran, the system followed. My only chance for freedom was to leave what I knew behind. I was sixteen by then, and it didn't seem quite as scary anymore.

Second, I knew who to blame for my mother. Her death lay on my father's shoulders. He provided her with the drugs, the child, the responsibility, and none of the support. I hated him, and I needed to watch him suffer, like I watched her, so many times.

Third in my life's education was the distrust of any organized system for the betterment of society. I was a product of the system, and I'd spent most of my youth alone and on the run. On top of that, the very system that is built to serve and protect barely raised a finger when my mother died. Was her dealer brought to justice? No, that coward ran free. If I wanted him to pay, I'd have to do it myself.

Based on those conclusions, my path seemed stupidly clear. Dad needed to pay for what he did, and my crazy mom had already given me the key to putting him behind bars. Only, I left the book in the apartment when child services hauled me away. Suddenly she didn't seem so stupid. I did.

So before I could chase after the bastard, I broke into the old apartment. It was in a low income, ready-to-be-torn-down building. Not surprisingly, everything was exactly how we left it. No one was going to move into that dump, not even the cockroaches.

After fifteen minutes of searching with no reward, there was a tick-tick at the door. Slowly and methodically, the lock opened up. With nowhere to run, I did the only thing I could-I hid. That was the first time I saw Christine Dru. She didn't look like much-just a wiry woman with high cheekbones and dusty blonde hair-but she picked the lock and tore through my room like a pro. Even with a limited view from my hiding spot in the closet, I knew what she was looking for. It was the same thing that I was looking for: my baby book.

Neither of us would find it. Dad must've grabbed it when he swiped everything else.

One year later, after following Christine and her daughter, Bree, across the country, I watched an SUV rip down an empty street toward them. I remembered how determined Christine looked scavenging through our apartment. The only thing worse than the crazed look in her eye was the terrified little girl at her side as the headlights closed in. I couldn't wipe Bree's face from my memory.

Mom must have written something awful about her in that book. Or maybe Christine just wanted to hurt Dad. I could relate. In either case, I had to save them. Bree was innocent and needed a mother. I needed to find out what Christine knew.

Then I died.

* * *

"Welcome to the afterlife, Seven Murphy-Collins," I read.

The message on the podium wasn't nearly as welcoming as it should've been. I read it twice, focusing on one word: afterlife.

"Lovely. At least they got my name right."

Behind the podium were gates. They stood about ten feet tall with a simple, unimposing style that reminded me of Midwestern farmhouses.

So these were the pearly gates of all that is good and holy. Pearly? They didn't look pearly. They looked porcelain. I stood before the porcelain gates of heaven. The entrance to the blissful afterlife, built from the same American Standard material used on toilets. Welcome to eternal happiness! Please don't pee on the gate.

I'd never been to Sunday school or church for the most part. The little bit of religion that I did know came from TV. It probably wasn't typical for an Irish kid. I'd seen paintings of heaven though. They usually included soft, fluffy clouds, bright rays of sunlight, angels, harps, and the toilet gates... can't forget those.

In reality, that idea of euphoric perfection couldn't be further from the truth. I'd seen, and stayed in, homeless shelters that were more inviting.

I wasn't standing on clouds. I didn't hear harps playing tranquil melodies in the background. I didn't even see the sun. It was overcast, silent, and the street smelled like stale beer.

A wall of red brick loomed behind the gates. Curious, I reached through and slowly ran my finger along the grey mortar. I wasn't sure what I expected, but tiny grains dusted off. Nothing jumped out and bit me. In a way, I was almost disappointed.

I stepped back and looked up at the building behind the gates. Near the top, a large rectangle held letters that cleverly spelled out: Heaven. I had to peek around a tall oak tree in order to read it. I'd think someone would trim that back or something.

There were also four banners. That's the part that finally gave it away. They were red, navy, red, and red. Each of them had a four-digit number on it: 1903, 1904, 1912, and 1915. I listened closely as they jostled in the wind. They weren't numbers. They were years. This wasn't heaven. I couldn't be dead. I was standing on Yawkey Way in Boston, Massachusetts.

"Fenway?" I whispered.

I'd never been to Boston, but I'd fantasized of seeing Fenway Park ever since dad sat me down in front of the TV to watch my first Sox game. That was the prick's idea of babysitting. Still, seeing those banners should have brought a smile to my face. It should've been a dream-come-true. It wasn't. There was no smile and I didn't break into an awful version of Sweet Caroline.

The silence was eerie. I knew something was off, but my head felt fuzzy. I tried to remember how I'd gotten there.

It came back in pieces. I could picture Christine and Bree falling to the curb as I shoved them away from the black SUV. I should've heard screams, but I didn't. What happened? Did it really hit me? I spun around, searching for some sign of life: a bum in an alley, a cop, even a dog would do; anything to prove that I was still alive. I peered down at my shirt, inspecting the dirty fabric for evidence of being mangled by an aluminum grill.

There was nothing, not even a scratch.

At the end of the street, past red and black awnings, a thick fog formed a barrier, a wall cloud to the world. Wind kicked up around me, blowing leaves across my feet as I followed them with my eyes up to an empty bar, with lights shining all the way to the brick wall in the back. Where were all the customers? There had to be more than half-a-million people in Boston. Someone had to be thirsty.

A sudden fear of being alone struck me, forming a knot in my stomach. I wanted to throw up. I probably would've if I'd had anything to eat in the past day or two, but I'd been starving for weeks. I had to get out of here, wherever here was. I ran... or tried to, but my feet were heavy, and my strides were sloppy. I tripped over curbs, slammed into trash cans, and moved in circles. No matter how far I got, I couldn't shake Fenway. Every turn started me back at the beginning, back at those porcelain gates. What is this place?

After a few of those pointless circles, I came to the thick fog. The grey curtain stretched further than I could see, but it seemed to part with each step. Peeling back, it revealed an image that squashed any hope of escape. A mammoth block of casinos lingered overhead, piercing the sky.

In no picture I'd ever seen of Boston did it include casinos like that. Oddly though, all the twinkling lights in the world couldn't hide the cold, deadness of the buildings. It was closer to a ghost town than Vegas, completely silent. I looked carefully, but I didn't recognize any of the buildings. Even the sign was different. It stood high and crooked, reading: Welcome to Sin City.

I stumbled back, rubbing my eyes and clenching my fists. "Where the hell am I?" I called out to no one in particular.

I raced down the block and onto the next one, away from the lights. It felt like I was running down empty halls, with no windows. I looked left and right, but every passageway was blocked. My mind grew skittish as my muscles burned, begging me to stop. I wondered what kind of sick joke this was. If I was dead, where was my guide? Why was I alone?

On the brink of rage and probable insanity, I finally heard sounds of life. They were faint, but I could hear conversation and laughter. I followed the trail until I reached a familiar sight. A small coffeehouse sat back from the sidewalk, with tall, asymmetric windows and a sign in the shape of a painter's pallet. I could hardly believe my eyes. It was Picasso's, a small coffeehouse I knew from St. Louis.

I pressed my face up against the window, trying to get a good look inside. I expected to find the same emptiness as the bars, but oddly enough, it was brimming with customers from all walks of life, just as I remembered. Everything from cyclists to grandparents scattered throughout, drinking their coffee. Just the sight of people got my blood pumping again. I was alive! I didn't know where the hell I was, but if they were alive, then I must be too. I immediately scooted across the front of the building, reaching for the handle to the front door, but my fingers found a large, rusted lock instead.

I yanked on the metal, knocking it around as I howled for someone to let me in. Who locks a coffeehouse? I stepped back and took a run at the door. My shoulder slammed into the wood, popping out of place as it collided with the thick frame. I screamed again, this time in pain.

Without thinking, I pounded on the windows with the bottom of my fist, yelling obscenities. The people continued their conversations, smiling to each other. Their faces had no reaction to the crazy kid in the window. They didn't even seem to notice. Then it hit me.

They couldn't see me.

My instinct was to get away as quick as humanly possible. I wasn't ready to die. My life had barely begun. How did I get in this mess? Why did I save those girls? Why did I jump in front of that SUV?

"They can't hear you," a husky voice called out from left of the gates.

He strolled from the alley, wearing a straw hat tilted back on his head. "The coffee people," he said, nodding at the windows. His old, brown overalls hung off him, grungy drapes with a black skeleton key hanging from his outside pocket. His formerly white, long-sleeve shirt was so big and puffy that he resembled a marshmallow, but I'm sure that had something to do with the anabolic balloons he called arms. I couldn't decide if he was a river rat, or a runway model; perhaps both.

I looked at him, bewildered briefly, before I recognized the once blotchy-faced kid I went to grade school with back in Vegas. "Jackson! Is that you?"

He grinned from ear to ear and raised his brow. "Seven Murphy-Collins... It's been a long time." He reached out and pulled me in for the half-handshake, half-hug. I tried to hold my place, but he barely noticed. It was as if I was being manhandled by a bear, without the fur.

"I haven't seen you in-"

"Four years!" he said, releasing me from the bear hug and slapping me on the back. Something didn't add up. He was seventeen like me, but he looked twenty-five. "You were still living with the Bergmann's back then."

I stepped back, afraid of another grappling. "Oh yeah, I remember. You had a thing for their daughter."

"Ahhh... Heidi... I miss her. After you left, I didn't have an excuse to come over anymore. You kind of killed my chances."

"Yeah, that's the reason you didn't hook up," I said, rolling my eyes. It once cost me ten bucks to have her call him.

"Why'd you take off, anyway?" The bench creaked in pain as he took a seat and leaned back. "They didn't seem all that bad."

"I, uh, had an uncle in St. Louis. He heard I was in foster care and demanded that I come live with him."

"Wow, that's excellent. I figured you just ran away again."

"Nope, it was my Uncle... My Uncle Bradley." I was a terrible liar.

"Bradley, huh? What was he like?"

I didn't like that he was using the past tense.

"He's rich-some kind of doctor, with a huge house in South County."

"Nice. Sounds like it would be tough to walk away from." There was a glint to his eye as he smiled at me.

"What are you grinning at? Are you saying I have to walk away from it?" I asked.

"I'm saying," he wiped crumbs from his mouth, "that by being here, you already have."

"Where the hell is here?" I asked, leaning against the light post.

"Oh come on Seven, you're a smart kid. Where do you think we are?"

I looked down at the street, sneaking a peak in Fenway's direction. "I have my suspicions."

"I'm sure you do." He got up and followed me as I walked up to the toilet gates.

I reached down and lifted the blue, rubber-coated chain. "Hey, do you remember when we stole your dad's mustang?" I asked, testing him.

He eyed me briefly before answering. "Dude, come on. Of course I do. He officially started referring to you as the asshole after that."

I laughed, thinking about his puffy father and how he always hated me. Only Jackson would've known that. We'd been through a lot together. We'd caused a good amount of trouble and always found ways of weaseling out of it, until now apparently.

"Speaking of dads, did you ever find your old man?" he asked.

I quickly tried to change the subject. "So, I'm dead?"

"Yeah, I was wondering if you remembered what happened," he replied.

"I remember an SUV and I remember shoving those girls out of the way."

"That's it?"

"What else is there?" I asked. "And how do you know about it?"

"I was there."

I turned around and cocked my head to the side. "You were there? How-" I shook my head, glaring through him. "You let this happen to me?"

"Let this? You've got to be kidding me. You're the idiot that dove in front of a moving vehicle."

I shoved him in the chest, tossing the key around, but he barely noticed. "You're supposed to be my friend!"

"And as your friend, I'm telling you that was a dumb move," he yelled. "Look, there are some things you need to understand. First of all, as you guessed, you are dead."

"This is heaven?"

"No, that is heaven," he said, motioning to Fenway, pointing at the letters etched into the cement.

"And if that is heaven, then the casinos are..."

"You never liked Vegas much, did you?" he asked, making little devil horns with his fingers.

My stomach twisted in knots as he confirmed my fear. "Fine, then where exactly are we right now?"

He looked up at the street sign. "I would guess Yawkey Way."

"Purgatory?" I guessed.

He nodded with a crooked grin, enjoying my predicament a little too much.

I quickly glanced at the coffeehouse, then back at Jackson. He caught my shifty gaze but abruptly changed the subject, fueling my curiosity.

"Things work a little differently here. For instance, aging doesn't occur. Here, my appearance is based on your perception, your imagination."

"Then I have one messed up imagination. Are you supposed to be a body builder?" I looked at his clothes again. "Or Huckleberry Finn?"

"I don't know for sure. Like I said, it's your perception."

"If you're here, then that means you're dead too?"

"About a year ago, right after my sixteenth birthday."

"How'd you die?" I asked.

His eyes grew cold and hard, like stone. "Drunk driver."

"Sorry man. It looks like you would've turned out all right."

"I would've." He paused.

"Did it hurt? Do you get to haunt the asshole that did this to you?" A bit of excitement crept into the corners of my mouth. I liked the idea of haunting people back on earth. I already had a list forming in my head.

He wasn't smiling with me. "I'm not a ghost, Seven."

"What are you?"

He smiled proudly. "I'm Death."

"What?" A sudden chill gripped my senses. "Death? Like the Grim Reaper?"

"I know. It doesn't make a lot of sense, does it?"

"Not really."

"Let me try to explain." His hands folded in front of his nose. He stepped closer and looked me in the eye. "Death is always shown in cartoons and movies as some faceless, black-cloaked, scythe-wielding ghost, right?" I nodded slowly. "As cool as that would be, it's not really accurate. You see, Death is actually a role, or a position."

I kept listening but leaned back slowly.

"You see, I didn't get in there," he said, gazing at Fenway. For the first time, I saw the strain in his forehead. He'd been masking it well.

I'm not sure I wanted to know, but curiosity got the best of me. "How'd you end up in hell?" I asked, glancing at the casinos.

He looked up and tilted his straw hat back. "I wasn't a good kid, Seven. You remember all the shit we did, all the trouble we caused. That might have changed as I got older, but I never had that opportunity. My time was up before I could mature."

I swallowed hard and watched him closely, realizing how my own fate was tied to his. He didn't avoid eye contact. He sought it out, like he wanted me to understand his remorse. For a brief moment he looked like my younger friend.

"So, if you're supposed to be in hell, how are you out here? Shouldn't you be burning or something?"

He finally turned away, exposing the key for the taking. "That's the thing, Seven. You are my second chance."

"I'm not following," I said slowly while sneaking another peak at Picasso's.

"Like I said before, the Reaper is a role. Each person has their own reaper, especially for them. You chose me."

"Wait, you're saying that of all the people in the world, I chose you to be my reaper?"

"For some reason, you thought I'd be the best person to pass your judgment."

"Judgment? So, you decide where I go? That's great! I have a man on the inside!"

"This isn't like cheating off a history test. If that's why you chose me, you're up shit creek. I have to be right about this, or I'll never get out of hell. This is for all eternity."

"You'll be allowed into heaven if you-"

"Like I said, you are my second chance."

I sat down on the bench and stared across the street at Fenway, taking it all in. Patches of light fought their way through the clouds and lit up the green metal seats in the distance. I kept thinking about Picasso's. Maybe the reason they couldn't hear me was because they weren't dead. Maybe that wasn't just a window to Picasso's. Maybe it was a window back to life. Jackson's key dangled inches from my grasp, taunting me.

"So, you're not going to make this easy on me?" I asked.

His eyes darted around, making me nervous. "Easy on you? Do you have any idea how much trouble you've caused?"

"What do you mean? I just died. How could I have caused trouble?"

"Hey dumbass! It wasn't your time," he growled. "Christine Dru and her daughter Bree! They're the ones who should be here. Not you. Why on earth did you throw yourself in front of that car?"

"Let me get this straight. Saving innocent people is a bad thing?" I asked.

"Things aren't always that simple. For all you know, she could've just robbed a bank," he replied. "Probably did," he added under his breath. "Look, events like death happen for a reason. Believe it or not, there's a master plan and any small ripple can have catastrophic effects on the future. Your little hero act created a huge mess."

"Well I'm sorry to burden you." I gave him an icy stare.

His chest expanded, pulling in a deep breath as I watched his patience dissipate. "I just spent the last year in hell! You don't know what that's like."

"It's not my fault you died early."

"No, but you're not exactly innocent either. And Lord knows she wasn't," he said.

"Why don't you just get on with it then? You've got me here. You know all there is to know. What are you waiting for?"

"Give me a second," he said. "I can't afford to be wrong and your heroic stunt has thrown the whole thing out of whack. On any other day, I'd just trot you off to the casinos, but I can't understand why you saved them, why you sacrificed yourself. Did you even know them?"

I stared at him blankly. "Let me get this straight. You're this close to reaching heaven, and you want to talk about some random girls with bad timing?"

His face scrunched into a sneer. "See, that's the thing. I'm not buying that they were random." His eyes grew big. "That's it!" You followed them all the way from Vegas. Did you really think Christine would lead you to your dad?"

"What's it matter?" I stood up from the bench, turning my back on him and walking to the gates. He followed behind, hissing over my shoulder.

"It matters if you sacrificed your own life to save someone for whom you've never met. That's a true act of selflessness. On the other hand, if you were still chasing daddy and they just happened to get in the way..." He sighed and cracked his knuckles. "We're both stuck here until you tell me the truth."

I reached down and grabbed the fire hydrant as I jerked to a stop in front of the coffee shop. "Well, it looks like we're going to be here for a while then."

He leaned in, angry desperation dripping from his chin. I met his stare, waiting for a response.

"I'm not going to waste away here for you!" His giant hand sprang out and grabbed my throat, slamming me up against the window. My body flew back and forth with each word. Sweat ran down his fingers, leaving a rotten cabbage smell in the air. "Tell me why you did it!"

"Go to hell!" I yelled, fighting back a chuckle. His fingers dug in deeper, cutting off my oxygen completely. I couldn't pry them away. My throat burned all the way down to my lungs. My vision clouded and my head grew dizzy. He threw me to the ground. My body landed with a thud at his feet.

"What are you going to do, kill me?" I coughed up a bloody laugh.

He smiled. "There are much worse things than death."

My sight slowly came back. The first thing I saw was the key, just above my nose as he scowled at Fenway.

That was my opportunity. I reached up and slipped it from his overalls, tucking it behind my back.

"I always wanted to beat the hell out of you," he said. His shoulders tensed and veins sprung from his neck. His hands balled into fists as he drew back to pound me into the concrete.

With my last ounce of energy, I sprang up and punched him, cracking my hand into his iron jaw. I used the key like brass knuckles, creating a loud, metal pop, cutting open his face. I was ready for the flush of adrenaline and instant swelling, but that wasn't it at all. My hand grew cold and lifeless, frigid even. The chill crept into my bones, making it near impossible to think.

While he was stunned, I slid the key into the lock with my other hand and twisted, but it wouldn't budge. I tried again, and again. Nothing. I jammed it in harder, desperate to get through that door. I rattled it in a panic, knowing my time was almost up.

Despite the nasty gash, he turned back, nostrils flaring. With one of his anvils, he threw me to the ground like a ragdoll and straightened up. He towered over me, ready to break my face into pieces.

"Did you really think it would be that easy? That the key would work for you?" He snickered. "Tell me something, why did you imagine me as a monster? Why would you be that stupid? You can't win this fight!"

If I couldn't break my way in, maybe Jackson could.

"Probably so I could do this!"

I jumped up and threw my shoulder into his gut, driving with my legs. The behemoth was caught off guard. A mighty groan sounded as he tried to push me back, but it was too late. After teetering back and forth, he fell like a redwood, smashing through the window and sending a howl through the street. A warm gust of air shot out and pulled us in, filling my chest with life.

Blindly following, I stepped into the light, and breathed in coffee.

* * *

A couple weeks had passed since Jackson and I crashed through the window, but not a day went by that I didn't question my sanity. Whether it really happened or not, bottling it up hadn't helped. I needed to tell someone the story, so I turned to the only person I could.

"Forgive me dad, for I have sinned."

"For the last time, I'm not a priest yet, and therefore, cannot take your confession. And if I was a priest, you'd call me father, not dad."

"Shut up and listen, holy man."

"The good lord sent you to test me, didn't he?"

"Well, if he did, you suck with flying colors."

"What'd you do, Seven?"

"I prayed to a false god that I whittled out of wood, while swearing in his name, on the Sabbath, and cursing my father. Then, I committed adultery with my neighbor's wife, stole her underwear, and lied about it. Oh, and then I murdered them both."

He was counting the Ten Commandments on his fingers. "Did you forget one?"

"I don't think so, but let's just assume I got all the checkboxes."

Gabe was not a priest. He had just turned eighteen, nearly a year older than me. He was preparing for seminary though, and there, he would fulfill his father's lifelong dream of having a son of the cloth. I, on the other hand, was Satan, pulling him back to a semi-normal life of teenage debauchery.

He found me homeless, hungry, and exhausted in the middle of a sweltering St. Louis summer. The temperatures roasted up to one-hundred degrees while the humidity hovered near eighty-percent. That number didn't make sense to me, growing up in a dry heat, but everything became painfully clear when the sweat engulfed my body.

Gabe took me in, and didn't ask questions. He didn't ask and he didn't judge. His parents applauded his generosity and even though they were nervous, they trusted him, and by extension, me. I'd never met people like that before. I didn't know they existed. And after three days, I took off. What can I say? It was in my nature.

That didn't deter Gabe. Giving up on people wasn't in his nature. He kept tabs on me, helped me out, even found me jobs, which I didn't take. He tried to help me find my dad, but Gabe wasn't exactly street-smart. His car came in handy though.

"So, what would you like to confess?"

"I thought you weren't a priest."

He let out a long exhale. "I have school tomorrow. I know that doesn't mean anything to you, but I gotta do good on my chemistry test. Look, are you hungry? Mom baked some lasagna for you. Here," he said, handing me a Tupperware dish from his bag.

"What does chemistry have to do with..." I didn't say the word, but I made the sign of the cross. I knew that pissed him off.

"I know you didn't ask me to come over here to talk about my future. So, quit with the games and tell me what's up."

"Fine, you grumpy bastard. But only part of it's a confession."

"What part would that be?"

"I stole something."

"Okay, what did you steal?"

"Calm down. Take a breather. I'll start from the beginning." He sat quietly and listened to my re-enactment of the events on Washington Avenue, until the part where I died.

"You... died?"

"That's not my confession. I haven't even gotten there yet."

"Yeah, but you're telling me that you died. I may not be a priest, but I'm not an idiot either."

"Is there much of a difference?"

He scowled at me. "Are you really intending on lying during a confession?"

"I'm not lying. For God's sake, just listen."

He closed his eyes and shook his head at the G-word.

"That one's on you," I said. "If you would've just sat there and listened like a good priest, I wouldn't have gotten all worked up."

He sat still, seething, but silent, so I continued. I explained the afterlife, heaven, hell, purgatory, and Jackson. Gabe would make a good priest, or psychiatrist. He listened, even if I was crazy.

"...And I came back, sitting in Picasso's." He sat, eyebrows working overtime, organizing questions in his head.

"Okay, let me start by asking if you're drunk, high, or just insane?"

So much for psychiatry. "I wish, no, and maybe."

"Do you believe that story?" His tone was more concerned than angry.

"I thought it was just a dream--"

"Thank the lord! I thought you were serious." He ran his fingers through his hair and leaned back in the dusty chair.

"Gabe, I'm not crazy, and I only thought it was a dream at first. I don't think it was a dream anymore. It happened. I died..."

I reached in my pocket and held out the rusty key. There was a flat circle, the size of a coin, where the skeleton head should've been. On the circle was a tiny carving of a sunset, dull, but distinguishable.

Gabe's jaw dropped slightly as he reached for the key.

"Where'd you get this? A cracker-jack box?"

"How old are you? Do they still sell those things?"

"Seven, you can't be serious. Do you want me to honestly believe that this key opens the door to the afterlife? A door that is, apparently, in the coffee shop across the street."

"Yeah, it's in the back, near the bathroom."

"Why wouldn't it be?"

"And what about this Jackson guy? You said he fell through with you. Does that mean he's alive again too?"

I ignored the tone. "He was unconscious when I woke up. I didn't wait around to find out."

He thought for a minute. "Have you told Joss this story?"

"Don't go there."

There was a moment of awkward silence.

"Why don't you just tell her how you feel?"

"I said, don't go there."

"Fine. I'm just saying that you may not have time to dream up these crazy stories if you had a girlfriend. It might be borderline healthy."

I thought about showing him the hand that I punched Jackson with, making him feel how glacially cold it was. It had been a couple weeks, but my fingers were still swollen stiff, cracking when I forced them to move. I really wanted him to prove me wrong, prove it was a dream. But, it sounded like he was more in denial than I was.

"Fine, you don't have to believe me, but can you at least help me out? If I've learned one thing from this whole adventure, it's that my time is limited. I have to take care of my dad before it's too late."

"Come on man, do you know how much gas money we've already burnt looking for him?"

"I know." I held up a torn page from the phone book. "There's a Joe Brown listed in Dogtown. He used that name when I was a kid. I remember him saying it on the phone."

"That sounds real flimsy." He was right. It was flimsy. But, it was all I had to go on.

He looked curiously at me. "Who uses a phone book anymore? Have you heard of the Internet?"

"That's good. Mock the homeless kid. I see how it is." I gave him my best guilt-laden frown.

"Sorry to bring up bad subjects, but honestly, I'm kind of glad we haven't found your dad. I mean, what were you going to do? Beat him up? Turn him in?" he asked.

I looked away, focusing on his key chain. It held a picture of Billie in a small soccer ball.

"Don't give me that sob story about Billie, either."

"Sorry, man, but I did introduce you to your girlfriend, whom you love. That's gotta count for something," I said.

"You didn't introduce us! You hit on her, feeding her some lie about you being the next Justin Bieber."

Sometimes my lies weren't thought out very well.

"Then, when she rejected you, she actually liked me because I was honest!"

"See! You wouldn't have seemed so honest had it not been for my lie."

"Whatever it takes to make you shut up. I'll help you find your dad and the book. Whatever, I don't care."

"Thanks man. I couldn't do it without you. Best confession I've ever had."

"Only confession you've ever had."

"So, do I need to say ten Hail Mary's or something?"

"Do you even know the words?"

"No, but I can fake it."

Chapter 2
JOSS

No matter how hard I scrubbed, I couldn't get the musty smell from my hair. It was ridiculous. Old mops smelled better. I wanted to blame it on the lousy hand soap I was using as shampoo, but I knew the truth. Months of sporadic showers in store restrooms like the one I was in left a stench that couldn't be washed off.

The experience of dying gave me the realization that my time was limited, and a sense of urgency to not take it for granted. I had a small window to bring my dad to justice before Jackson found me, but I'd never forgive myself if I didn't take a shot with Joss. Gabe was right. I couldn't sit around any longer. If I was finally going to ask her out though, I couldn't do it smelling like a musk ox.

After drying off with hand towels, I pulled the scissors from my garbage bag of toiletries. They were bent and rusty, but they'd get the job done. I took a long look in the mirror. Was this really necessary?

I took a putrid whiff of my bangs. Of course it was necessary. She was a few years older, ridiculously hot, and perhaps the nicest person I'd ever met. To say that she had better options would've been an understatement.

Gritting my teeth, I slid the crooked sheers in and clipped. A long clump of greasy hair dropped into the sink. I stared at it for a minute, wondering if I'd made a mistake. Maybe, but there was no turning back. I methodically mowed over the rest of my raggedy mane, trimming everything I could.

When it was over, I ran my hands through the short mess, brushing away any strays. My head looked oblong and uneven, but cleaner.

If only the bookstore had installed a shower... It was quiet though, which was all I could really ask for. Nothing was worse than having someone walk in while I was buck naked at the sink.

I used some car air fresheners as deodorant, rubbing them underneath my arms. The convenience store would never miss them. My shirt and pants could use a cleaning too, but it was cold and I didn't have any way of drying them, so I passed.

I was still too tall for my own good, making it hard to steal clothes that fit. My nose was still crooked and my cheeks still sunk in like a skeleton, but it was an improvement. If Joss was going to shoot me down - and she would - at least I'd know that I gave it my best shot, as pathetic as that was.

I kept working though different ways of asking her out as I sat down in Picasso's, nervously tapping on the pedestal table. I didn't know why I was nervous. There was no chance that she'd say yes.

A couple of private school brats sat across the room, snickering in my direction. They had blue and silver lettermen jackets on. One of the baristas, Mandy, strolled by, noticing the taunts but paying no mind. She never liked me anyway-accused me of lurking. Of course, she was right. I'd usually sit there for hours, especially when it was really cold. On any other day, I would get up and leave. But, not today. Today, I was waiting for an angel.

I met Josslyn Gordon a year ago in a homeless shelter. I'd just left Gabe's house and needed a roof to stay dry. I didn't really like the idea of staying in one of those places, but she was standing on the curb, ushering people in, a blond Mother Theresa.

It worked. The richest men in the city would've lined up at those doors.

"Sugar, do you need a place to stay tonight?" she asked.

I'll always remember the thoughts racing through my head when I heard that Southern twang behind me for the first time.

Please don't be hot. Please don't be hot.

Of course, she was. My karma came in the form of big, teardrop eyes. She had a button nose, with golden locks trickling down from her blue-knit hat. Despite being stunned, I kept my head high and made up some story about doing research for a documentary. It was amazing that I found a way to spit out the English language. She didn't buy my stupid story, but smiled politely and welcomed me in.

I shuffled through the doorway, finding my way to one of the open cots laid out on the gym floor, soaking in the despair of my homeless neighbors. That night, I felt alone. It was near impossible not to drown in depression. I swam in it-the long, desperate looks, the tired eyes, the injuries, the tears, and even a few screams. It was paralyzing, and it forced me to think about my life, or lack thereof.

I'd been on the road, chasing after my dad for nearly a year. I'd always found my way, and that's how I wanted it to be. I didn't need much to survive and I hated being a burden, almost as much as I hated the idea of holding a job. Clocking in and out was for the birds.

That's why I left Gabe's place. I'd stayed with families before, and I knew how it ended. I'd lash out when they tried to send me to school or get a job. I didn't want that same fate for them. They were too good for that. It was better for everyone that I left.

After an hour, I started packing my stuff back up. Self-reflection wasn't my thing anyway. It had a way of stealing your balls, making you think about stuff you're just better off not worrying about. I was nearly ready to go when a little songbird crooned in my ear.

"That must be the world's shortest documentary," she said. "Or maybe you're that good at research." I could hear the smile in her voice. It was warmer than a blanket, and even less judging.

"Yeah, I got what I needed..." I exhaled and brushed two dark strands from my eyes. "You and I both know I'm not shooting a documentary."

Another smile. She handed them out like lemonade. "What's your name?"

"Seven." And the pause. I learned to do that. It gave people a second to soak in the number. "Seven Murphy-Collins."

"Well, that's an interesting name. I mean, how many times do you hear two classic Irish names hyphenated like that?"

We stared at each other before simultaneously bursting into laughter. "Do you mind?" she asked, motioning for a seat on my cot.

That's how we met. It was simple, like Joss. She liked simple. She loved people, and she believed in them-even me. For some reason, intrigue or disgust, she kept asking me questions: where I was from, what I wanted to do, all the stuff she was trained to ask. It reminded me of the foster care agents back in Vegas. She told me about the soup kitchens, low-income housing, and places that were hiring. She went over the job openings twice. Then, she looked down at the pamphlets but surprisingly, never handed them over.

"I could give you these, like I'm supposed to, but something tells me they'll be in the garbage before you leave."

It felt like a test, an important one.

I held onto her eyes and tried to sound sincere. "I don't know. I may surprise you." It may have been an innocent response, but it came with herculean effort. I wanted to ask if her number was going to be on them, but for some reason I bit my tongue. It's a good thing. It wouldn't have been smooth. It wouldn't have been dashing, or debonair. Creepy. Creepy was how it would've sounded.

"I hope you do." Simple.

I knew in my heart that I didn't have a chance in hell with a girl like that, but I went back a few times anyway. Every time I did though, she stayed up with me through the night. It's funny, because I went there for rest, which was the one thing I never got. We didn't talk so much as play twenty questions. She loved questions, lots of them. Where were you born? How pretty is the desert? How tall are you? What's your favorite season? What do you like about baseball?

She treaded cautiously around anything that could touch on family or foster care. It was as if she sensed the danger any time we got close.

That's usually when she'd throw a softball like: What's your favorite color?

I knew she was analyzing my answers but I didn't mind. I never minded with her. Just the chance to hear some more of that beautiful accent was enough to keep me going. Some people had a strange way of making the world seem brighter. That was Joss. Everything around her was bright and if it wasn't, she made it bright. I envied her in that way. To see the world like that must be nice.

It'd been nearly a year since then and even though we hung out, we never seemed to cross that invisible barrier. We played along it, crossed a toe over once in a while, but never more than that. It was frustrating and painful at times, especially when she spent so much time at the homeless shelter. The girl never took a break. Sometimes, I wish she'd just quit volunteering, but that was part of what I liked about her. She was a few years out of high school, with an associate's degree from community college. She was young, smart, and beautiful. She had options but still gave back, trying to make the world a brighter place.

I knew that if I ever wanted her to take me seriously, I had to separate myself from the homeless pack. I was sure the last thing she wanted was another leach. Somehow, I had to show her that I wasn't helpless. I didn't need her to make me bright. I just needed her.

I pondered how to do that as I stared out the window, wondering if she'd blown me off. Maybe she sensed the desperation in my voice. Maybe she was sick of dealing with me. Maybe she didn't feel like driving all the way out to St. Charles from downtown.

Despite the cold, people filled Main Street's sidewalks, stopping into the small French Colonial shops. Every once in a while, one of them would try to enter through Picasso's main door, which was locked. It made me chuckle. Anyone who'd ever been there before knew the actual entrance was the tiny one on the side of the building. That was the right of passage. You had to look like an idiot once before you could become a regular.

On the other side of the street, an elderly couple stopped in front of the abandoned bank where I'd been staying. It was an old cement block with high ceilings-horrible for the winter, but still better than a park bench or the homeless shelter. The electricity was hooked up for some reason, and it was full of old, dusty furniture. Despite not having running water, it was a gem. I found it a few days after I took off from Gabe's house. The fire escape window was broken, allowing me to climb in and claim my little palace. My only companion in that big, drafty place was Rusty. I found him roaming around the neighborhood a few months ago and decided to keep him at the bank.

The most interesting part of that ancient cave, though, was the bank vault in the basement. It was still in great condition, and it became my own personal scavenger hunt to get inside. Of course, I had it set in my mind that there was money inside. After weeks of searching, I finally found a yellow notebook in the back office. Someone named Joanne had conveniently scribbled the combination on the third page. When I cracked the door open, there was a row of metal bars that needed a key. Another month went by, but when I finally found the key and got inside, there was nothing but some transaction receipts from the fifties, a bench drilled into the floor, and shiny walls with three tiny slits near the top, barely big enough to slide a piece of paper through. I assumed they were to prevent suffocation if you got locked in.

A sweet symphony interrupted my train of thought. "At first I thought you were just ignoring me. But after a few minutes, I figured I better say something."

I jerked back from the window, slamming my knee into the table leg. My face flushed with embarrassment. "Ignore you? Not possible. I didn't hear you come in."

She had her hair tucked into a maroon wool hat today. If I didn't know any better, I'd swear she knew how that drove me crazy. Something about wool hats reminded me of how innocent she was, warm and inviting.

"No problem, sugar. Have you ordered anything yet? I'm starving."

Little comments like that burned me. I knew Joss was trying to find out if I'd been eating. It was her way of offering to get me something. The irony wasn't lost on me. I invited her for coffee so I could ask her out. I should be the one offering to get her something, not the other way around. It proved my point of how she saw me.

"Let me get that for you," I said, getting lost in her surprised smile.

"Seven, you don't have to-"

"I want to."

"Seven, I have a job. I can pay for it myself."

"I do too. I'm a ticket scalper," I said, standing up a little straighter.

Her round eyes drew closed. "You are? When did that start?"

"A while ago." I smiled. "Now what do you want to drink?"

Still looking skeptical, she replied, "Tell you what, I'll let you pay next time." She got up and slid around the corner to order a latte. As she disappeared, some confused stares pierced the side of my head from across the room. The wise guys from the table were whispering something about Joss, but I couldn't make out the words. Not sure that I needed to. It wasn't hard to imagine what those two meatheads would say about her.

"What've you been up to? I haven't seen you at the shelter in a while." Her accent was a glorious gift from Alabama, but I had no idea where her Barbie-doll looks came from. She didn't talk much about her family either.

"I've been pretty busy, selling tickets and all."

"Really? That's great!" Her voice was excited but her face was full of concern. I knew she'd be torn. Ticket scalping wasn't exactly an honorable profession, but Joss had this crazy notion that a job, any job, was commendable.

I scowled slightly. "Joss, I'm doing fine." Except for the fact that I died and pissed off Death in the process, I thought to myself.

"I'm sorry. It's just that I've been worried about you. It feels like I haven't seen you in a long time."

"Three weeks." Saying the time out loud actually hurt. I couldn't believe I hadn't seen her in three weeks.

"Yeah, a lot can happen in three weeks," she said.

"You don't have to tell me. Look, I, uh, well, I missed--"

"Josslyn, your latte is ready!" someone yelled from the front counter.

Flustered, I nodded and looked down. More laughter rose from the assholes across the room. My cold hand started to itch as I clenched my fist on the table. I could hear the bones popping.

She sat back down and took a sip, sliding a small cappuccino to me. I wasn't expecting her to get me something and shot my hand up to catch it. I wrapped my fingers around the mug and held it up with a smile.

"Isn't that hot?" she asked.

"No." I gawked at my hand. My fingers were bright red, flaring up at the touch against the ceramic surface.

It was scalding.

I slammed it down on the table and rubbed my eyebrow like it was nothing. My skin scorched my forehead, but it couldn't feel colder in my bones. How was this possible? What was happening to me? Did Jackson do this?

"You were saying?" Joss asked, leaning in.

"He was saying he needs a new shirt," one of the guys at the table whispered loud enough to be heard.

I didn't have to look down to know they were talking about a hole along the right side. I glared over at them, but that only seemed to egg it on even more.

"Hey, I brought you something," she said with a grin, pretending she hadn't heard them.

"I told you to quit bringing me food. I'm fine."

"I'm choosing to ignore that statement. Anyway, it's not food." She handed me a small brown box, complete with a tiny yellow ribbon. I bet she made the bow herself.

"If this is an engagement ring, I think you're supposed to be on one knee."

"Will you just open the thing?" She had this way of fiddling with her hands when she was anxious.

I smiled as I unfolded the lid and slid a silver lighter into my cold palm. "Awesome. I always wanted a Zippo. Hey, you realize I don't smoke, right?"

She tilted her head and sighed, "Flip it over."

"Okay."

Artfully sketched into the opposite side was a large number seven. "That's funny. Jack Daniels No. 7?"

"Yep. I saw it in the gas station and thought of you."

"There's a line if I've heard one."

"Whatever, it's cute. Get over it and stick it in your pocket."

I obeyed and tucked it into my pants pocket, making sure there wasn't a hole in the bottom. I didn't want to lose it. She took another long sip and the pressure started mounting again in my head. The room seemed to grow silent. Even the guys in the corner were suddenly quiet. I bit the inside of my lip and went for it.

"You were right earlier, it has been a while since I've seen you and what I'm trying to say is that I've been-"

The barista turned up the volume on the TV overhead, drowning me out. My blood pressure started to boil and I took deep breath. I turned to look over my shoulder at the screen, wanting to throw a rock through it. There was a slick, grey-haired goat in an expensive suit with a purple sash across his chest. He was delivering a fiery speech to the Senate, repeatedly using some word I'd never heard before: Religiment.

"Nice Sash, Miss America," I mumbled.

"It's Senator Abraham Grey. He's kind of crazy, trying to start some cult movement in Texas," she explained. "He's been all over the news, even more than that coke dealer."

"Sounds like a typical government nutjob. Wait, what coke dealer?"

"You know, Jericho Splitzer. Heck, he's from your neck of the woods. I thought you would've heard of him. They think he's here in St. Louis for some reason."

I was barely listening. All I could think about was telling her how I felt. I couldn't miss this opportunity. What if Jackson caught up with me? What if I never got the chance to tell her? What if she actually felt the same way?

"Joss, I've been--"

"Hey dude, I've got to know where you got your haircut," letterman-jacket-number-one said, snickering. "I really like all the funny angles. It's like a drunk bobbed and weaved on your head."

"Do you have a problem?" I yelled back, jumping to my feet. Pains shot through my right hand, the one I punched Jackson with.

"Yeah, I'm trying to figure out what that girl is doing here with you," he said, eyeing Joss.

I jumped up from my chair and started for their table.

Joss quickly got up from her seat and grabbed my arm. "Seven, come on, let's just go."

"I'm serious kid. Did you drug her or something? Honey, are you feeling okay?"

"I'm quite fine, thank you."

"Oh, that you are. Why don't you stay here with us and let him crawl back into his dumpster?" he said.

It was tough to hear because it was the truth, and Joss was hearing it firsthand. She kept tugging at my arm, desperately trying to lead me out of the place. That's when Mandy popped her head out from behind the counter. "You two, you have to go! Now!"

It was the first time I remembered being glad to hear her voice, until I looked up and realized she was pointing at us. "You can't be serious! We didn't-"

"I've had to chase you off too many times. If you're going to be in here, you need to buy something. So, be gone. Don't make me call the cops."

My eyes fluttered to the meat-heads, then Joss, and finally back to the barista. I couldn't get out of there fast enough. I practically ran out into the street, not even looking to see if I'd be hit. A tear peaked out from the corner of my eye, but I wiped it away before it had a chance to fester. Did that really just happen? Did I just leave Joss back there?

Screw it. I already knew what she was going to say. There was no need to go through more humiliation. I circled around to the fire escape on the back of the bank and slammed the door open. My tears turned into fury. My head felt light, almost empty. I grabbed the closest wooden chair and flipped it across the room, splintering open against the counter. The muffled explosion felt good-so good that I grabbed another one and swung it into the banister, breaking it in pieces.

"What are you doing?" Joss said from the doorway. "Those guys are hardly worth getting worked up over."

I hung my head and exhaled a long breath, dropping the broken pieces to the floor. "They weren't saying anything that wasn't true," I said. "I don't understand why you hang out with me."

"Seven..." She trailed off, breathing loudly. "What is this place?"

"It's the First National Bank of St. Charles, or it used to be anyway."

She looked around and up to the high ceilings. Light snuck through the dusty windows and made her hair a bright orange color. "Okay, what are we doing here?" she asked.

"I live here now."

Her eyes followed the boundaries of the ceiling. "Okay, I guess I understand why you haven't been coming to the shelter. This place is awesome."

"Well, yes, that's why I haven't been to the shelter. But this isn't why I wanted to see you."

"Why did you then?"

This was it. I had her undivided attention. All I needed to do was ask her out. Pretty simple. Her golden face patiently waited for me to do just that, but instead of doing what I set out to do, my jaw locked shut. I tried to open it, but it was stuck. The awkward silence began turning rude. I had to say something. Panic set in. Everything I could ever want was right in front of me, but so was the harsh reality of how she'd react.

Would it scare her away? Would she shriek in terror, or break into a fit of laughter? Either way, I knew that I'd never see her again once I crossed that line. What was I thinking? How could I push her away?

Finally, my lips began to move, and I asked her the question, but the words didn't add up to what I'd thought about in my head.

"I had something I wanted to ask you."

"Of course sugar, what's that?"

"I've been trying to track down my father. He took off when I was young. Anyway, I've got a lead."

What the hell was that? That wasn't asking her out. Where did that come from?

She stopped what she was doing and bore into me, brushing back her silky locks. It felt nice to be the focus of her world, even if for a second. I could stay in that moment forever.

"I was hoping you could come along and help," I added.

It wasn't the whole story, of course. But I'd already seen how one person reacted to the whole death/afterlife story. She'd already been reminded how pathetic I was. I wasn't about to risk sounding crazy on top of it.

"We've never really talked about your dad. I didn't even realize you were looking."

Her tone, suddenly sharp, surprised me.

"Yes, for a while now," I said, cringing at the potential onslaught of questions.

"Do you want to tell me about him?"

I recognized that she hadn't answered the question yet. "Not much to say. He abandoned me after Mom OD'd."

I looked down, not wanting to get into it. She'd just feel sorry for me, which is exactly what I didn't need. I wasn't a child. I didn't need her pity.

"So, this is a revenge kind of thing?" she asked, her big eyes pouring through my skull.

That wasn't the question I expected. I didn't answer.

She reached out to grab my left hand, sending a shock through me. "Hurting him won't bring your mom back. You know that."

Normally, Joss grabbing my hand would turn me into a gooey mess. Not this time. All her sympathy was pissing me off. Nothing was going right.

"What would? Because you let me know and I'll be all over it. Until then, the bastard's gotta pay." Anger bubbled up to the surface as my voice rose. I took a deep breath and tried to keep my cool. "My mom's dead. She's never coming back. I refuse to let him walk free."

She looked at my chest with a deep line across her forehead. Her eyes were working overtime. I could already see her gearing up for more questions. "I don't think I'm ready to talk about it. Is that alright?" I asked, cutting her off.

She must've understood the thin line she was treading on because she didn't push any further. "Alright sugar, you tell me when you're ready." Her hand wrapped tighter around my fingers as she leaned in, kissing me on the little spot where my jaw met my ear. A prickle of excitement started in my gut and surged up my neck, making my head woozy. She smelled like caramel.

"I'm going to let you cool down. I've gotta get to the shelter, but just say the word and I'll be there." She squeezed my good hand one last time and walked out the door, taking my breath with her. Simple.

It wasn't the date I was hoping for, but it was a date nonetheless.

I'd never thanked God for any of his creations, but as she walked out onto the street, I felt the need to thank him... and the state of Alabama. I also cursed Jackson. I hoped all of them were listening.

Chapter 3
FAT SATURDAY

I really hated hockey fans. Most of them were two beers north of a twelve pack and the others complained about the weather. It was March in the Midwest. What did they expect? Nevertheless, I hadn't scalped any tickets since the night I saved Christine and her daughter. So after a week of living off scraps, there I was, standing on the corner of Chestnut Street, a few blocks north of the arena, surrounded by rednecks in hockey gear.

Pink sneakers flashed through my head while I dangled a cardboard sign in the bitter cold. A little girl skipped by, trying to keep up with her father's long strides. I looked down and rubbed my eyes, convinced that I was going mad. Her shoes weren't pink at all. They were green.

My stomach constricted and groaned as I leaned against the light post. I could feel the walls collapsing as it slowly ate itself. My ribs were starting to push through my sweater. I really needed some protein, or a double cheeseburger.

Normally I didn't mind scalping, but starvation wasn't good for a sales pitch. Also, it was Fat Saturday, as I was told to call it.

Most people didn't recognize St. Louis as the second largest Mardi Gras celebration in the States. Neither did I. My guess was that every city, outside of New Orleans, claimed the same thing. Regardless, selling hockey tickets was the last thing I wanted to be doing. I didn't have a choice though. If I wanted to act like a normal teenager for a few hours, I had to make some money and I had to get something to eat.

Surprisingly, the day started off pretty well. I acquired four tickets and unloaded three in the first half hour. Some couple from Minnesota went for my asking price on the two-hundred level seats. It was an easy seventy bucks, but I hated selling on the first offer. It meant I probably should've asked for more. I immediately walked over to the hot dog guy and bought two jumbo chili dogs. It was the best breakfast I'd had in a long time.

I sold another ticket to a drunk who said it was for his wife, since he already had one. Feeling a little better after eating, I said I would swap him tickets so they could sit together. He gave me a dirty look like I was crazy and said, "Son, you've never been married."

Good guess, since I was only seventeen and could barely work up enough courage to talk to Joss. It had only been a day, but I couldn't get her out of my mind. Was that kiss on the neck just a friend saying goodbye, or was it more than that? I've never seen her do that with anyone else. Definitely not Gabe or Billie.

I wished she wasn't at the shelter today. I briefly played with the idea of stopping in to see her, but quickly squashed that thought. I didn't even want to present the idea that I was at the homeless shelter for any other reason but to see her. I needed to completely distance myself from that place.

Across the street, a man resembling an over-inflated football was making his way over to me. He had smooth, stylish strides like he owned the street. He smiled at everyone, and his booming voice could be heard for blocks. "My man, my man. What's going on, young friend?"

Darren was my de facto father in St. Louis, if I had one. He showed me the ropes of scalping after a brief misunderstanding where I tried to rob him of some tickets. Most guys would've beaten the poor, homeless kid, but not Darren. He was a good guy, an honest soul in a devilish occupation.

"It looks like I might be in and out today," I said.

"Oh, that's just the whine of the lazy. You gotta get the green while it's hot!"

"So, it's hot today?" I asked, chattering my teeth.

"'Course it is! That's what happens when there's one less player on the field." The scalpers referred to it like they were playing a sport.

"What are you going on about? Someone's sick or something?"

"Shit yeah! Mike's sick with the brown bottle flu if you ask me." I didn't, but that never stopped Darren. "He's weak, but more action for us. I like it!"

"He's a lifer though. He doesn't have a nine-to-five. He must really be sick to not show up for a game."

"Well, the word is that nobody can find him. His girlfriend says he's missing. She called me, hysterical little thing. He'll show up. He's probably passed out in one of the strip clubs on the east side." Something caught his attention back at his corner. An older couple was standing there, looking around with confused faces. "Gotta go! The fish are jumping!"

I watched him strut across the street, slinging his hands out as he greeted them like old friends. I used to think Darren was too nice to do this for a living. It took me a while to realize that he wasn't too nice. He was just happy to be there. He called it a sport, because that's how he saw it. It really was his field of play.

I refocused on the task at hand when a group of girls walked by with purple and gold beads, feathers, and ribbons. They were already a few drinks in and laughing hysterically. Part of me was jealous; jealous of their freedom, their normalcy, their chase for some fun. The other part reminded me that they were probably stuck up, spoon-fed caviar since birth. That made me feel a little better.

The last ticket turned into six when some guy walked up with a desperate look. He mouthed the words on my cardboard sign that clearly read: I need tickets.

"Hey man, do you need some tickets?"

I glared, pulling my eyebrows to a point.

"How many are you looking for?" he asked.

Clearly, he wasn't aware how this worked. I only needed tickets that I could buy cheap and sell for a profit. Fighting back the need to wink, I replied, "How many do you have?"

"Well, I have four, but how many are you short?"

"Short? I think you're confused. Do you want to sell the tickets or not?" I didn't even know where they were or how much he wanted.

"Yeah, they're in the three-twenty-six," he stuttered.

"Great, how much?" I asked gruffly.

"Well, the face value is-"

"I'll give you fifty." I really wasn't in the mood to hear his sales pitch. The puck would be dropping in about twenty minutes.

"That's not even half the face value."

I wanted to slap the side burns off his face and beat him with this jean jacket. "Maybe you should be on your way."

"No, no. That's fine. But I actually have five tickets. How about seventy for five?"

"Of course you do," I grinned. "I'll give you sixty, or you can walk."

"Fine. Here, take 'em." He looked over his shoulder at someone and smiled. He knew that I just robbed him, but it wouldn't be the story he told his buddies.

With the remaining tickets, I cleared two hundred for the day. It wasn't bad for a few hours of work. I could live off that for a couple of weeks, no problem.

"Are you selling tickets? I need eight, all together. Can I get those in the two hundred level? I'll give you five bucks for each." Gabe's scratchy voice was impossible to miss, even on a crowded street.

"Sure, let me bend over for ya," I replied. "Can we at least cuddle afterwards?"

"Really? Why'd you have to go there?" he asked, sticking out his tongue in disgust.

"Okay, enough with the bromance. It kind of creeps me out after a while. I'm afraid I'm going to walk in on you guys one day," Billie said, stepping between us. "And I really don't want to be caught in the church's next scandal."

Billie had been with Gabe for over a year now and I didn't expect that to change anytime soon. There were only so many girls that would put up with his quirkiness. She was naturally beautiful and an athlete, the-girl-next-door that looked better dressed down. I struggled to recall a time when she wasn't wearing a t-shirt and jeans with her brown hair pulled back in ponytail.

"He wishes. Let's face it, I'm a solid eight. Gabe might be a five on a good day," I said.

"So humble of you, dude."

I shrugged my shoulders. "What can I say?"

"So, if you're an eight, and he's a five, than what am I?" Billie asked.

"Careful..."

I smiled and put my arm around her. "Honey, everyone knows Gabe out-kicked his coverage with you. When are you going to quit wasting your time with this guy and be with me?" I asked sarcastically.

"Honey, if I truly believed you were an eight, I might be interested," she said, jabbing me in the ribs. "Now, back to the question. What am I?" she asked, folding her arms across her chest with a scowl. I didn't dare lowball her.

"Billie, you know they haven't come up with numbers high enough for you yet," Gabe said.

"Enough... Before I have to throw up." She pulled Gabe back to her side.

Truth was, I couldn't think of Billie like that. She felt more like an older sister, or at least how I'd imagine one to be - always trying to keep us in line.

"So, what's the story? Did you sell those tickets?" she asked, arms still folded.

"Of course. I was done hours ago. I've been waiting for you guys to show up."

"You're such a liar," Gabe said.

"And where's Joss?" Billie asked. "I haven't seen that girl in over a week."

"She's at the shelter," I replied, hoping it would end there. Billie had always been a little more vocal, like most things, about my slow movement.

"Again?" she asked.

I ignored the question. If I continued to think about Joss, I'd end up at the shelter, looking pathetic.

We headed south toward the Soulard District. It was a twenty-minute walk but I didn't mind. It was better than standing on the corner like a working girl.

In the winter months, St. Louis reminded me of the casinos from my post death experience. The entire downtown area closed as soon as baseball season ended.

We wandered through empty streets, around an empty stadium, and by empty restaurants before we started hearing signs of life. I knew we were finally getting close because we passed the farmer's market, hearing zydeco music with heavy base. Lovely.

"Since I've never been to one of these things before, what should I expect?" I asked.

Gabe grinned at me. "Well, imagine a city, starved of summer, baseball, and everything it holds dear for five months, then let the gerbils out of their cage and surround them with alcohol."

* * *

Gabe was right. Soulard wasn't an old St. Louis neighborhood on Fat Saturday. It was a town on a bender. Wading through a sea of drunks, we had no choice but to blindly push our way to McGurk's, an Irish Pub, just southeast of Lafayette Square. The gated doors were packed sardine tight, sturdier than the decrepit brick walls, slowly crumbling to the street. The herd of men in winter clothing, women in summer clothing, and the cheap, plastic beads drawing them together kept us at least twenty feet from the entrance. I'd probably have to fight someone to get any closer.

"This is so exciting! Where are my beads boys?" Billie shouted over the noise.

"What kind of crap is that? You've got to earn them!" I yelled, swiping some purple, yellow, and orange necklaces from the redneck to my left. Some of them had logos from years back and tiny lights that didn't work anymore.

It may have gone unnoticed to the redneck, but Gabe saw. I thought he was mouthing a prayer. "Seven, I could have bought some."

"Do you want orange or purple?" I asked, cutting him off. He grumbled something only Billie could hear and reached out for the orange ones.

"Now that we have that settled," Billie said, trailing off. "Do you seriously want me to flash people? Because I'll do it!"

Gabe chuckled as he skipped over a puddle in the concrete. "Of course not," he said, wiping away the grin to sneer at me.

"Good, because I really wasn't going to flash anyone," she said.

"Speak for yourself, I was looking forward to the show," I replied.

She glared up at me as I studied the street, snickering quietly.

"Fine, but remember... Don't cry to me when you don't have any beads." Before she could respond, her foot slid on the slushy concrete, throwing her body awkwardly horizontal. I reached out and caught her, nearly falling myself.

"Cut her off. She's had too many," Gabe said.

"Ha, ha. A lot of help you were. Thanks Seven." She stopped and stared, running her fingers through her ponytail. "Did you seriously just stick an ice cube down the back of my shirt?" Twisting back and over her shoulder, she reached down her sweater, trying to fish something out.

"What?" I peeked down at my hands, immediately realizing the answer. My hand-the same one I'd punched Jackson with, held her up. She was right. It was an ice cube, a big frost-bitten brick. It prickled at first but shooting pains quickly followed. I shoved it in my pocket and shook my shoulders.

"Sorry, I've been standing outside for a while. It's freezing." She hooked her eyebrow and smirked, clearly not buying my flimsy excuse. I could see a blue mark along the back of her neck where I touched her bare skin. It could pass for a bruise, if not for the brush of charcoal skin along the edge.

"I really wish Joss was here," she said, straightening her shirt.

"Me too," I said.

"How are you ever going to be with that girl if you're scared of her?" Gabe asked.

The irony was ridiculous. "Are you sure you're the best person to ask that question?" I asked, glancing at Billie.

"Dude, that's not cool."

"Let's explore shall we?" I asked, hoping to avoid reliving my latest failure with Joss.

I didn't want advice from the happy couple. Listening to them go on about Joss was verbal diarrhea. They had no idea how hard it was to talk to her. All she had to do was smile and I turned into an idiot, stumbling over my own name.

"Okay, but we need some ground rules," Billie said, scratching her neck. "If we're going to do this, we're going to do it right. First: There are seventeen beads between the two of you. If I can get seventeen beads before you give those away, I win. If you give those away first, you win. Second: I have to approve any giving of any beads. None of these flimsy excuses like: she was hot, she was nice, or she bought me a drink." Her loopy impression was uncanny. "If the girl wants beads, she's gotta show the goods."

I loved this game.

"Third," Gabe cut in with a concerned expression. "You, on the other hand, can't flash anyone for beads. You have to earn them the old fashioned way, with charm."

"Fine," she said with a slight hesitation.

"And... lies," I added. "She can lie. She can't be totally handcuffed."

"Agreed." She looked relieved.

"Fourth: the person who's doing the worst has to get drinks."

"Agreed," we said in unison.

"I'll go first," I said. Nobody argued. Let's face it, getting alcohol at a place like this wasn't hard. The trick was not to make a scene. The cops couldn't catch all the underage drinking, so they had to focus on the rowdy ones, the idiots among idiots. Jackson's dad taught me that back in Vegas. I assumed it was universal.

We made our way down Russell Boulevard, enjoying the live entertainment; adults acting like teenagers, teenagers acting like adults. Alcohol might as well have been flowing from the Mississippi River. That's how it smelled.

After a couple blocks, I spotted what I was looking for. A large, metal tin sat to the right, overflowing with ice and beer. Next to the tin was a tiny, makeshift bar with prices listed across the front in faded marker. A toasted ravioli booth stood beside it, a St. Louis favorite. With no one in line and only a few people in the vicinity, it was the perfect little oasis.

With all the excitement of my find, I nearly missed her. She was impossible to miss though, a skinny gypsy girl with short, dark hair in a semi-chaotic mess. Hissing obscenities and chucking ice, she dug through a cooler of frozen ravioli behind the booth. When she noticed me standing there, she slid upright with her hand on her hip, tapping her fingers.

"Well, what the hell do you want?" she asked, motioning to the bar. Faint, purple tones tugged at her eyes. Skin clung to her cheekbones with the all-too-familiar look of severe hunger.

Not wanting to call her out on obvious thievery, I played along. "Three beers."

She didn't exactly smile but pursed her lips crookedly and eyed me up and down. I just saw her scavenging for food in some restaurant's cooler. How far was she actually going to take the bartender act? I waited for the obvious question, "Can I see your ID?"

It didn't come.

She continued to stare at me with an inquisitive look. There was a natural intensity in her eyes; such a light shade of blue they almost seemed white. It had an unnerving effect that made me squirm.

"You're not twenty-one," she said matter-of-factly.

Not willing to give up just yet, I took a wild guess. "Neither are you."

"True, but I'm not a bartender. Here, take these." She held two ice-covered beers in her tiny hand.

"If you're not a bartender, who's-?"

"Who cares?"

I glazed over, realizing my mind was a complete blank. Silence is always impressive. Girls love that creepy, stalker gaze. I silently took the cold, aluminum cans. Her fingertips lingered a split second longer than necessary but she quickly turned away with a roll of her eyes.

"Not to complain, but I did ask for three," I finally muttered.

"No, you shouldn't complain... and I heard you. Here's a tip: always ask a girl what she wants to drink instead of assuming she's down with the same swill you and your buddies choke down." My not-bartender turned to Billie and asked, "What's it going to be?"

"What are you having?" Billie asked in reply, failing to hide her distaste.

"Tequila and Coke."

"That sounds good. I'll have one too."

"Sure thing, ponytail" she said, glancing at me with an I-told-you-so-look.

Back to the bar, she quietly made herself at home. Her white tank top and tattered jeans looked two, maybe three sizes too big. The jacket had to have been from goodwill, or a bowling alley.

"So, is that your thing?" I asked.

"You're going to have to be a little more specific."

"Bartender posing."

"Is that your thing?" she asked.

I tilted my head and smiled. "What's that?"

"Lurking around like a stalker."

"Are you selling ravioli too?"

Her hand locked around the glass. "Quick to judge, tough guy, aren't you?"

"I'm not judging. I've been there."

"Ohhh... You have, have you? Is this where you give me advice? Tell me how you were able to pull yourself from the ashes, how you collected some rich kids for an entourage," she motioned to Gabe and Billie. "Please, wise man, tell me your secret to life. Save me from my wrongdoings."

"What's your problem?"

"Apparently, the tall jackass in front of me. You're a ticket scalper. Do you really consider that an honorable profession?"

"You saw me earlier," I said, connecting the dots.

She handed Billie a dark concoction, "To dimly lit bulbs," she said, clinking her glass. After taking a long pull, she noticed Gabe. "And the mute, is he yours?"

"He's not a mute. He's probably just thrown off by how rude you are," Billie said.

All he could muster was an empty grunt. Brilliant.

"It's fine darling, someone's gotta wear the pants in the relationship. You probably didn't have to take it so literally, though."

"What's your name?" My voice ripped through the air, before Billie killed her. She hated the tom-boy stereotype.

She spun around and slunk close to me, smelling like booze. "Hmmm... guess."

"Guess? Your name?" I heard a deep chuckle from the mute. "How do you guess someone's name? It's impossible."

"No it's not. What do I look like? I'll give you a hint, it's not Mary."

"Oh, well now that it's narrowed down... Chastity. Is that your name?" She smirked, closing her eyes so tight they formed frosty lines.

"You were so, so close." Her hands found her waist again. "I bet I could guess yours. Hold on. Let me think." She stepped back, holding her hand to her forehead.

"Let's see. Is it Five? Or were you number Six?"

"Funny... very original."

"If we didn't have names, how would you introduce yourself? We would have to be creative. I think that would be better."

"Have we met or something?"

She paused, rolling her tongue behind her lips. "If I could introduce you today, I would say, hello, this is the rebellious Captain of Befuddlement."

"Well, you got the befuddlement part right."

"We haven't met. You were busy hitting on some blonde rag at the time."

I took a long drink of my beer rather than owning up to it. Based on appearance, I assumed she'd been at the shelter. Although, I'm not sure how I could have missed her, even if Joss was around.

"Seven... Sounds like a serial killer. Did you know that most serial killers like oranges?"

I closed my eyes. "What? Are you calling me a serial killer?"

"So why'd they name you that?"

"Dad loved craps. He said I was lucky." It was my prepackaged response.

She took a sip from her straw and looked up at me with a v-shaped, wicked grin. "No he didn't. Loving fathers say shit like that, not the dad of an obvious runaway."

I faked a smile in return, trying to figure the best way to rip her head off.

"Not to interrupt this interesting debate, but how about you hand me my beer?" Gabe reached between us and snagged his drink.

"No problem. I was getting bored." Without warning, she moved inches from my face, bumped into my chest, and plucked purple beads from my neck, all while standing on her tip-toes. She disappeared into the crowd before I could respond.

Perhaps it was Joss lingering in my head, or maybe I wasn't as dumb as I used to be, but I fought every instinct to chase after her. They were just beads. I could feel Gabe and Billie's eyes on me, asking questions without words.

"Was that girl for real?" Gabe finally spoke up. "Aren't you going to..." He motioned with his head to follow her.

"Nope. We're going to Hammerstone's," Billie replied quickly, pushing me forward. "I see some open space on the patio near the space heaters."

She led us through the mass of people flooding the street. There was a line in the front, but she was right. The patio was surprisingly sparse.

"Dude, that was pretty darn funny. That chick was psychotic, even for you," Gabe said. "I've never heard you stutter so much. Duh, duh, duh..."

"She was a piece of trash," Billie said. "And don't think I'm letting that one go. She didn't flash anything. Why didn't you bring Joss?"

I seethed at the little tomboy. How dare she compare the two? Gabe caught my eye, pleading me to let it go. Against my better judgment, I did. Billie didn't understand.

"You're right, I did break the rules. It's my turn to--" Deep in my pocket, my fingers rubbed against each other where paper bills should've been. I pulled out the material, looking to the ground in case my money fell out. It didn't. It wasn't there.

My eyes exploded. Heat rippled up my spine. "That little bitch stole my money."

Both of them stepped closer. "Are you sure?" Gabe asked.

"Of course I'm sure!" I stomped to the patio edge, but they both locked on, pulling me back. "What the hell are you doing? Let me go! I'm going to kill her!"

"Dude, you know if she did steal it, she's long gone from here. I'll buy the round, no worries."

"Yeah, cause the booze is what I'm pissed about. That's what I was going to live off of for the next few weeks."

"We'll help out. It'll be okay. Right Billie?" he asked.

She nodded in agreement.

"I don't need your charity. I need to rip her spiky little head off."

"I'll say it again," Billie said. "You should've brought Joss."

"Enough! Mardi Gras is probably the last place in the world Joss would want to be," I growled back. "Besides, as I told you earlier, she's volunteering at the shelter today!"

As hard as it was to avoid, I couldn't think about Josslyn Gordon right now. A little gypsy stole my money and I had to get it back. A bunch of options came to mind; all of them resulted in some kind of broken limb.

I didn't like it, but we stayed on the patio the rest of the afternoon. I wanted to go gypsy hunting, but slowly, the party came to us, distracting me of my predicament. People piled in as the street became too crowded. Dancing broke out but I wasn't sure how. At any given time there were about eight different songs blaring from different directions: the bar, the apartments next door, the restaurant across the street, the radio van at the corner. It's amazing what people heard when they stopped listening.

Billie and Gabe moved with the crowd. Actually, Billie was dancing. Gabe was trying. If it was possible, he might've been a worse dancer with alcohol than he was sober. That was saying something, considering he made up songs and dances to everything like he was five.

The bouncers were outnumbered, trying to keep the peace. Random scuffles broke out, usually over a girl, usually nothing more than some overblown shouting. We learned to ignore the scrum and keep our distance, but it got worse as the day went on.

I was watching some joker strike out miserably with a blond princess when a commotion I couldn't ignore broke out behind me.

"Hold it right there, you little thief!"

"Get your slimy hands off me!"

I recognized that hiss.

"Not until you give back my wallet, bitch."

I whipped around and pushed my way through a baccalaureate party. A wide-bodied mullet had his back to me, wrestling with my thieving non-bartender. Maybe she wasn't that smart after all. Either that or I didn't scare her enough to worry about getting caught. I wanted to believe it was the first.

Rather than piling on, I kept back, eager to watch him slap her around. I'd get my money when he was done.

A small pocket of air opened around them. I scanned the room, but I couldn't see any staff shirts. Perfect. She really was going to take a beating. I was hoping for the backhand. I could already hear the pop in my head.

She flailed everywhere, trying to shake his vice grip as rose blotches flushed her forearm. Her squirming just seemed to piss him off. She clawed at his arms and pinched his skin, but she was barely half his size. I'm not even sure he noticed.

"You call this a wallet? You don't have a dollar to your name! All you have is a miserable picture of...." Her eyes shot back up at the bruiser. "How do you know Christine Dru?"

I froze. So did he.

"The question is, little girl, how do you know Christine Dru," he said, yanking her back by the hair.

A blurry image of a frightened mother filled my head, followed by a flash of light and a sickening crunch. Damn it.

"She's my parole officer."

Even I didn't believe that one. I ducked behind another walrus, trying to stay out of view, but close enough to hear. She jammed a key in his face, almost stabbing him in the eye. Another scream. He didn't hit her though; just bore down on her forearm again, squeezing so tight she sank to the floor. Tears ran down her cheeks as she kicked at his ankles.

What if he beat her? What if they both got arrested? How would I find the book then? As much as I hated her, I needed her. She was suddenly the only lead I had.

She bent over to the side, still with one arm in the air as he reached for her hair. "Dear, you're acting like a child. It's time to go home," he said, trying to diffuse the crowd.

"Dude, I don't think she wants to go with you," shouted a skinny stocking cap to the right.

"Back off kid."

Something snapped. She leaned in and pulled up the bottom of his jeans. Teeth drawn, she sunk into his hairy ankle. His scream was only half as putrid as the look on her face. I didn't want to imagine how that tasted. His face drew beet red. He hopped on one leg and raised his arm across his chest, palm facing out.

I scanned the crowd. The do-rag next to me, the overalls drenched in sweat, the mini-skirt, none of them were going to jump in. They were just there for the show.

His hand bobbed as he flexed his shoulder. Her face was sticky with tears, still trying to break free. I didn't want to help her. I didn't. But as the back of his palm came down, I slid in and caught it with my left hand. I couldn't stop him completely, but it was enough to break his concentration.

He stumbled back and lost his grip on her hair. It took him a second to process what happened, but when he did, he clocked me with his other hand. Why was I taking punches for this girl?

His fist felt like a wooden mallet with hair. I stumbled to the side, my mind already going blank. I caught my weight before reaching the ground, slowly turning back.

"Hold on! You look-" He ripped the wallet back from her and pulled out a different picture. It was an old image of me and dad. I must've been nine or ten in the photo. "Is this you?" he asked, shoving it in my face.

I couldn't hide the shock from my face. Why did he have a picture of Christine? Why did he have a picture of me? Did he know what I did? How could he? The only people who could know were Christine and

Jackson. Or the driver... The SUV driver would know. Was this guy the driver?

"You are, aren't you?" he asked. "You're Seven," he said. His stubby finger poked me in the chest.

"No, are you eight?" I could have fun with the name too, spitting blood between my teeth. If he was the driver, how would he get a picture of me when I was ten? How would he know my name? He couldn't be the driver, which meant he was someone else. That wasn't comforting. Who else could possibly know who I was?

"Jericho's been looking for you. Where's your dad, kid?"

I tilted my head to the side, trying to figure out how to respond. Did he mean Jericho Splitzer, the drug dealer Joss mentioned? I wonder how dad pissed him off.

Slap!

Her blow to his scruffy face rang out across the patio. His head spun, immediately showing a red hand print on his cheek. Fury flushed over his face, but he looked past her and back at me.

"Get out of my way darling. I need a word with your boyfriend." His arm swept her aside and without thinking, my right hand braced her waist. She was lighter than I expected, and warmer than her personality. I could feel her skin pressed against my palm where her jacket rolled up a few inches. I smiled, knowing how cold it must feel.

"Thanks." She cringed but didn't say anything about the ice cube propping her up.

When I looked up, he grabbed me by the side of my head, tossing me to the ground. We both crumbled into a mess on the floor, body parts tangled.

Adrenaline masked the pain as my eyes rolled back to their normal position. I stared at the little hellion beneath me. Part of me wanted to hit her instead of the guy, but I didn't. I stood up caveman style, beat my chest, howled at the moon, and swung my club. I gave up about thirty pounds on him but my club was more effective than I realized. As my knuckles slammed into his jaw, I felt it.

When I hit Jackson, there was pain. It was natural. There was blood, and swelling. Then the adrenaline stopped and all I felt was cold. I felt death. As I hit the goon, I didn't feel pain and I didn't feel death.

He did.

There was a surge of electricity in my fingers - not like the cold waves I'd been getting used to. This was a release of energy that almost burned as it ripped out from my skin. I watched his eyes flush grey. Connecting with his face, I felt his blood pumping, and I felt it stop. He dropped like a weight in water; a body on a patio casket.

I fell next. Only when I landed, my hands touched a new cold. Steel rings clicked around my wrists and I heard someone shouting something about my rights.

Chapter 4
JAILHOUSE BLUES

I wiped away the blur to focus on metal bars, inches from my nose. The side of my face stuck to the cement floor in a substance I didn't want to identify. A sheet of smoke hung below the dingy tile ceiling, creating a rancid mix of cigarettes and stale coffee. As I pulled up to a sitting position, my head swam with a hazy throbbing. I heard the buzz of people around the corner and phones ringing off the hook.

The police station swarmed with partygoers still hung over from Mardi Gras, but I was in a cell off to the side, away from the action. I nudged closer to bars, trying to look around the corner and get a better view. How long had I been there?

I played back the sequence of events but everything went dark after I slugged the goon. I peeked down at my cold right hand. What was that? Did I just shock someone to death? Did Jackson do something to me when I hit him? Does punching a reaper kill your hand? Why did I pass out? I don't think anyone else hit me. Did they? I guess I wouldn't be surprised if he had a crew of wannabes. Maybe someone hit me from behind. I felt the back of my head, looking for a raised area, a bruise that would explain my blackout.

"I tried to pick you up."

I spun around to see the little gypsy spread out on the bench against the back wall. A tiny mole on her left cheek danced as she smiled. I hadn't noticed it until just then.

"Too heavy for you?" I asked.

"No, I just thought you looked better drooling into that green puddle," she replied.

"That and you'd have to give up some of your bench." She wasn't big enough to use it all anyway. Maybe the voices in her head took up the rest of the space.

"Yeah, I wouldn't want to do that." She stretched out and yawned. "I'm not ready to share a bench with you."

"Where's my money?"

"I spent it," she said, rolling away to face the wall.

"You're nothing but a thief. I should've just let that guy beat on you." I buried my face between my knees.

Anger tugged at the back of my throat but the words felt empty. Something was holding me back from truly ripping into her.

Flipping back over, she coiled to a sitting position. "Why didn't you? What was it? Damsel in distress? Fancy yourself as the knight in shining armor, saving a helpless little girl?"

I avoided her face, afraid that if I met her eyes, she'd see my hesitation. I couldn't understand why, but when I looked at her, the scraggily little thing, I couldn't stay mad. Why? She didn't deserve my pity. Pity... It didn't feel like pity.

My stomach rumbled something fierce but not from hunger. I caught myself staring at her left leg, dangling below the bench. Her skin was a cool grey tone, tightly wrapped over bone and a little muscle. Her dark hair contrasted perfectly, setting her white eyes on fire. She was beautiful in a way.

A silver chain hung loose around her ankle that didn't belong there. I wouldn't think a girl like her, if I'd ever met one, would own or even care about jewelry.

She probably stole it, which reminded me why I hated her.

"How do you know Christine Dru?" I asked, getting back to the reason I defended her from the goon in the first place.

She smiled, brushing dark strands behind her ear. "You heard that, huh? She's my parole officer."

"If you want to stick to that story, fine. I really don't care. Just tell me where I can find her."

"What's it to you?"

"If you tell me where she is, I won't finish what the sweaty redneck started."

She crossed her eyes and stuck her tongue out. "I'm already bored with this. Besides, judging by your appearance, you have nothing else to offer."

"Tell me about it... Kyle," I said, reading the tag from the bowling shirt that hung off her like drapes.

"She lived next to me for a while. What's it matter?"

"Lived?"

"I don't live there anymore. See, I'm a bit of a nomad." She jumped up and turned around to get a look out the window.

I guessed that was because no one would put up with her long enough to stay in one place. I'd be afraid she'd slit my throat in my sleep. For once I was glad to be broke. I had nothing she'd want.

"Is that all you can tell me? When was the last time you saw her?" I asked.

"You think all thieves hang out together or something? It's not like we had sleepovers and painted our nails. Why do you care? Does she owe you money?" she asked. "Because if that's it, good luck. You'll never catch her."

Blood rushed to the new welts on my head. "The only person that owes me money is you."

"I don't know what you're talking about," she shrugged, wrapping hair around her finger. "Anyway, Christine was nice, but she was obsessed with finding some guy from Vegas. Last time I saw her, she was going on about how she found him."

My eyes burst open. "She found him? Where?" I asked, hardly containing my excitement.

"It was some apartment in Wood River, across from the baseball diamonds." I didn't trust the curl of her lip. It had to be some kind of tell, but I couldn't decide if she did it when she was lying, or in the rare occasion she was telling the truth.

"Did she say anything about a book?" I asked.

"Nope. I don't think so." She waved her hand in the air. "I don't know. I lost interest and stopped listening."

Figures.

Regardless, this was too good to be true. I suddenly didn't care that my body felt beaten and bruised or that my hand was having hot and cold flashes. I would've taken a hundred beatings like that if it meant I could finally make him pay.

Then, like someone just punched me in the gut, all the air drained from my lungs. I thought about what she said. This is the same girl that had just robbed me. Wasn't it convenient that she was telling me exactly what I wanted to hear?

"How can I know you're not lying to me?" I demanded, watching her closely.

"You can't." She closed her eyes and put her head back down. "Deal with it."

I wanted to get mad but she was right. There was nothing she could say that would make me trust her. I had to hope that it wasn't a lie.

"How long have we been here?" I groaned.

"I don't know... Half a day, maybe more." Her words may have been nonchalant but there was a sharpness to her tone. I pictured her stewing in the cell while I was passed out.

"It's Sunday?"

"Ahh, our first night together."

"Was I a complete gentleman?"

"Yeah, a complete bore. And here I wore my sluttiest outfit and everything." She rolled her eyes to the ceiling, revealing a hint of periwinkle in the light. She really would be pretty if she wasn't psychotic. Maybe if she took a bath.

I took a short sniff as I looked down at my shirt. The odor burned my nostrils a bit. Guess I didn't have room to judge.

"What happened to me? Did someone hit me from behind or something?"

"No. Right after you hit that jackass with the 70's chops, you passed out. It was real manly, very impressive."

"Well maybe if I didn't have to save a little girl from getting clobbered for thinking she weighed more than a buck-o'five."

"You're one to talk, skinny. Anyway, I didn't ask you to help me. Maybe I wouldn't have this interesting blue scar on my back if you hadn't." She sat up and twisted to look over her shoulder, showing off an athletic figure beneath her tank top. Sure enough, there was a light blue mark, like a bruise where I'd caught her. I looked down at my hand, which still felt tingly.

"Do you ice that thing down or something?" she said, glancing at my right hand.

I could tell her the truth. Sure. I died while saving a couple of girls from being run over by a car. Then, I punched Death in order to escape purgatory. Ever since then, my hand feels like a freezer. That's the reason you have a weird, blue mark on your back.

"It was freezing outside," I said. "Why are you in here?"

A gruff voice spoke up behind me. "I can answer that. After you cold-cocked McIntyre, I cuffed you. Then your girlfriend, Ms. St. Claire, assaulted a police officer."

Standing outside the cell was a thin, middle-aged guy wearing dark slacks and a maize dress shirt, both wrinkled. There was a badge attached to his belt, nearly as tarnished as his wedding ring. It said Officer Remy Boudreaux in small black letters. His charcoal goatee matched his thinning hair. He leaned awkwardly against our cage, trying too hard to be casual, tapping the bars with a clipboard and clinging to a cigarette butt.

"For the last time, I'm not his fucking girlfriend." She paused. "I could be yours though," she hissed, licking her lips.

"I might have kicked him in the balls," she said to me with a shrug.

"Mr. Murphy-Collins," he said, grabbing my attention. "I don't have all day. Do you know why you're here?"

"Did I steal your car?" I always wanted to ask a cop that. She snickered behind me.

"Did you steal my...? No, you didn't steal my car. You almost killed someone."

I tried to hide my look of shock. Was he talking about the same thug? All I did was hit the dirtbag. I'm strong, but I couldn't kill someone with a punch. Could I?

The rest of the events came flooding back to me. I remembered the thrill that ran through my body after I punched him. It wasn't that I actually landed the wild roundhouse. It was deeper than that, like a cold shot of adrenaline. I don't know if I had blocked it out on purpose, but I quickly recalled the flash of fear in his eyes as they glazed over.

"Nothing to say? Is that your defense?" he asked. His dark eyebrows pushed down on his face to hide his eyes.

"You said almost. That means he's still alive." It was as much a question as a statement.

"He is."

"Then why am I here? Some thug tries to beat up a girl and I'm the one locked up. Brilliant."

He lowered the cancer stick from his mouth and grinned. "That's the law, son. If you assault someone, you get arrested."

"Assault someone? Did you even see what he was doing to her?"

"No, but let's talk about that. What did Dane McIntyre, a well-known hit man for Jericho Splitzer, want with a couple of kids?"

"Jericho Splitzer? The drug dealer guy?"

"The drug ring's only half of it. Do you know how dangerous he is? He's also wanted for murder, money laundering, theft, and a host of other things. Mr. McIntyre is an associate of his. Now, back to my question. What does a guy like that want with you two?"

We sat in silence, staring at nothing in particular. I knew the truth - that Piper was the one who found him when she tried to steal his wallet and for some reason Jericho wanted my dad - but why would I help this pig? He'd probably just use the information to keep us longer.

"That's how it's going to be? Fine. You can rot in here until you decide to talk." He stepped away, tucking his hand in his pocket.

"You can't keep us in here!" I'd spent enough time in the system in one way or another to know that I hadn't been charged with a crime. He couldn't lock us up indefinitely for nothing.

"You're right. I can't. But I can make your lives extremely painful. Let me tell you what I think. You have quite a track record for seventeen." He flipped through some pages on the clipboard. "Theft, vandalism, skipping from foster family to foster family--"

"What do you want?" I said, standing up. I had at least three inches on him, like most people.

He took another drag and ashed on the floor next to my foot, grinning. A waft of smoke seeped from his lips. "I want to speak to your father, kiddo."

I rolled my eyes. "I'll add you to the list."

"Are you refusing to help a law enforcement official?"

"No, I'm telling you to get in line. Dad hasn't spoken to me in years." I leaned against the bars, fighting the pain in my fingers to lash out and tear his head off. "You don't know a damn thing about me. You should be thanking me, not locking me up. I did your job, since you couldn't catch that guy on your own. Let me out of this cell."

"You know what, you're right," he said with a sly grin. "You're a modern day hero. You saved the girl and caught the bad guy."

"Let me out," I repeated.

"Of course," he said, sliding open the door.

Huh? Did that work? I cautiously walked through the door and thought about bumping his shoulder. That wouldn't have been smart. He probably would've called it assault too. The door slammed shut and I looked back. She had already laid back down on the bench; her tiny little frame landscaped the cement wall. She winked and shut her eyes like she was going to sleep.

"If you had to, how would you introduce me today?" I asked, unsure why.

She rolled her tongue as she thought. "If I could introduce you today, I would say, hello, this is Alice, the rabbit chaser."

I laughed at the image. "Does that make you the Mad Hatter?"

"My name's Piper, Piper St. Claire," she said quietly before I could follow-up, never opening her eyes. "And no, you're not getting your money back."

"Enjoy your time in jail, sweetheart," I said, taking one last look at the mysterious little gypsy before turning back to the amused cop.

Detective Boudreaux guided me through the station. The main room smelled like booze. Looking down at the floor, I wondered how many times it'd been puked on. That was the part of Mardi Gras they left out of the brochure.

Through the doors of the station, I stepped out to an unseasonably warm day. The sun blinded me momentarily but a huddle of shadows quickly blocked it out.

"Hold it right there," Boudreaux said. I faced the street, looking from left to right, wondering my odds if I made a run for it. They weren't good, considering I was still in cuffs.

"Are you sure you can handle him?" he asked to someone behind me. "The press already knows it was one of Jericho Splitzer's men, damn vultures. You'll have to move quickly."

"I'm sure I can handle it," she said.

I knew that voice, but I didn't believe it. My ears were playing tricks on me.

Boudreaux whispered in my ear as he undid my cuffs. "I'll be seeing you soon, Seven. Tell your dad I said hello, and if you feel like saving yourself from a life behind bars, give me a call." He slid a card in my back pocket. "This nice lady is going to take you from here, hero. She's going to find a good family to take you in."

A swarm of reporters and cameramen were instantly in my face. Their voices blended together, impossible to make out one question from the other. A dark trench-coat covered my head, and before I knew it, I was sitting in the back seat of a car.

The driver side door opened to a sea of clicks. The seat barely moved with the added weight, leaving the interior in silence. The cold, leather seats smelled like I imagined a new car did. Soft, rhythmic breathing ensured me the driver didn't get out. A key inserted in the ignition, beeping into a purr of a new engine. I strained to see through the jacket, but it was no use. The fabric was too thick.

The car reversed quickly, leaving the commotion behind and jerking to a stop. The engine roared to life again, this time jolting me back against the seat.

"You can take that jacket off now."

I didn't want to. I was afraid of what I'd see. The twang in her voice had to be a coincidence. It was the most beautiful sound I didn't want to hear. Treachery and lies shouldn't sound that graceful.

I couldn't see her face when I pulled the jacket down. I didn't need to. White-blond hair curled over the headrest, exposing Joss' identity. Every image of perfection shattered in an instant. How could she do this? Who was she? Boudreaux knew her. What did that mean?

"You bitch!"

It was hardly poetic. Leering through the rear-view mirror, her face glistened with tear stained cheeks. She'd been holding them in until now.

"That's not fair," she said through a whimper.

"Not fair? You've been lying to me since day one! I thought you were a volunteer! You're one of them!" It came out in a snarl. "You work for Child Services!"

"Not exactly. I do, but only because I run the homeless shelter." The car jumped into fifth gear as she tore down I-70, heading west.

"How could you not tell me? Is this your thing? Do you get some kind of twisted pleasure from messing with homeless kids? Were you going to figure me out before you turned me in?"

"No, it was never like that. I'm not turning you in. As soon as I heard your name on the radio, I drove downtown. I couldn't let you go back into the system."

I wanted to strangle her from the back seat. It would be easy. I could wrap my forearm around her throat. Maybe I could grab her face with my frozen hand. Would it knock her out like the guy at Mardi Gras? No, that would be crazy. There had to be some other explanation - one that didn't make me sound psychotic. Maybe he had a heart attack.

She pulled to a stop in bumper-to-bumper traffic. Peering out the window to the South, I could see the university, which meant the Metrolink station was within walking distance. Guilt ran through me, but only for an instant. I couldn't look at her. It felt like the first night in the shelter. I was suffocating, but instead of her coming to the rescue, she was the one causing the pain. I was actually afraid I was going to hurt her. I had to get out of that car and this was my opportunity. I knew the safety locks would be on the door, so I leaned back on the upholstery. My legs became a springboard, crashing through the window and throwing shards of glass on the highway.

"Seven!" Joss screamed, still crying.

I didn't waste any time climbing through the window. Glass cut through my jeans and blood dripped from my calves, but I was too furious to feel it.

She fumbled around, unbuckling her seat belt and unlocking the door. It was too late. I was already over the median.

I dodged cars on the freeway, barely noticing as they whipped by, inches from my face. I was done with her. All of it, ever since the beginning; it was all lies. She never cared about me. I was just another charity case, her little project. It was worse than that. She knew me. She knew where I was squatting. I climbed the platform stairs two at a time and jumped on the train.

I didn't even look out the window as it sped off. Instead, I stewed in murderous thoughts for the remainder of the ride home.

Home... the bank wasn't much, but my chest ached at the idea that it might not be safe anymore. I shouldn't have shown it to her. On top of that, the homeless shelters wouldn't be safe either. They'd probably have my picture behind the front desk. In one move, she screwed me out of two beds. The best hookers in Vegas couldn't pull that off.

I hoped she cried as she watched me disappear. There's a reason I didn't have a lot of people in my life. People let you down. Everyone had their own agenda, their own angle, and their own skeletons. Joss was too perfect to believe, and I made the mistake of believing.

When I finally got to the bank, I was eager to get inside and check on Rusty. It'd been nearly two days and I'm sure he was dying of hunger. I climbed up the fire escape, checking over my shoulder as I went. She couldn't have moved that quickly. I probably had at least a few hours before the cops showed up.

It was stupid to tempt fate like that. I pushed the door open, but the hallway didn't seem right. My jacket was on the floor by my feet. I know I left that in the lobby. My foot slid back, shuffling back out the door.

No. Something told me to keep moving. I couldn't just abandon everything. I left some money inside. I needed that before I could take off.

Reluctantly, I crept through the dark hallway. Overhead lights would've been handy as I waded through the mess, picking up clues as I went. My shoes were scattered around like a closet threw up. I found old tickets, some shredded, some crumbled up, all thrown wildly about. The few clothes I owned were everywhere: hanging from doors, on top of dusty desks, wadded up in corners. The cushions from the green couch where I slept were lying on the counter where the bank tellers used to sit. Even the trash cans had been sifted through.

When I reached the lobby, I hesitated. If someone was there, I'd be walking out into the open. Maybe I should turn back and grab something. What would I grab? It's not like I had a baseball bat sitting around.

My foot hung in the air before resting on the dark, mahogany floor. That floorboard always had it in for me. It screamed as soon as my weight rested on the ball of my foot, sending an unmistakable creak through the entire building.

I didn't have a choice anymore. If someone was there, they definitely knew I was too. I didn't want to make a break for it. I didn't want to turn my back. I'd rather face the bastard head on.

Screw it. I kept moving forward, peeking my head into the lobby, which was useless. It was darker than the hallway. The only source of light was the moon, slipping through the slits in the torn blinds.

The extension cord I swiped from the bar down the road would be on the floor beneath the outlet. I had a clear path to it through the maze of random crap, but could I make it? A curious thought ran through my head. If someone was there, wouldn't Rusty be making some noise? I looked around again. Did Rusty make this mess? Did he get out? Did someone break in and let him out? Why would they do that?

"Rusty!" I called out. "Is that you?"

No response.

My muscles relaxed a bit, releasing an edge of tension. I walked quietly, almost sliding across the lobby floor, heading for the extension cord. I bent down to find the black plug. I found the chord and traced it... to the outlet. The chord was plugged in.

Click.

The lamp on the desk behind me flipped on, throwing a long shadow across the dusty floor.

Chapter 5
BREADCRUMBS

I didn't want to look up. Was it Jackson? Had he already found me? Joss? Was it Detective Boudreaux? Was it one of Jericho Splitzer's goons? Who else had I pissed off?

I looked at the broken chair by the door, hoping I'd find some kind of weapon: a letter opener, a stapler, anything with a sharp edge. My personality wasn't going to be enough.

"Dude, you're free!"

That awkward stance was the most welcome sight I could think of. Gabe's look of shock mimicked my own. I could feel my heart slowing back to its normal pace.

"Dude, you scared the crap out of me." I exhaled. "Yeah, I'm free, for now."

"I don't understand. The last thing we saw was that cop throwing you in the back of his car. How'd you get out?"

I started to answer, but the mess distracted me. "Did you tear up my place?"

"No, it was this way when I got here."

"What were you doing here?"

"I was hoping you'd be out of jail."

I leaned back, folding my arms across my chest. That didn't add up at all. One minute he was surprised I got out, the next he was waiting at the bank in case I did.

"Sorry, you know I can't lie. Joss called Billie and told her the whole thing. I came here to check on you. When I saw the mess, I figured you took off."

"She called you?" I leaned over and picked up my shirt.

"She's really torn up over the whole thing. She thinks you hate her."

"Joss doesn't get to be worried. Backstabbers forfeit that right."

I could hear Gabe step closer as I had my back turned, peaking down the stairs, wondering about Rusty. "She got you out of jail. Doesn't that count for anything?"

I laughed, stepping closer to force him back. "Nope."

I could barely picture her making the call to the station, explaining how she would come down to pick me up. I wondered if she'd really felt bad doing it, knowing that she'd have to come clean. Did she really care? Was the crying just part of the act? What else had she been lying about?

I guess I should be thankful she got me free, but there was no way in hell I was going to spend the remainder of my days in foster care. I'd be a sitting duck for Jackson to come find me.

"What are you going to do?"

"Did she tell the cops about the bank?" I asked, looking around the ceiling.

"No, I don't think so."

I breathed a small sigh of relief. "Then, nothing for now."

"You can't just--"

"What? What do you think I should do? Tell me! Go ahead, dad. What would Jesus do?" I shoved him in the chest, knocking him into a banister. "Oh, that's right, you can't make a decision to save your life. Why would you start now?"

Silence filled the room while I turned on another lamp.

I tried to calm down but every time I took a deep breath Joss' face appeared. I was all jittery and my chest felt tight. What if that was the last time I ever saw her? I remembered when she kissed me on the cheek. It was simple, but her lips were so soft and she smelled like a light caramel. I pictured her smile and how much her eyes lit up when I was near.

Was she that good of an actress?

I looked at Gabe and felt bad for snapping at him. It wasn't his fault. He didn't have to be there. He was just trying to help.

"That sucks, dude," he said, almost too low to make out.

"Look, you know I didn't mean that. I'm just pissed off."

"Quit backtracking. You're only saying what I deserve."

Shit. I got him in depression mode. "What's going on?"

"Billie knows I'm waiting to hear back from Seminary. She thinks I'm going to get in."

"Are you?" I cringed, knowing I'd just opened the door to his internal debate.

"Probably. Dad thinks I'm a shoe in. He's practically written to everyone except the pope. Actually, he probably wrote him too."

"Does that mean you're going to go through with it?"

He smiled and looked over my shoulder. "I'm not sure I could do that to her, you know?"

"Will you seriously listen to yourself? You're thinking of doing it so you don't disappoint your dad. You're thinking of not doing it so you don't disappoint Billie. It's your life, not theirs."

"That's the wrong way to look at it."

"Oh really?"

"Yeah, it's not about whose life it is. It's about choosing the best way to serve. Am I better to serve in the church, or to stand by Billie?"

"You know what serving gets you? A tip." I couldn't help laughing at my own joke. "Stop worrying about everyone else. You're eighteen, not thirty. Jeez, in the last couple of weeks I died, broke out of the afterlife, nearly killed a guy, went to jail, and found out the girl of my dreams was nothing but a liar. But I still get depressed listening to you."

He chuckled at the floor. "Sorry, you're right. I came here to check on you, not to whine about my dilemma."

I filled him in on Jericho Splitzer, Detective Boudreaux, and Piper. He barely moved a muscle while I rehashed the events.

"That's why you stood up for that girl! In all the commotion, I thought you were attacking her for stealing your money and the guy was trying to save her, not the other way around." His mouth twisted as he thought.

"So, wait a second. You spent the entire night with her in a cell?" he asked.

I nodded.

"And did you get your money back?"

My eyes narrowed. "No."

The corners of his mouth curved upward and he let out a short grunt.

"What?" I demanded.

"You wanted to kill that girl. She literally stole everything you had. Why didn't you get your money back when she was cornered in a jail cell?"

Now I was smiling. "I was more interested in her information at the time."

"Right. And it wouldn't have anything to do with the fact that she's incredibly hot and wilder than a jackrabbit?"

"Wilder than a jackrabbit?" I blurted out. "Who says that?"

"Quit trying to deflect. Why didn't you take the money back?"

"She's not that hot. I mean, she's okay." He grinned wider. "But she's too skinny and she's a liar."

"Too skinny?" he laughed. "That's all you got?"

"I don't have a thing for the gypsy!"

It caught me by surprise when I yelled. My fingers tingled. A shiver ran up my spine. My temper was out of control. Deep breaths weren't going to cut it at this rate. I had to calm down.

I didn't understand why I'd be worked up about accusations of liking Piper. I didn't. It was absurd. The only thing he was right about was that she did in fact steal my money.

"Okay, dude. I believe you," he stuttered. "So, who do you think broke in here?"

I shrugged.

"Well, Jericho is the only one that could've trashed the place, considering the other three were at the station with you."

He had a point, but my head was still spinning.

"You think it was your boogeyman, don't you?"

I threw a shoe down the hallway. "I know you think I'm crazy, but yeah, I do. I really did die, kind of."

"Alright, then what do we do?"

"I think we go to Wood River," I said.

His face scrunched. "How is finding your dad going to stop Jackson?"

"I don't know. How do you stop Death?" I shrugged. "I can't control that. I can bring my dad to justice."

My baby book flashed in my head. The cover was sky blue with a small picture of me in the middle. I remember Mom's handwriting. It was scratchy and compact because she pressed too hard. I used to trace it with my finger. There were more pictures of us inside. I'd give anything to see those again. I barely remember what she looked like.

It hurt to think that those were the happiest times of my life. Through all the drug highs and lows she'd been scared for her life, scribbling down facts in a baby book. It made me feel selfish for not understanding what she was going through.

"Jericho and Boudreaux, they're looking for your dad too?"

"Apparently."

His face scrunched as he rubbed his forehead. "Why is your dad so important?"

"I wish I knew. The stubborn bastard never told me a thing."

* * *

I was doing my Rain Man impression, counting cobwebs as I lurked around the lobby, munching on stale bread. Patience wasn't my strong suit. Gabe needed to get his lazy ass up. He had to be some kind of champion sleeper. How someone could snooze across two wooden chairs was beyond me.

"Wake up!" I kicked the one at his feet, jolting him awake.

"What? Why would you do that?"

"Because I'm a jerk, and it's nearly nine. You said you'd take me to Wood River, remember?"

He sat up, wiping his eyes. "No, I don't remember saying that."

"Well, you are," I said firmly. "Besides, if you're right about Joss, then Boudreaux won't know that I escaped."

"It's not going to be that simple!" Billie was standing in front of the fire escape exit, blocking the sunlight. Gabe stumbled to his feet, suddenly eager to be awake.

"Let yourself in, by all means," I replied.

"Thanks, we will."

"We?"

She strolled down the hallway and into the lobby. Joss nipped at her heels, wearing the same shirt from yesterday. Eyeliner stained her cheek and blond strands stuck to her face. All that and she was still beautiful, striking down to every last tear.

"You can come in. She can go home," I said, trying to be tough.

"Seven, you don't own this place. You can't tell her to leave."

"You're right. I can't." I picked up my shoes and moved for the front door. Gabe jumped in front of me, hands up, palms out.

"You too? One Judas is enough."

"You can't tell me the words to Hail Mary, but you can reference Judas?" he asked.

"Just hear us out," Billie said, throwing her gym bag on the chair. She made herself at home quickly for never having been in the bank before.

I looked at both of them, then the liar. "Fine, let's hear it," I said, leaning against the wall.

Joss kept her eyes on the floor, a sad Barbie, badly in need of a shower.

"Look, it's not a matter of whether Boudreaux knows that you escaped. It's a matter of when."

Billie grabbed her Mac from the bag and flipped it open to a page on YouTube. I'd seen YouTube and Facebook before but I didn't quite understand how they worked, or why they were so popular. It probably would've helped if I had access to a computer.

"I'm not really in the mood to watch a video of some kid dishing on Hollywood."

"How about watching some kid dish on you?" she replied with a grin. My body tensed up even though I didn't quite follow. She hit refresh on the page.

"You have horrible Wi-Fi access here. I barely have a connection."

"No problem, I'll just call my Internet provider," I said, smirking at her.

Once the page finally came up, it showed a shaky image from what looked to be the back seat of a car.

"Hey, that's--" I didn't have to connect the dots completely before Billie started nodding. It was Joss' car, coming to a stop in heavy traffic. The video quickly cut to a shot of some dark complected kid with a round face with trendy glasses, sitting in a basement.

"Hey guys! Welcome to Lance TV! Today, I've got a great one for you. For those of you who've watched before, you know I'm from St. Louis. Now don't get me wrong, I love my town, but nothing, and I mean nothing... happens here. So, when a local kid took down number 28 on the most wanted list for manhandling some girl, St. Louis was suddenly on the national scene! It's awesome!

"Anyway, I've been told his name is Seven Murphy-Collins, and apparently, he's a runaway. How do I know? Well, after the cops were done with him, they turned him over to DCFS-child services. I know, I know, most of this has already been in the news, for those of you who trust such sources. Anyway, I bet you're wondering why I'm showing you a video of a car on the highway. Let's watch and find out."

The choppy video resumed, showing Joss' white sedan stopped in traffic. It was difficult to see inside the car, but I knew what to look for. My foot kicked up from the seat, breaking the window and throwing glass on the street. My body wriggled out the window and I played Frogger across the highway. I have to admit, it was pretty slick. I looked like I knew what I was doing, despite the truth.

"Did you catch that?" he asked. A blurry still popped up, showing my face up close. "Now, compare these images." Another image appeared next to the blurry one. It was taken from the St. Louis Post-Dispatch website, showing half my face. The other half was covered by a trench coat. It must have been taken when Boudreaux was shoving me in Joss' car.

"It's the same kid! That means Seven Murphy-Collins escaped! I don't know him, or his story, but I think that's awesome. I'm happy that he's free. More to come as the story unfolds, but Seven-if you're watching, I've got your back!"

"Who the hell is that joker?" I asked.

"What's it matter? It's YouTube. Obviously, this kid thinks he's some kind of reporter. That's not the issue."

I looked at Billie blankly, feeling dumb.

"Look at the hit count," Joss whispered.

Again, feeling dumb, I stared at the number. "Twenty-thousand people watched this?"

"Yeah... How long do you think it will take for the police to figure out you escaped? Or DCFS?" Billie asked.

"Or someone else?" Gabe added, looking me squarely in the eyes.

He didn't even have to say it. He was thinking about the break in. Maybe it was too late already. Maybe Jackson already found me.

"Twenty thousand people? That's insane. Why would anyone care?" I groaned, suddenly pissed for how attached I felt to the bank. I'd squatted in plenty of dumps, shacks, holes in the wall, but for some reason I really didn't want to look for another place, or go back to the homeless shelter. The bank was perfect, beyond perfect. It was one thing when I thought Joss was going to rat me out, but now some YouTube kid decided to blast my story all over the internet and cost me a bed.

No. I refused to leave - not for the mere chance that someone might see the video, might recognize me and might follow me to the bank. I'd take my chances.

Gabe spoke up. "It's a pretty interesting story-fighting drug dealers and escaping government agencies."

"Yeah, except the government agency was her," I said, waving at Joss. "Hardly daring."

"Give her a break. She was just doing her job," Billie said.

"I'm sure she was."

Billie was staring me down but I learned long ago to avoid her scolding. It wasn't just me. No one wanted to feel mother hen's wrath. My eyes kept steady on Joss.

"Speaking of that," I added, "this place was wrecked when we got here. What else did you do?" Accusation filled my voice.

"I didn't do it. I went to Billie's after you ran," Joss said. Her body slumped into the banister, forming a curvy s-shape. It hardly seemed fair. Guys were wired in straight lines and she was too hot for words. I couldn't stay mad with my tongue hanging out.

Billie nodded in agreement. That meant it had to be Jackson and I was running out of time. He'd find me long before some crazy video blogger and his followers.

"Forget about the mess for now," I said. "Forget about this YouTube thing. I've got more important things to worry about."

"Seven, do want to go to juvee?" Gabe said. "I think--"

"I know," I interjected. "There's nothing I can do about Boudreaux right now. If he finds the bank, so be it. We need to go to Wood River."

"Wood River?" The question rang out from the girls in unison.

"My dad has an apartment there," I said.

I stood up, grabbed my jacket, and pushed them down the hallway. Joss followed behind. I wasn't sure how I felt about that.

"Seven, how is that more important?" Joss asked.

Stopping mid-step, I spun and slammed my hand into the wall. "You don't get an opinion! You shouldn't even be here. Go home!"

I watched as more tears welled up before turning to see silent, somber faces.

"What?" I demanded.

"Well, she may not, but I do get an opinion," Billie said with her hand out. I braced for the ensuing fight. "Where exactly is this place? And how did you find it?"

"The gypsy girl from Mardi Gras knew Christine Dru. She found my dad at an apartment in Wood River, across the street from the baseball diamonds," I replied.

I could see Billie's wheels spinning. "This is the same girl that robbed you?"

I nodded.

"And you trust her?"

"Of course not, but what other choice do I have?" My fists clenched into balls and I could feel my skin turning warm. "My dad is going to pay for what he did. Screw the risks. If you don't like it, you don't have to go either."

Gabe's head dropped. "What? You agreed to help," I said, glaring at the coward.

"She's got a point, dude," Gabe said. "I've been thinking about it all night and it seems strange that all of a sudden you're willing to blow off getting arrested on a hunch from someone you can't trust."

I believed Piper, but I understood their point. I wanted to believe her. It meant I still had a trail to follow. I also understood where Billie was headed. If I fought back too hard, she would accuse me of having feelings for Piper. And that was not the case.

I stepped back and scoffed. "I trusted her and look where it got me," I said, pointing at Joss, then feeling bad about it. "Look, that goon at Mardi Gras worked for Jericho Splitzer, the drug dealer from the news."

"Really?" Billie asked. "That's interesting but what does it have to do with anything?"

"Jericho and Detective Boudreaux, both of them, are looking for my dad. I need to find him and my baby book before they do."

"Why? What do they want your dad for?" Billie wasn't about to let this go easy.

"I don't know. That's what I want to find out."

"And then what? What will you do then?" she asked.

"I'll figure it out then. Come on," I said, leading them down to Gabe's car. I could feel the hesitation, but they eventually followed.

As I opened the passenger-side door, I stopped in my tracks. I'd forgotten to feed Rusty. "Hold on a second, guys, I'll be right back." I ran back inside and downstairs, threw him the last bit of bread, and found my way back outside, making sure all the lamps in the lobby were out along the way.

When I got back, Billie had grabbed shotgun. I sneered into the window and reached for the handle to the backseat. It was full of sweaty soccer gear.

"Sorry," she whispered from the front seat, "Gabe gave me a ride to practice yesterday." I caught Gabe rolling his eyes in the mirror.

* * *

A gut-wrenching smell of airborne turpentine covered the hard-working, refinery town, trickling its way into my nose and sticking to the walls of my lungs. Worse than the smell might have been the smog, covering Wood River in a smoky grey, depressing blanket.

The two-lane highway led us to 6th Street, past the junior-high, the local bar, and all the way through town. When we reached the baseball diamonds, we realized we'd gone too far. Gabe circled back and found a group of four apartment complexes on the right. They were set back off the road, each with their own muddy courtyard. They had to be the ones Piper was talking about.

"Is this really it?" Billie asked.

We parked out front, behind some overgrown bushes near the sidewalk. Gabe leaned over the seat and smiled, "Okay, I got you here. The rest is up to you."

"Damn heroic of ya."

"I'll stay here with Billie. You two can have fun in the creepy buildings."

"I'm not a little lady to take care of," Billie said, glaring at Gabe. "We're going too."

I hadn't come all that way to chicken out. Stepping out of the car, we headed for the dingy entrance of the brick buildings, stumbling over the crooked sidewalk. I glanced up through the trees at the apartment windows. Most of the blinds were drawn, showing little sign of life.

Resting my hand on the broken knob, I took a deep breath and pushed the heavy door in. A waft of air immediately engulfed us in a haze of cigarette smoke, dancing around a smoke detector like it wasn't even there.

"Oh! The air in here is worse than the refineries!" Joss said behind me. "How can you even see your way around?"

I couldn't. I was kind of hoping she could. My eyes were on fire. I was practically putting my hands out in the dark, hoping to hit a doorknob.

"You're not helping. Go back to the car," I said to Joss. She didn't listen.

"How are we going to find the right apartment?" Gabe asked.

"Don't they have those mailbox things?"

I was right. There was a row of rusted metal mailboxes with names scribbled in black marker. Brushing aside the smoke, I leaned in and found the one with Collins across the top.

"333. There are three floors in this dump?"

"Why are we doing this? You should be leaving town. It's the only way. The police will eventually figure out that you're not in foster care. Boudreaux will try to put you in juvee. I'm not sure how, but he will. You don't know him. He's relentless. He'll never let this go," Joss said.

"Maybe if you were better at your job, we wouldn't be having this conversation right now. I'd be stuck with yet another foster family. How do you know Boudreaux, anyway?"

"He comes by the shelter every once in a while, looking for fugitives," she said under her breath.

"Well I'm not scared of him. Maybe running is your answer, but it's not mine, not until I finish what I came here for."

Gabe and Billie stood back, giving me just enough room to strangle her.

I climbed up the creaky stairs and followed the hallway to the end. Dad's door was the last one on the left. The door wasn't locked, or even latched. Upon closer inspection, the frame was broken.

"Someone broke in," I whispered. Thank you Captain Obvious.

What were the odds that both of our places were broke into at the same time?

I slowly pushed the door open, sending a loud creak down the hall.

"Are you sure we should be going in?" Joss asked. Her fingers dug into my arm as she peaked nervously down the hall.

"Would you like to ring the doorbell?" I asked, glaring back at her.

"What if he's home?"

"Then this will be very interesting," I snapped.

"I got ten bucks on Seven," Gabe whispered. I heard a soft thud over my shoulder, followed by Gabe's chuckle.

As we edged through the doorway, the smell of dried ketchup jumped to my nose. Fruit flies swarmed my face.

"I don't suppose you brought a flash light?" Billie asked.

"Or a bat?" I joked. She didn't laugh.

The apartment had nasty brown carpet. We were staring at the back of a sofa in the living room as we stood on the small, linoleum threshold. The walls were bare and there was no TV to mention.

"I need you to understand that I never meant to hurt you," Joss whispered.

"Now?" I whispered. "You want to come clean now?"

Her big blue eyes washed away my resolve. It was just so hard to stay mad at her. I shook my head, but I wasn't going to let her off easy.

"Either you're lying and you really meant to hurt me, or you're telling the truth and you're that freakin' stupid. So, which is it?"

Her bottom lip quivered as she pulled at my arm. "I was terrified to tell you the truth. I didn't know how you'd react. You've been through so much. All those nights at the shelter... I wanted to tell you, but I knew that you'd never talk to me again."

The putrid ketchup smell was coming from the kitchen. A paper plate sat on the counter with dried, crimson patches next to cold french-fry crumbs. The rest of the kitchen was spotless. Someone must've left in a hurry, or never left.

"Why would it matter?" I asked. "I was just some homeless kid that you could practice your child psychology crap on. Why would you care?" I glared back at her. "Just another one of your charity cases."

"Is that what you think?" Red blotches filled her cheeks.

"I don't know what to think. You're super model girl and I'm a runaway. I have no idea why you'd possibly want to hang out with me."

Her jaw dropped a bit before she looked over her shoulder at Billie and Gabe. I didn't care if they were there. I was angry enough to finally get it off my chest.

"Maybe we should talk about this later," she said.

I peeked around the counter to see the same linoleum floor throughout the kitchen. The garbage can was empty, with a clean bag lining the inside. Dad wasn't this clean. He couldn't have been here long.

"No, you wanted to talk. I'm sick of putting it off. Why have you been slumming it with me?"

She scrunched her face at the suggestion, which made me feel better.

"I never thought you were a charity case. You have to understand how much I..." She stepped back, swallowing hard. "I don't want to lose you."

Shaking my head, I slinked back to the living room. Some yellow tickets were on the floor. I leaned over to pick them up. They were for a play at the Hound Theatre."

"Wicked?" I read it aloud.

"It's a musical," Joss replied.

I was distracted by the ticket, still thinking about what she said. "So, here's your chance. If you really don't want to lie, start now. Who are you, really?"

Her eyes danced around the room and she ran her top row of teeth against her bottom lip, grinding back and forth in the dim light. "I live in a small loft off Washington and I don't volunteer at the shelter. I work for DCFS. I've been running the shelter for a year now, since high school. I don't have any family to speak of, so I know a little bit about being on your own."

"Yeah, you're a regular Mother Teresa." I trailed off and stood up before she had time to react. I was more interested in the dark hall leading to what had to be the bedroom.

"You see, that's why I never told you. You want to blame the system so badly. I didn't want you to blame me too."

Suddenly, the spooky hallway looked inviting. I fought the urge to turn back with each step, but there had to be more. I kept looking around for something I'd recognize. He took everything from Vegas. Where was it all? Where was the book?

"And lying about it was going to make me trust you?" I asked. "All that does is prove you're one of them."

The door to the bathroom was open, revealing a strangely untouched space. I started to question if he'd actually stayed here.

"That's a pretty narrow-minded view. DCFS has helped a lot of kids," she said.

Something hit me. "Did you do a background check on me?"

It was like I hit her with a bat.

"My job required me to," she finally whispered.

I heard Billie take a deep breath. My hands balled into fists and my chest pulled tight like I was about to explode.

"I wished I hadn't. I didn't know we would... Seven, you weren't, you aren't, my job. I know that if I want to know about your past, I should've asked you myself, but it was too late."

I spun around, watching Gabe and Billie stare at the floor, looking awkward. Joss' big eyes were full of tears. "So you already knew about my parents? And you've been lying, playing dumb, ever since?"

The only thing I could hear was my own teeth grinding as she nodded with tear-filled eyes. If I ever could have hit a girl, I would've then. I had to turn around and focus on the task at hand or I might've anyway.

The bedroom door was shut, with a tiny bit of sunlight sliding underneath. The handle stuck as I tried to turn it but eventually gave way to a muffled click and a long whine. Inside, it was more of the same, nearly empty, almost untouched. The bed had been slept in though, with a couple of stuffed animals tucked in the mangled covers. There was a book, but not the one I was looking for. It was porn, torn and tattered on the bed. That definitely could've been Dad. I went to reach for it, but something stopped me.

A second screech echoed through the empty apartment, sending a pulse of fear through my body. Someone had just opened the front door. I pulled them all behind me and stepped in the closet, sliding the door behind us.

I covered Joss' mouth with my left hand as she started to whisper something. I couldn't hear the footsteps I was waiting for. Who could it be? Were they following us?

The heavy footsteps finally came, smashing the carpet with each thud. I could hear one set, moving through the kitchen and then the living room, just as we had. The feet became secondary though. With each step closer to the bedroom, the breathing took over. They were short, deep breaths with a methodical pace, perfectly in sync with every other step.

The intruder came to a stop in the bathroom. It was silent, so I leaned in closer to the wall. Joss' hands braced me from behind. I couldn't hear anything. Where did they go? I shifted closer, stepping on some abandoned shoes. My face pressed closer to the wood, near the hinges. I tried to peak through the tiny crack where the frame met the door but it was too dark to see anything.

The bedroom door flew open, throwing light everywhere. The handle slammed into the wall near Billie's face, forcing her to step back.

"Ahh!" she yelled, losing her balance.

Whoever it was had to have heard us. The slow footsteps moved directly in front of the closet. It was hard to see through the slotted doors, but the figure was huge. His crusty breath sounded like gusts of dying wind. It had to be Jackson. Did he see us come in?

He turned away from us, looking at the bed. My eyes had adjusted enough to where I could see Joss' face, silently screaming at me. I searched for a weapon along the floor. All I could find were shoes, and some dirty socks on the ground. Maybe I could beat him with a shoe. I accidentally grazed her leg as I momentarily lost balance. I almost fell through the door in the process.

There was a grizzly chuckle as Jackson set down the old book. He slowly circled the room and came back to the closet, inches in front of us. I stood up straight, an athletic beanpole. That's what Mom used to call me.

His hand reached for the closet door. How could he not have heard Billie's stumble? Was he just toying with us? My life should've been flashing before my eyes. I guess that doesn't happen if you've already died. I only had one option that I could think of, and it wasn't a good one. It was more like a Hail Mary.

The door jostled, slowly sliding to the left as it did. Gabe put together my plan and tried to stop me, but it was too late. He couldn't hold me back. I flung everything, every pound, every ounce at the folding closet door. My half-jump, half-shoulder move broke it right off the hinges. The quick snap of the flimsy wood was followed by a sickening crash of bones, bodies, and muffled groans.

As I lifted my head off the door and peered through the broken pieces, I caught a look at him. It wasn't Jackson. It wasn't even close. It was an older, rounder guy, with a beard that hadn't been trimmed in weeks. He was strung out, with a faded tattoo of a bird on the side of his neck. He had two silver beads pierced above his left eyebrow, like he was reliving the nineties. "Who the hell are you?"

"I'm the guy who's gonna slit your throat, little maggot."

He punched me wildly in the ribs, heavy hammers pounding at the bone. I fell back in immediate pain, grabbing my side and reaching for a broken sliver from the door. Before I could get a grip on one, his knuckles cracked into my orbital bone, sending me into the wall. My head slammed into the trashcan.

I lifted my head off the floor and opened my eyes, but all I could see was red. My face was covered in blood, dripping to the floor and filling my nostrils. I could hear him toss the door to the side. I didn't have time to gather my bearings. The next punch would be my last. I couldn't take another shot.

"I can't believe Jericho wants you alive," he seethed.

That was the window I needed. Before he could hit me again, I swung my frozen right fist. I couldn't see, so I went for the source of his voice. My knuckles slammed into a cactus of facial hair. The same chilled adrenaline ran through me as when I punched the guy at Mardi Gras. I felt the thumping in his chest slow to a crawl. His lungs seemed to deflate. His breath stopped.

His body fell flat to the floor. I reached around for his throat, flinging blood from my eyes. There was no logic to what just happened. I shouldn't be able to feel his heart. I shouldn't be able to take his breath.

"You want to kill me?" I yelled.

Blind anger and rage washed over me. The urge to hurt him again, to kill, sunk in. Why shouldn't I? He'd do the same.

"No!" Before I could follow through, a much smaller, more petite body shoved me off his unconscious frame, freeing me of my dilemma.

My eyes felt heavy as I wiped the blood from them.

"What are you doing?" Joss asked. "What are you doing? Are you seriously going to choke him to death? Hey! Stay Awake!"

"I am awake! I'm fine!" I yelled but there wasn't any force behind it. She was right. For some reason, hitting him zapped the energy right out of me.

Snapping out of it, I looked down at him, then back at her. "What do you care what happens to him? He just tried to kill me!"

"You don't get to make that judgment."

"Why the hell not?" I yelled.

"Come on! We have to get out of here," Gabe yelled. He pushed Billie through the door and tugged at my arm.

I looked back at the worthless scum, passed out on the floor. The decision seemed easy. Bad guy equals death. How difficult was that? If I left him there, nothing would happen. The question swirled around in my head before I conceded, against my better judgment.

"Hold on." I leaned over and grabbed the book from the bed with my free arm.

"Wow, I must have really pissed that Jericho guy off."

"All the more reason to get out of here. He probably wasn't alone."

We found our way back outside and before we could open the door, Joss saw two more guys roaming around the courtyard. They were doing a sweep of the buildings. They must've followed us.

"What did you do to that guy?"

She was right. Even for a guy like Jericho, this was an overreaction. "This doesn't make sense. All I did was hit that guy." My mind starting running wild, imagining what Jericho would do if he caught me. I remembered hearing stories of guys like him back in Vegas. They all ended the same way, with silent victims, buried in the desert.

There had to be something we were missing, but it would have to wait. We had to get out of there. I looked back to the other end of the hallway and saw a back door. Without exchanging words, we hobbled to it and spilled into the alley. As the door opened, sound exploded from crowded streets. Vehicles, kids, and megaphones blared from 6th Street. Where did all the noise come from?

We came around the far side of the apartment complex, behind a dumpster, next to a small, Italian restaurant.

"Where'd you leave the car?" Joss asked.

"Great question," Gabe said, scanning the road.

I heard footsteps on the gravel near the first building. "We have to keep moving." I led her around the dumpster and found the source of the noise. There was a parade on 6th street.

"Damn! We circled around the wrong way. It's on the other end of the complex, near the ball fields."

Joss looked at me for a second and then started wiping my face with her sleeve. "You won't blend in if you're covered in blood." Her fingers traced the ridge along my brow, pausing briefly at my eyes. "That's good. We can slip into the crowd."

She moved quickly, cutting through the parade-watchers. We crossed the street in between a float of guys dressed up like oil rig workers and a smaller float with a bunch of kids in yellow shells. Some little bastard hit me with a sucker as they launched candy into the crowd.

I was about to ask what the parade was for when I heard the booming voice behind me. It was the guy from the TV, Senator Grey, still wearing that stupid purple sash.

"Are you tired of your government ignoring your religious beliefs? Are you tired of your religion ignoring the current issues? Why do you have to be pulled in separate directions? Wouldn't it be great if these two factions learned to get along? To work together? Trust in me! Unity starts with a choice!"

I wasn't sure what he was preaching about, but it was clear this wasn't a parade. It was a pep rally.

Joss froze, stopping near the middle of the street. A snarl seethed from her lips. If I hadn't seen it, I wouldn't have believed her face could contort that way.

Looking around, I felt like we were standing in a sea of drones. Flashing lights and colorful streamers washed away the sanity of the little town.

I stared up at the lunatic. His frizzy, grey hair and well-groomed beard felt natural for his charcoal suit and purple tie, matching the sash. His skin was a dark shade of peach, perfectly set in between most races I could think of. His voice carried naturally, challenging the microphone itself. His eyes were kind, in stark contrast to the force behind his words.

"Come on, we have to get out of here," I finally said. She resisted slightly, but eventually gave in. I didn't have time to contemplate her hatred for the Senator.

We slid in between the drones, now chanting the word religiment like Grey coined in his speech to the Senate. We were in a bad zombie movie.

"Look," I whispered in Joss' ear. We ducked behind a large group of people, avoiding the trees growing through the sidewalk. Across the street, in front of the apartment complex, three men huddled around a body, slumped up against a tree in the courtyard.

"That didn't take long."

They were slapping him lightly in the face, trying to wake him up. The tallest of the men, turned in our direction and scanned the crowd. His eyes caught mine, despite my attempt at hiding. He motioned for them and they jumped to attention. The goons cut through the sea of people and crossed the street, fanning out in the process.

"Have any ideas?" I asked.

"One," Joss quickly replied. "But you're not going to like it."

They were closing in quickly and I didn't like the look in her eye so I pushed a few people to the side and pulled her along. I could see Gabe's Chevy in the distance.

The tallest guy was only about thirty feet behind us. The other two were working their way through the edge of the street.

There was a clearing of bodies up ahead to the right, but it wouldn't stay that way for long. If we could get through the passage before it closed, we might be able reach the car. I put my head down and pushed forward with my dead hand in front, pulling Joss with the other.

Rude was an understatement. I shoved, groped, even pinched any obstacles. I half-expected an angry husband to jump out, pissed that I grabbed his wife's ass.

I thought we were going to make it for a few fleeting moments, but the mass kept getting thicker. Right as I stepped around the last couple of drones and reached for the skinny sapling near the fence, Joss jerked back. I heard a grunt and a whimper behind us.

He had Billie, the tall one, using her hair like a leash. I sprang back, mindlessly. I fought through some stoner kids and got within arm's reach of him. He was bigger than I anticipated, easily having forty pounds on me. I was already beaten up pretty bad and my eyes were bruised over and stinging from blood. It wasn't going to be pretty.

"Get your hands off her! Rape!" Joss screamed, piercing my eardrums in the process. Her shrill cry was doused in desperation and fear, which sold it beautifully. The zombies snapped out of their trance and growled angrily, reaching for the tall drug dealer. His face was priceless, shocked with fear. I wished I owned a camera.

Billie quickly broke free and I pulled her through the closing passage. Gabe took her arm and made sure she got in the passenger's seat before he climbed in to start the car.

I motioned for him to go, and quickly ran to the door; yanking it open and shoving Joss in. "Get us out of here!"

"Who were those guys?"

"More of Jericho's thugs," I answered. We were nearly a block away but I kept checking out the back window.

I couldn't see Gabe's face but I could read the worry in his voice. "So, after all that, we still don't know anything?"

"I wouldn't say that," I replied. Holding up the porno, I opened the page to the bookmark, but it wasn't a bookmark at all. It was the yellow ticket from the apartment.

"Anyone feel like going to a show?"

Chapter 6
WICKED

"Why are you here?" I asked, staring at my purple eye in the bank bathroom. The cut on my forehead had closed up, but the rest of my face was puffy and sore.

Billie scooted through the dusty lobby, leaving a trail of clean in her wake. "This place is disgusting. Someone has to clean it up."

"Why?" I asked.

"Why clean?" Billie asked. "Are you serious? I mean, beyond general hygiene, how do expect to be with a girl like Joss, living in a dump like this?"

"I'm not with Joss."

"But you'd like to be."

"She lied to me. She can go to hell."

"Give me a break. You're not fooling anyone. If that girl sneezed, you'd race to buy her a handkerchief, or in your case, steal one."

"Don't you have practice?" Her ponytail was wet and she was wearing a sweat-stained jersey underneath a long sleeve t-shirt. She must've had four layers on but still looked skinny.

"I did this morning, while you were snoozing." She kept milling about the room. I watched her closely, wondering what she was up to. Something wasn't right. Why did she care so much about me impressing Joss? Was it just her way of creating her perfect double-date scenario? Or was it more than that? Did she truly think it was her job as mother hen to get us all together?

"Why are you are here? And don't say cleaning."

"I told Gabe that I'd pick you up for the show. I can't believe we're going to see Wicked."

I leaned against the pole, arms folded across my chest, staring her down while she dusted.

She stopped wiping down the chair that hadn't been used since I moved in. She turned slowly. "Can't I just want to help out?"

"I'll never understand girls."

"Neither will I," she said. "So, this thing tonight-what exactly do you expect to find at the theatre?"

The thought felt heavy, weighing down my shoulders. "I'm not sure. I guess I'll try to find out when we get there."

"Okay... Let's say your dad shows up. Does that mean you're going to get him?" She put an emphasis on 'get.'

After my encounter with Jericho's thugs in Dad's apartment, 'get' had a whole new meaning. That was the second time something strange came over me. I had to face it. Crazy or not, there was something wrong with me. But what? What did Jackson do to me when I hit him?

"Let's not go there," I said, referring to my dad. "I'm sick of that discussion and I don't know what I'll do. Besides, I need the baby book if I want to turn him over to the cops."

"Fine. It's just that it sounds kind of funny."

"What does?"

"Well, you've followed the guy halfway across the country, but you're still scared of him."

"Scared of him? Why the hell would I be scared of him?"

"Why else wouldn't you commit? If it were me, I'd want to kill him."

Want to kill him? I'd be lying if I'd said it hadn't crossed my mind, but it felt like a trap, like she was fishing.

"I do, but you're not me, and don't pretend you know how I feel because you're adopted. It's not the same."

With her back to me, frozen in place, a tiny shiver shook her body. "And you, asshole, don't have a monopoly on family drama. Don't pretend you know how I feel because your parents were garbage. At least you know who they are."

"Were," I said.

"Whatever."

She was the only one who could, and would, stand up to my bullshit. I had a theory on why she was so controlling. She put it on herself to keep everyone together because she was too young to do it for her parents. That's when they gave her up for adoption. Billie was three. To this day, I thought she blamed herself.

"What would you do?" I asked. "With my dad."

She looked at my feet. "I don't know."

"Thanks. You're a big help. Why are you here?" I asked, again.

Her eyes were still glued to the floor.

"Ahh, so that's why you're here. It's Gabe." I grinned. "What did he do this time?"

Her middle finger flew up as she picked a rag off the floor.

"You didn't drive across town just to fluff my pillows."

"There's a euphemism for ya," she replied. "This isn't a booty call."

"Okay, but if you don't come clean, that might be the story I spread," I chuckled. "Yeah, Billie came over wearing some skimpy lingerie. What was I to do?"

"You wouldn't even know what to do with it," she said, throwing a rag at me.

She had a point. I probably wouldn't.

"Fine, yes, I'm worried about Gabe," she finally gave in. "This whole Seminary thing. I always thought he'd lose interest and drop it. He barely even goes to church! But here we are, on the brink of college, and I don't know what he's going to do." She picked the rag back up and wiped down the long counter against the wall.

"It's kind of funny."

"What?"

"Well, you have this tough front, but you're still scared to death of him," I said, winking.

"Touché. But seriously, the kid doesn't even like going to church. How's he going to make it through Seminary?"

"Don't act like it's ever been about him. He's scared to death of disappointing his dad or hurting you. He's screwed either way. That's why I keep telling him to do what he wants, not to worry about anyone else."

She looked hurt. "I kind of thought you'd help me out."

After a few seconds of dusting the Las Vegas Sun clipping on the counter, she read it aloud. "Mother Dies of Overdose, Husband on the Run." She took a deep breath. "It's quite the family portrait."

She knew how to piss me off. She'd seen that picture before but never said a word. I knew how this worked. Once her little claws started twisting, they wouldn't stop until she got her way.

"Do you really want him not to go?"

She didn't even flinch.

"If you really want to stop him, just the play the girl card."

"The what?"

"If going to Seminary would hurt you more than the alternative, he'll stay."

"The girl card? Really? You want me to lie?"

She could act innocent all she wanted, but I knew lying wasn't beyond her if she really wanted something. "It's not lying. It's acting," I justified.

"Aren't you mad at Joss for doing the same thing?"

A surge of heat rose up to my head and prickled the hairs on my neck. I couldn't tell if it was anger or embarrassment. I should've seen her little trap coming.

She set the rag down on the windowsill and tried to look innocent. Glancing out the window, she stopped.

"Hey, isn't that the girl from Mardi Gras? The one who stole your money?"

I jumped to her side, peering across the street. The day was bitter cold with a tease of sunlight fighting through the otherwise overcast sky, partially blinding my view.

The strange little pixie sat in the cold with her feet up on the table. "Did you ever get your money back?"

"Her name is Piper, and no, I didn't," I said, swinging the door open.

She sat quietly at a sidewalk table, munching on some toasted ravioli. There were a couple to-go boxes folded at her feet.

"What are you doing here?" I yelled, stomping across the brick road with Billie right behind.

"Me? I'm just having a snack. Are you following me or something?" Her fingers ran through the dark, messy weave on her head.

"I live here."

She smiled and looked around. "Where exactly? In that old building? That's kinda creepy."

All the reasons I wanted to strangle her came flooding back. So did the other, more confusing feelings. She was wearing a dirty white tank top and some orange cargo pants that barely hung onto her waist after she cinched them tight. It was attractive, forcing my eyes to trace her torso.

"Oh, the boyish one, is she your girlfriend? I thought you were with the goofy guy, honey," she said, looking over my shoulder.

"My name is Billie, and I am with the goof--I am with Gabe."

"So, you have a boy's name too? They didn't give you a chance, did they?

I could hear a long exhale. Before Billie could lunge at her, I tried to change the subject. "Where'd you steal those from?" I asked, motioning to the boxes.

She tossed a ravioli up in the air and caught it in her mouth. "Why do you assume I stole them?"

"Because you did," I said.

"Do you realize how many people forget to take their to-go boxes with them?" she asked with a mouthful of food.

"I see. And naturally, that means you swiped them when they weren't looking."

Piper snickered. "Are you saying you never steal?"

"Not like that," I replied, grinding my teeth. I was sick of being called out.

She smiled patiently, waiting for my response. "Shouldn't you be locked up right now?" I asked. "How'd you get out?"

"I had to sleep with Detective Boudreaux," she said nonchalantly, pulling another ravioli from the top box.

Billie's mouth flew open. I had to hold onto a chair to avoid falling over.

"Relax," Piper said. "I posted bail."

"So, that's where my money went."

She answered with another snicker and kicked a chair back from the table. "Did you find daddy-o?"

The invitation had teeth, but I reluctantly took a seat.

"Seven, we really don't have time to--"

"Relax Johnny, it'll be fine," Piper said, sneering up at Billie. I fought every instinct to let the girl fight ensue, but I wanted to know what Piper was up to. I caught Billie out of the corner of my eye and looked back at the bank.

"Whatever. When you're done with the little tramp, it's time to go. The show starts at six," she said.

Before she made it across the street, she turned around. "Is Joss coming?"

My head held steady but my eyes were screaming at Billie. She just wanted to say Joss' name in front of Piper. She already knew Joss wasn't coming.

"No, she has to work." As usual, I wanted to add.

She didn't even give me the courtesy of listening to my answer before she marched back the bank.

I turned to Piper, who was holding a ravioli out in my direction. "Relax, loverboy. You can play Ken doll later."

I fought the urge to take the bait and snap back. It didn't take a genius to figure out she loved to fight.

"Thanks," I said, taking the potential poison. I was hungry.

"Nice face. Who beat you up this time? Girl scout?"

I forced a laugh. "You sent me into a trap."

"I didn't send you anywhere. That was your own dumbass idea."

"The apartment was empty."

She shrugged. "He must have moved."

"It looked like he took off in a hurry."

"Very odd," she said, eyes focused on her food.

I stared up at the awning, wondering what I was thinking, talking to the psycho. "Tell me something. Why did you steal his wallet?"

"You're going to have to be more specific."

"Of all the people at Mardi Gras, you stole from the one guy who worked for Jericho Splitzer. Why?"

"You know what I find interesting?" she asked.

"What's that?"

"You find out that one of the most dangerous men in the country is looking for your father, and what do you do? You listened to a stranger who might know where your dad was. Why? Why are you looking for him? It seems to me that Jericho's the problem."

"Are you serious? You're saying I should be looking for Splitzer?"

"Yeah. Quit trying to be the savior. Just take out the asshole, problem solved."

"That's got to be the dumbest idea I've ever heard," I said, crunching loudly as she stared through me with pale eyes. "Seriously, I'm a seventeen-year-old kid. What am I going to do to Jericho Splitzer?"

"Apparently nothing, coward."

"Is that why you're here? To recruit me for some suicide mission?"

She grabbed the to-go boxes and set them on the table. "Don't you care that he's going to hurt your dad?'

"Nope. Somebody should." I shrugged.

"What do you think he'll do if he finds him?" she asked.

"How the hell am I supposed to know? His goons didn't exactly say what he wanted."

She swiped the boxes from the table and glared at me.

"How'd you find me?" I asked.

"Please!" she scoffed. "You're plastered all over the Internet and you have the nerve to ask me how I found you! Get over yourself!" She walked off before I could come up with a clever response.

More bait, I thought to myself. She kept trying to get me to chase after her. I was smarter than that.

* * *

Standing in front of the Hound Theater could be a training session for the running of the bulls. Old, rich people are rude. They sneer at anyone who doesn't meet their ridiculous standards. Some old broad looked at me like I was going to steal her silver jaguar when they pulled into the handicap spot. It made me want to steal it.

On any other night, I would've thought about it, but I had a mission. I had to find out why Dad had a ticket to this show. He didn't care about musicals. What was going to happen here?

"You look out of place, kids!" Gabe shouted from other side of the lot.

I couldn't argue with him. "Nice of you to show up," I replied.

"It's not my fault. I don't know what to wear to these things. Girls have it easy."

Billie scoffed. It wasn't her typical tear away pants and baggy t-shirt, but she pulled off the purple, open-back dress surprisingly well.

"You do!" he continued. "Look, you have to wear a dress-easy decision. Guys have to figure out how formal to be. Do I wear a tie? Just a jacket and no tie? A full suit? Maybe it's casual and I can get away with dark jeans and jacket."

He shook his head like he was exhausted, but Billie and I weren't joining in on his confusion. He looked down at her and then at me like I, of all people, should agree.

"Dude, I'm homeless. I have about five total outfits. You're witnessing the only button up shirt I own and dress pants that I stole from a dumpster."

He didn't have an answer for that. No matter how close we grew as friends, we'd never get past the worlds we grew up in. He'd never showered in a mall bathroom.

"Where's Joss?" he asked. "I figured you'd bring her along for this little mission.

Billie turned to me as I scanned the crowd. "Yeah Seven, where is Joss?" she asked in her best Southern twang.

"Enough guys, I don't want to hear it. You both know she's working."

I knew they were trying to be funny, but it sucked to hear that question every time I saw them. It justified the nagging feeling in the back of my throat - that Joss, despite what she said, didn't care enough to take off work. All of her tears about not wanting to lose me, yet she chose to work for DCFS instead of helping.

All of my insecurities rushed in. I bet if I wasn't some piece of trash runaway, she'd make the time. What was I doing - thinking she'd really want to be with me? It was self-torture. Even if she did, what next? My days were numbered. It was only a matter of time before Jackson found me. She was better off without me.

"Did you get tickets yet?" Billie asked.

I welcomed the change of subject. "Not yet. Darren's gotta be around here somewhere." I looked for a small group of people, huddled around a big guy with a voice that could carry through a sand storm.

"How do you know this guy again?" Billie asked.

I smiled. "Well, I tried to steal some Cardinal tickets from him."

Her eyes tripled in size. "You did what?"

"I wanted to see how much tickets were going for, so Gabe asked the biggest guy he could find."

"Yeah, except you didn't tell me you were going to lift them while I was asking." Gabe punched me in the shoulder.

"Anyway... the guy was deceptively quick and nearly broke my arm," I said, smiling.

"Idiot. Did he kick your ass?" Billie asked.

"No. He's a big teddy bear. He let me go and taught me the ropes before I got myself killed." Billie rolled her eyes.

"Guess that was a wasted lesson," I mumbled under my breath.

"Is that from the guy in your dad's apartment?" Gabe asked, touching the back of my head.

"Probably," I said, trailing off. It was getting hard to keep track of my injuries. I finally spotted the ogre. He was standing under a sidewalk tree, talking quieter than I expected. I gladly used him to change the subject. "There he is. Come on."

As we walked up, the small crowd dispersed. The big guy, who always looked hammered, lifted his head to the side with a grin. He made eye contact while he talked to someone behind an obese couple.

"Five, Six, Seven! My man, how's it goin?" His megaphone-like voice was low and relaxed, which meant he was talking to a woman, a hot one. He thought he was slick like that. His hand held out so I could shake it, but I knew that was for show too. He liked people to think he knew everyone. I'm pretty sure he lived alone. I shook it with my left hand, which was strange, but easier than shocking him with my frozen fingers.

"What's the action like tonight? Makin' any money?"

He glared at me like I just blew his cover. "It's not about the money, my friend. It's about getting out there and being with the people, enjoying the city." His voice was cool, but his eyes said, "I'm going to hurt you."

I couldn't help but laugh. Despite his size, he might be the gentlest person I knew.

The couple in between us finally moved out of way, revealing the young woman he was working over. She wore the same orange cargo pants and dirty tank top, underneath an unbuttoned, plaid shirt. Showing how little she cared about social protocol, was Piper.

"Sorry bud, this pretty, young thing just bought the last of my tickets."

Those ivory eyes looked up at me, setting the back of my head on fire. "What do you think you're doing here?" I demanded.

"Dude, that's no way to talk to a lady."

She turned back to Darren. "I'd expect nothing less from him. Actually, Darren, did you know he hit me?" She said, running her tongue between her teeth.

"He did what?" Darren's voice cracked.

Her pixie smile came back like a flash, almost sparkling. "Just kidding. He is kind of a jerk though."

Darren relaxed, looking dazed. I knew the feeling.

"Thanks Darren. I appreciate a man with integrity," she cooed.

I rolled my eyes and nearly threw up in my mouth as I watched him melt. "Please, you wouldn't know the first thing about integrity. How many tickets did you steal from him?" I asked.

"Steal? Why, I wouldn't do that," she said, feigning innocence.

Billie fake-sneezed the word bullshit.

"What's going on here?" he asked.

"You can't trust this little gypsy, Darren. She'll steal the shirt off your back when you're not looking."

"I'll have you know, I just paid him," she said matter-of-factly.

"Yep, she bought my last four," he said.

"What are you up to?" I asked, fists clenched.

"I thought about what you said earlier. I decided to help you," she said. "Now, what's your dad look like?"

"I don't want your help." My voice was razor sharp.

"Fine, then find your own way into the show," Piper said.

"Here you go," Piper said, handing them each a ticket. "Let him get his own."

"I already have my own ticket," I said, holding the one from Dad's apartment.

"Good, then you can sit by yourself. Have fun," she said, turning her back on me.

I angrily took a step closer when Darren's big paw shot out, holding me back. "Hold up, fella." I had five inches on him, but he outweighed me by a hundred, easily. If he wanted to hold me back, I wasn't going anywhere. "I think you need to apologize to the lady."

I looked at Darren, hoping he'd give me the benefit of the doubt. No such luck. He was putty in her hands.

"Traitor," I whispered.

"Come on Seven, I don't feel like standing out here all night," Gabe finally piped up.

Why was everyone suddenly against me?

"What do you want?" I asked, turning to Piper.

"Apologize," she said.

"Apologize? For what?"

"For accusing me of stealing," she said.

I gritted my teeth and hung my head sarcastically, "Sorry, dear."

Piper bounced to my side, wrapped her arm around mine, and headed for the front entrance. "There. That's much better, dick."

It took every ounce of energy not to wring her neck, but she was too busy looking over her shoulder to notice. "Thanks Darren," she said with a twisted smile I didn't need to see. Her head nuzzled against my lower shoulder as we walked. Snakes were more welcome.

"So dear, how was your day?" she asked.

"I contemplated the value of staying alive," I replied.

* * *

The gigantic, black awning, with gold letters and winged lions didn't even begin to do the Hound Theatre justice. Walking through the entrance was like stepping into a palace. Thick, blood red pillars outlined the cavernous hall, complete with gold decorations in every corner. It wasn't a theatre, but a place of worship to the god of music. I stopped mid-stride, confused as to where I was. Was I still in St. Louis?

Joss would've loved it. Even though I was pissed at her, I couldn't stop thinking how I wished she was the one at my side. I hated myself just for thinking it.

"It's pretty incredible, isn't it?" Piper asked.

"I'm not sure I have words to describe it."

"And that's coming from someone who grew up in Vegas," Gabe said. "Don't some of those crazy casinos blow this thing out of the water?"

"When you think about me back in Vegas, what do you picture? I was just a kid, and it's not like I lived on the strip."

"He's a little slow, isn't he?" Piper asked.

"Enough with the girlfriend act. What are you up to?" I demanded.

"I like Wicked."

It was fitting, but I didn't believe her for a second. "Seriously, why'd you come?"

"What are you so worried about?" she asked.

"Every time I see you, I end up with a new injury. Why do bad things follow you around?"

"Maybe it's not me. Maybe it's you."

"I highly doubt that."

"Look, someone had to pay for your tickets. What were you going to do, steal from your friend?" There was an edge to her voice, but it wasn't judging. It was warm, almost expectant.

"I wasn't going to steal from Darren. I would've floated him an IOU. Who are you to lecture on stealing?"

"Get me a drink. I'm thirsty," she said.

Before I had time to react, she was on her way to the bathroom. It killed me when she disappeared like that. Billie quickly followed, leaving Gabe and I standing around like morons. He was smiling like a schmuck.

I looked down and shook my head. "Don't start with me. I don't know what she's doing here."

"Uh-huh. She just showed up? I hate it when hot chicks do that. It's like they won't leave me alone sometimes," Gabe said.

"Come on. Let's snoop around."

"Whatever you say, boss."

I shuffled my way through the line, grabbing a drink for Piper. I couldn't believe I was buying a drink for someone who robbed me. I counted out three quarters, two dimes, and a nickel on the counter.

"Do you know what I'm supposed to be looking for?" Gabe asked.

The crowd had grown to fill the room in its entirety. I scanned through it but like Gabe, I wasn't sure what I expected to find. Why would Dad go to a musical? Why this musical? Or was it the location?

I weaved my way to the middle of the room and looked up at the Asian-themed decorations along the wall. I checked out the entrance, the exits, the stairs leading up to the balcony levels, and some of the private rooms off to the side. I had to be missing something. The room was so loud that I could barely think.

Maybe that was the point. "Hey!" I yelled into Gabe's ear. "Maybe he picked this spot because it's so busy. It would be easy to blend in."

"You got that right! I think they just opened the doors to sit down," he said, looking back over his shoulder.

The sea of people gushed over the red carpet, nearly swallowing us whole. There was an announcement overhead that the curtain would go up in ten minutes. Ushers began pushing from the entrance, instructing everyone to find their seats.

A raspy voice announced, "The concession stands are now closed. Please make your way to your seats." A hand gently touched my shoulder. "Sir, please find your seats before the performance starts."

"Wow, these people are serious," Piper said, sliding her arm around my waist.

"Tell me about it. What'd you find out?" I asked.

"I found out that the girls' bathroom is down a huge flight of stairs, and nasty."

"That's what you were doing the whole time?"

"Hey, it's a long show. Besides, this is your quest, not mine," she replied.

"I thought you were here to help me."

"I thought you didn't want my help. Where's my drink?"

I wondered if we'd get thrown out if I poured it on her head. Begrudgingly, I shoved it into her hand."

"Thanks, dear."

"Seven, come on!" Gabe said. His hands were up in the air like he'd given up. Billie was leading him through the sea.

The seats were actually very close. We might've been ten or eleven rows from the stage. "And you accuse me of stealing? How much did Darren want for these?"

"Attention is often the best form of payment," she said quickly.

"You paid him with attention?"

"She flirted," Billie translated. "Girls do that. Apparently she does too."

An angry hush came from a few rows back. "We're going to get kicked out of here if you guys don't keep it down," Gabe whispered.

"Oh, look who's interested in watching the show now," I said.

Another angry shhh spit out.

"I'm going to--"

Before I could stand up, Piper's fingers wrapped tightly around my hand, my cold hand. We both jumped at the touch, but I kept my eyes forward. Maybe she thought it was just static electricity. No such luck. The little pixie was burning a hole in the side of my head.

I couldn't come up with any explanation for why my hand was ice cold. There was nothing that made sense. What was I going to say?

Luckily, the room went black, the curtain raised, and a bright light filled the stage, highlighting the countless motifs, statues, and golden deities. It was near impossible to avoid being pulled into the performance, but I fought it for a while, trying to work out my dad's plan in my head.

He picked this place for a distraction.

The thought sizzled in my head. I couldn't worry about the little gypsy sitting next to me. I could figure out what to tell her later. I looked down at my watch. Fifteen minutes until intermission. Now was my chance to snoop around without the crowd. I shifted in my chair, sat up, and twisted to spot the closest exit. Looking around, I found three sets of eyes, wider than the spotlights flashing across the stage.

"Dude, what are you doing?"

"I didn't come here to watch a play." Still looking, I found the face most likely responsible for the shushing earlier. It belonged to a slick, mid-thirties hotshot with a red tie. Yep, he was my guy. I stood up, fully blocking the stage to a smattering of hisses. I looked him in the eyes and mouthed something about meeting me outside. He pointed at his watch like a tough guy-didn't want to miss the show.

Surprisingly, three embarrassed friends followed me up the aisle and out into the lobby. The red room was filled with the smell of fresh popcorn and chocolate. "You guys didn't have to come along."

"You're kidding right?" Gabe asked. "We're your friends. We're not going to leave you hanging. Even if that means we have to follow along in your delusional crusade."

"It's hardly a crusade, but I appreciate the help." I hesitated, realizing they were waiting for some kind of instruction. "I think we need to split up and watch the crowd as everyone spills out for intermission. If my dad was meeting someone, they'd do it during all the commotion."

It was thin, but it was worth a shot. I was starting to get excited at the possibility, and appreciated the help, but before we could break up into search parties, a man in a suit with a silver name tag walked up to our pow-wow.

"Excuse me, but is there something I can help you with? We don't usually encourage our patrons to get up from their seats between intermissions."

"We're just looking for someone," I said.

"How can I help, young man?"

"My father was supposed to meet me here, that's all."

He paused, looking down at my shoes, and then over the rest of the group. His nose quickly found its place high in the air as his tone changed, like he suddenly realized he was talking to kids. "Well, we'd usually report lost children on the public announcement system at the intermission."

He quickly straightened his tie and grabbed a stack of fliers from the nearest ticket desk, handing one to me. "Please make sure you join us for our upcoming shows. I'm sure there will be some more to your liking," he said. "In the meantime, I do ask that you move closer to the entrance so as not to interrupt the patrons who are actually watching the performance."

Before I could reply, a scratchy voice, like cats playing on velcro, interrupted.

"Seven Murphy-Collins. When I was told you knocked out ol' Dane at Mardi Gras, I didn't believe it. You were such a skinny little worm last I saw you. Well, you're still skinny, but not at all like the little tumor hugging his mother's leg."

Behind Billie, only a few feet away, stood a man I'd never met, yet his face was unmistakable. He was almost as tall as me, with straight blond hair hanging to his chin, sporting a beard to match.

His blue denim shirt was unbuttoned halfway down, showing off some kind of bird tattoo across his chiseled chest. Jericho Splitzer didn't fit any drug dealer stereotype. He should've been a ski instructor, or a mountain climbing guide. Definitely not number nine on the FBI's most-wanted list.

"I didn't expect to see you here. Where's your dad?" he asked smugly.

"Probably rotting in a hole somewhere, Jericho" I said. "Why'd your man attack me?" A pair of tiny fingers pinched the back of my arm but I was too focused on the bastard that tried to have me killed.

He chuckled, stepping closer and resting his hand on Billie's shoulder. I could feel her flinch as his fingers wrapped tight around her collarbone.

Gabe's face wasn't hiding anything; a mix of rage, fear, and a recklessness I didn't realize he possessed.

"Are you familiar with how leverage works?" he asked.

"If you knew my dad at all, you'd know I don't mean shit to him."

He scratched his head. "Is that so? Well, the apple doesn't fall far from the tree. Got some spunk in you!"

"What do you want with my father?" I asked.

"You're a little too young to be diving into the family business, kid. Let's just say he owes me some money and he was supposed to return it to me tonight. I'd like to get that back." He lifted his hand off her shoulder and shifted closer to Piper, smiling at her. "Now, just tell me where he is and I'll be on my way. You can run along and we don't ever have to see each other again."

I could see Billie's mind working overtime, trying to work out some kind of escape.

My cold fingers were suddenly itching beyond control. I tried to scratch them with my other hand, but it didn't help. "How should I know where the bastard is? Why do you think I'm in St. Louis? I came here to find him myself."

"I thought you were looking for some book."

"How do you know about the book?" I asked.

"You're mom wasn't as sneaky as she thought. Junkies never are. The book's worthless, full of incoherent ramblings that can't be proven."

He had to be bluffing about wanting money from Dad. I refused to believe the book was worthless. He was just trying to trick me. If the book could incriminate Dad, then it could probably take him down as well. How many people knew about the book? How much had Mom witnessed?

"I don't really know what you want with some worthless book, but that's not why I'm here. Where's your dad?"

Now I knew he was lying. Why bring it up twice if he didn't care about it?

"The thing about leverage is that it applies to everyone. You, for instance. Which one of these pretty little things means more to you?" he asked, taking a long whiff of Piper's hair. I hoped it smelled like sweat.

I wanted to say Piper but I don't know what he would've done. Could I let him kill her? I didn't need to look at her face to know that I couldn't. I may want to hurt her, but I couldn't let someone else do it.

His hand wrapped around the back of her neck. Her face was sickening, like his very touch was so putrid that she might hurl right there. "Let me put it this way, even if you make lousy leverage, I have this funny feeling that you can find him. So just make it easier on all of us and tell me where he is."

"Gentlemen, I don't really care what business you are discussing, but I need you to clear out of the doorway before the intermission begins." The snooty usher shifted around the circle, with his arms extended out.

"You really don't want to piss me off, kid. Just tell me where your father is," Jericho continued.

"Sir, I must insist," the usher said again. He shuffled even closer, trying to push us out into the lobby.

Jericho's irritation visibly bubbled over as he looked to the ceiling. Without hesitation, he jabbed a knife into the man's midsection, spilling blood on the red carpet. The usher's face went ghost white as he fell forward. His head slammed against the carpet, bouncing twice before flopping to the side in a sticky mess.

We stood in shock, unable to move. Jericho, on the other hand, didn't flinch. He coldly wiped the blade on the usher's jacket and turned to me.

He stared me down, playfully fondling the knife. "I don't want to hurt you kid, but I will, so tell me where your father is."

He reached for me before I was ready.

Crack!

With his attention focused on me, a kid from across the hall grabbed one the banisters that roped off the ticket counter and swung it like a baseball bat at Jericho's ribs.

Just then, the doors behind us opened and a rumble of theatre-goers filled the hallway. "Run, Seven!"

I didn't wait to see who it was, but I heard the kid's voice as I shot through the closest door. "That was Seven Murphy-Collins, the Mardi Gras kid!"

Piper shook her head as we veered down a very ordinary hallway, staggered with brightly lit offices. "I hope you're enjoying your fifteen minutes of fame," she said.

"It came in handy back there, didn't it?" I replied. "Who ever said the Internet was a bad thing?"

"Seven, where are we going?" Gabe asked.

I turned right into a small break room and then through the far door in the corner, which lead to another skinny hallway. "Does it look like I have the faintest clue where we are?"

I threw my shoulder into the last door and it opened to a stairwell. "There has to be an exit at the bottom."

Skipping down the steps, I could hear heavy footsteps fumbling toward the door.

"Ahh!"

Billie stumbled, sliding down the stairs and taking out Gabe at the ankles. I turned to help but Piper pushed me forward. "Keep moving!" I hesitated, but the pounding steps overhead were getting closer. Each thud grew louder, more determined. The door would swing open any second and Jericho would be on top of us.

How could Billie fall? She was the most athletic of the group. What the hell was she doing?

The sign on the concrete wall said level four, then level three. With each subsequent flight, the light dimmed and a stale smell slowly enveloped us. We weren't quiet. I'm sure it sounded like a herd of elephants falling down the stairs. Not exactly covert.

At the base floor, the exit light cast a red hue on the oversized double doors. I reached for the handle, but Piper nearly tackled me into the corner, covering my mouth. There was a crazed look in her eye. I didn't want to know what she was thinking.

I reached for the door again, but she slammed me back against the wall.

"What are you doing? Are you insane?" I whispered.

She slowly glanced over her shoulder at the exit, finally hearing the creak of the stairwell door above. "This is your chance!" she said. "He's alone. You can end this right now."

"Get a hold of yourself! Unlike you, I really don't have a death wish." I picked her up by the waist and moved her to the side.

The exit opened up to the backside of the building along a narrow alley. Without waiting to see if Jericho was still on our tail, I ran to the left, ducking under rusty metal scaffolding. I trusted that everyone was behind me, not wanting to turn around.

At the corner of the building, I made another left, hoping to find a straight shot to the parking lot. My muscles were tight. I was straining to move faster, to pull speed from anywhere. All I could think of was the hope that we might find more people, taxis, any chance for escape.

Instead of safety though, the bitter reality of my grave existence came at me. My stomach turned, and my lungs deflated. A round, motionless object blocked the path. I didn't need to get closer, but I couldn't stay away. Darren's body, cold, broken, and stiff, sprawled across the alley in a lifeless heap.

"Check the other side. Some of Jericho's guys are down there," I said, barely thinking about the words coming from my mouth. As they scattered in the opposite direction, I hung back, creeping close along the edge of the building.

I covered my mouth, keeping my eyes on his. Their color was gone, as was his smile, barely resembling my large friend. His skin was grey and wrinkled, loosely bunched across his wide frame. Slowly reaching down, my finger grazed his ashen forearm. I snapped back. It was sandpaper to the touch, but frigid and loose.

"No, this can't be happening," I whispered.

"What would cause that?" Piper asked.

I turned to the gypsy, the liar, the thief. She'd been hovering behind me, alone. Rage filled my veins as her question sank in. I sprang to her throat with my left hand and smashed her back against the wall. The thump of her skull against the brick felt so good I did it twice.

"Great question," I seethed.

"I didn't do it! I was with you, remember?" she yelled back. "Why would I want to kill the dope?"

"Don't call him that! He's my friend."

"No, he was your friend. Now, he's an oversized baseball mitt."

I took a deep breath and slowly let go of her neck. My knees found the concrete next to his body, trying to make sense of it. I closed his eyes with my shaky, cold hand. He wouldn't notice if his eyes turned blue.

Who would want Darren dead? He wouldn't hurt a fly. "Poor, dumb fool," I whispered.

It wasn't the funeral he should've had. It wasn't the fate he deserved. He was going to suffer for my selfishness and as that truth became clear, it dug at my chest. My skin, my muscles, everything was on fire. Vengeance consumed me. For the first time since my mother died, I found greater hate than I had for my father. Jackson, Death, whatever he was... He was behind this. It had to be him.

Breaking away from her fingers, I found my feet. "Seven, we have to go. Jericho..." Piper whispered. "Come on, it's time."

I turned around, suddenly very aware of our surroundings, and our company. It was easy to hate her, to blame her, but I knew she was right. We had to get out of there.

"Excuse us over here, but what is going on? Is that Darren?" Gabe asked, holding Billie back.

"It had to be her," Billie said, pointing at Piper. "All of this started after you showed up!"

"Don't get your sports bra up in tizzy. I'm not the liar here," Piper snapped back.

"Are you saying that I am?"

"No sweetheart, I don't think you have any angles at all." Piper slid in front, putting Gabe and me on the ends.

I was too shocked to think straight. All I could process was getting out of there. I didn't want to be around if Jackson or Jericho found us in the alley.

A smattering of screams and a roar of footsteps sounded out from inside the building. Someone must've found the usher. "We don't have time for this! We're leaving," I said.

Heading back the way we came sounded like a death wish, so I cut to the end of the alley. From there, we circled around the set of buildings and found the parking lot on the north side of The Hound.

"Do you think Jericho would stick around? The cops have to be on their way." Billie was already on to the next thought. "Look, there's a Metrolink station right there!"

"Forget that noise! Do you see what I do?"

The silver jaguar was like a beacon, shining brightly. The old hag from earlier popped into my head. I smiled crookedly as I recalled the scowl on her wrinkly face. She assumed I was a thief. I wouldn't want to make a liar out of her.

"What are you doing?" Billie cried.

"We don't have time to sit around and wait for a train. On second thought, go ahead. You do that," Piper said, slithering between the rows of cars. People were spilling out into the street. Our window was closing.

"I'm not going to be part of this," Gabe whispered to me. "You know this is wrong."

Piper smiled, nodding her head. She didn't have to say a word. "You act like this is the first time I've stolen a car," I said.

"It's not! But it is the first time I have!" Billie cried.

I looked at her, then Gabe, then back at Piper. She was leaning against the car, arms folded, still smiling.

"Then don't. No one's twisting your arm. You'll be safer this way. He's after me, remember?"

I could see the tears begin to well up, but I didn't care. Jericho and Jackson weren't chasing her. They were after me. "Gabe, can you get home?"

"Of course, but are you sure about this?"

"It'll be fine," I reassured him.

My elbow broke through the window, spraying shards everywhere. The owners were so untouchable that they didn't even bother with an alarm.

Billie's face pulled tight. She spun and yanked Gabe toward the station. The door popped open and Piper jumped in.

I went to work on the wires and was about to start up the car when my conscience struck. I hesitated, looking forward at the Hound.

"They're my friends. I can't just leave them."

"You said it yourself, he's not after them," she said.

"Why should I listen to you?"

"You're not. If it were up to me, we'd go back and find that bastard." She leaned against the windows, putting her elbow against the seat. "Aren't you sick of running?"

The engine roared to life, shaking the seats. "You're right. I'm not listening to you. Let's go."

Chapter 7
THREE STEPS

"It smells like mothballs in here." Piper crawled into the front seat, shoving some bags around as she went.

I drove away from the theatre in a dizzy haze, picturing Darren's face. My fingers dug deeper into the steering wheel with each thought. No matter how hard I tried, I couldn't get away from it. How could he be dead? How could I just let him die? That stupid bastard had no business being there. He should've just told Jackson where I was.

"Keep heading east on the Interstate," Piper said.

"Oh, you have a destination in mind?"

"I do, in fact," she said, grabbing a small purse from the glove compartment like nothing had happened.

"You're serious?" I could feel my irritation coming back, although slower than before. "Fine, where am I headed?"

"Just stay on the highway until you see the Wood River exit." Her eyes lit up as she pulled a big wad of money from the olive clutch and tucked it into the waist of her pants. She caught my grimace in the mirror.

"What? You have something to say? You're not exactly in a position to judge." Her eyes circled the stolen car with a wicked grin.

"It has nothing to do with the money," I grumbled.

"Look! Are you paying attention? That's the exit." Her finger scraped my cheek as she pointed at the sign.

"I'm going to throw you out of the car."

"That's not nice."

"Why are we going to Wood River? I think I've had enough of that place."

"Relax. We're not going into town. I have somewhere else in mind."

"What's that?" I asked.

"It's a great place to clear your head. You'll see."

"Do you really have that problem? Clearing your head?"

I ducked as she whipped a pen at my head. We both laughed for a minute, taking the time to breathe.

"You know who did it, don't you?" she asked in a solemn, low voice.

I looked out the window, silently watching the lights as we sped through the exit. How did I get here? I left home with a mission, plain and simple: find my father, get the book. Somewhere along the way, everything got complicated: first Gabe and Billie, then Joss, now this strange pixie next to me. Darren died because of me. What was next?

I followed the ramp to a four-lane road, heading to the southeast side of town. We hung a right at the stoplight across from the grocery store, than another right at the credit union. We ended up on a back road that led away from town, past a dimly lit subdivision. At the top of the hill, we passed open fields and a few dying streetlights. The road had been paved, but not in the last decade.

I looked around the creepy scene. "Is this where you kill me? In a corn field?" I asked.

"There would be much more poetic ways to do it."

"That wasn't a no."

She snickered. "There-turn left and park across the street from the last house."

I did as she said, but all I could tell was that we were on the edge of a golf course, surrounded by farms. It was too dark to see much of the course itself, but I could make out a No. 2 flag tucked behind some trees across the way.

Piper was out of the car quickly, tracking dark, muddy footsteps across the green. The option of leaving crossed my mind at least a few times. The girl was clinically insane, and mostly I wanted to cause her physical pain, but something made me stay. Perhaps it was just morbid curiosity. Everyone likes a train wreck.

Taking a deep breath, I jumped out of the car after her.

"Look up!" she yelled, laying down in the fairway. "There's no better place to see the stars in the entire city."

I scratched my head and looked around.

"Come on pansy; don't tell me I have to make you."

It wasn't peer pressure, but a constant threat of violence, from a girl half my size. What the hell? We already stole a car and ran from a crime scene. Getting arrested for trespassing seemed like the natural progression. I swallowed my pride and laid down next to her.

The ground was freezing, sending chills down my back. She was right about the view. It was amazing, like looking into a field of diamonds.

"Wow, you're right. It reminds me of home. The desert always had so many stars."

"Do you miss home? Vegas, right?"

"Yeah, that's right, but I don't miss it."

"Why?"

"Because nothing good ever happened there. What about you? What's your story?"

"Oh, I have a home."

"Do tell."

"It's a mansion. You know the kind with a really long driveway, lined by skinny Christmas trees? It's like that."

"You don't say." She was homeless, and a liar. I checked to make sure I wasn't looking in a mirror. I wasn't, but apparently I'd make a very pretty girl.

"So, what's up with your hand?"

"What's up with your hand?" I replied.

"Mine's fine, see?" She held up her right fist, extending her middle finger near my face.

"Nice."

"Seriously, what's up with your hand?"

"Nothing."

"I have a dark blue handprint on my ass that would prove otherwise."

"That wasn't your ass. It was your back."

"Whatever makes you sleep better, but it sure seemed like you were copping a feel."

"I wish," I blurted out before thinking. Shit. Blood rushed to my cheeks and heat filled my head.

I caught the twist of her lips as she continued to stare up at the stars. "I don't think shelter girl would appreciate that little slip," she said.

"What do you have against Joss?" I asked, surprising myself.

"What do you? Every time her name comes up you get really defensive. What are you defending?"

"I think we're done talking about Joss."

She exhaled for a few seconds and groaned. "I know you're lying about your hand." She reached over to swipe at it but I jerked my arm away. "That guy from Mardi Gras dropped like a rock when you hit him."

"I must not know my own strength," I said, happy to cause her some aggravation for once.

"Yeah, you're the strongest. How's that black eye?" She got up before I could come up with a clever quip.

"What now?" I asked, climbing to my feet, losing patience.

"Now, I'm thirsty. Come on." Her feet bounced with each step, making me nervous.

"Has anyone ever tested you for ADD? What are you going to do? Drink from the water hazard?"

She disappeared behind a group of trees. I was still wondering if I should jump in the car, but I followed around the cart path, over the wooden fence, and down the hill. She hummed a low, creepy tune as she bounced in and out of the trees.

"So, you know about my family, thanks to Boudreaux. What about yours? How do they afford that big house with all the Christmas trees?" If nothing else, I figured her answer would be entertaining.

"They're great," she said quickly. "Tell me about your friends, the preachy one and the dyke."

"He's not... well, he is. Gabe's going to be a priest."

She rolled her eyes.

"Billie's not a lesbian though. Why do you hate her so much?"

"How well do you really know her?" she asked, swinging around the base of a tree.

"Better than I know you, thief."

"That's true, but did you actually see her trip in that stairwell?"

"You're saying that she fell on purpose?" I leaned against a wooden sign, curious to hear her response.

"You should be a little more careful about who you hang out with," she said, trying to look me in the eyes from her tip-toes. It wasn't even close. She hissed and jumped on a bench, smiling down as she tried to make her point.

"Speaking of who we hang out with," I said. "Tell me about Christine Dru."

Piper stopped in place and spun on one foot to lean against a tree, looking cuter than I expected. For some reason, I tried to imagine her all dolled up, like Joss. It didn't work. She wouldn't look right with make-up. She didn't need it. Her raggedy clothes hung off her in a way that left a lot to the imagination, in a good way. Her messy hair hung over her face, making her snowy eyes mysterious. And when she did smile, it almost made me forget about how she had robbed me. In her own way, she was much prettier in her just-rolled-out-of-bed-don't-care-what-you-think style.

"Christine was a piece of work," she said, leaning down to get my eye contact. I quickly looked away, as if I hadn't been ogling her. "I remember the time she was robbing the landlord in order to pay rent. He caught her in the act, which I could tell was a rare occurrence. She had a knife on him before he could blink."

It wasn't the single mother I'd been picturing. "What'd she do then?" I asked.

"Bree started crying and distracted her," she replied. "He was able to break free but she clocked him with a phone."

"Sounds like a doll," I said.

"She was a good mom, always fed Bree first. She hated living in that apartment, but the subway is no place for a five-year-old to sleep while her mother lifted wallets. You know?"

Suddenly my mother didn't look quite as bad.

"Do you know why she was so determined to find my dad?"

She eyed me closely, tucking some hair behind her ear. "She said the guy from Vegas knew too much, things that she couldn't talk about.

Christine never shared much, but whatever that guy had, spooked her pretty good. Which was weird, because I couldn't imagine many things that would spook that woman."

Things started fitting together in my head. Christine must've worked for Jericho. I wondered what she stole for him and why it scared her so much. Mom must've seen what she took and written it in my baby book.

"Is that where we're headed?" I asked, pointing at circular building down the fairway.

The clubhouse had a banquet room that sat behind the first tee box, throwing light across the parking lot. Laughter rolled out in waves when anyone stumbled out for a smoke. The air smelled like beer and cigars. A few guys stood outside, shutting down a hot dog grill and staring into the darkness of the course. A few of them were pissing into the bushes by the practice green.

"Now," she said, "there are three steps to clearing your head."

Words started to come out, but I couldn't put them together into cohesive sentence.

"Here's the first step. Ready?"

"My head's clear. No steps needed," I said, stuttering.

She raised her eyebrow and looked at my forehead. "Nope, not buying it. The first step is simple: lie to a cop."

Without warning, she walked up to the overweight guy behind the aluminum table. The transformation was deadly. In her most girly, not-Piper voice, she seduced him with eight words. "Hey sweetie, can I get a few drinks?"

That's all it took. He indiscreetly tried to straighten his blue tank top and reached for the nearest cooler. "Sure, honey. What can I get for ya?"

"Two tequila tonics. Can you put them in those big glasses?"

"The glass ones?"

"Yep, those are perfect."

He threw me a skeptical look but I tried not to respond. I'm glad I wasn't the only one who thought she was crazy. When he bent over to grab the clear bottle, a badge dangled from under his belt. I went to grab her arm, but when I did, she pulled me in closer and wrapped her arm around my waist.

"Do I know you, honey?" he asked.

"I'm the new dispatcher. The name's Claire. I don't think we've met yet."

"Oh, sorry about that," he said. "You got a name?" he asked, looking back at me.

"Collin. What's yours?" I asked, trying to fake a yawn.

"I'm Pete McKay. Nice to meet you. Look honey, don't let the Sergeant give you a hard time. He's usually rough on new people."

"Thanks! I'll keep that in mind," she said. "Hey, when Detective Boudreaux comes around, can you tell him I said hello?"

Piper leaned over and pulled the money roll from the inside of her jeans. He shook his head with a grin and rubbed his goatee. "Sure thing."

"We're gonna take a romantic walk on the course. Thanks, love."

I took her lead, quickly scooting away, trying to seem nonchalant.

"Step one: done," she whispered.

"Are you crazy?" That was a dumb question.

"Loosen up, will ya?"

We took the long way around the outside of the banquet room, sneaking glances inside when the bushes allowed. Leftover food and drinks were scattered everywhere. Crunch sounds from golf shoes echoed off the walls. It was some kind of tournament but I couldn't make out the sign behind the front table. Then it hit me. It was their dress that was throwing me off. Most of them had badges, but a handful were also wearing purple sashes. I started to count, but the branches got in the way.

"Did you see those sashes?" Piper asked.

"Is this your idea of a good time? Do you realize what will happen--"

"God, you whimper like a little girl." She nudged me with her hip and grinned. "You're so uptight. Here, take this." She held out my drink.

I grabbed the glass and looked forward, shaking my head. I was slowly learning not to ask why. As we got to the other end of the building, the parking lot opened up to a maze of red and blue lights, sending a violent storm of fear through me. My feet jerked to a stop and I grabbed the back of her shirt.

"Piper... This has to be some kind of fundraiser for the police station!"

"Seriously, will you just calm down? Breathe. It's going to be okay."

"No, it's not. There's a reason I'm not stuck in juvee right now. This is insane."

"Are you calling me insane?"

Flint Ory

"No, well maybe, but staying here would definitely be insane. I like my freedom."

"A little insanity can keep you sane. You're really uptight."

I started to laugh. "You know, I've been called a lot of things, but that's definitely a first."

"Please! You're wound so tight, it's not even funny. So what if you're hungry a little now and then. Get over it. You're free to do what you want, when you want. Nobody's checking on you, making sure you're following the rules, home on time, staying out of trouble. If you'd just loosen up, you wouldn't be afraid of Jericho."

"Did you see what happened tonight? That usher might be dead."

"All the more reason to take him down."

"How is that my responsibility?"

Her frosty eyes grew big with excitement. "How is it not?"

I didn't want to know her logic behind that question. "And you think I could hurt him, with my hand?"

A pink hue immediately filled her cheeks. "How would you know unless you try?"

"You really have it out for that guy."

She scrunched her nose. "Fine, forget about the hand. Forget about Jericho. You should have a little fun though, lighten up, and unwind," twirling in place as she said it.

"My friends would disagree."

"Life's too short to let Gabe and his hypocritical nun drag you down. I'd think you, of all people, would get that."

"I'm not uptight!"

"No?"

"No," I growled.

"Okay, I'm going to need you to prove it."

"Prove it?"

"I told you. It's a three step process."

I was too exhausted to argue anymore. "Fine, what's the second step?"

Still grinning, she jumped on the cement parking block, and then onto the tree planter made of thick railroad ties. She looked over at me, then at the top of the police cruiser to her right. Her foot hovered over the top of the car, dangling inches above the roof.

"The alarm's going to go off."

"No it won't. You just have to keep... balance." Her sole came to rest on the surface, right behind the lights. She took a quick breath and smiled at the clubhouse. She shifted her weight and placed her other foot on the hood. Beaming with triumph, she waved at me to join her. "Come on. Step two!"

My tough exterior felt flimsy. I looked back at the banquet hall. What the hell was I thinking? I couldn't throw everything away just to see if I could live up to a dare. She was completely nuts, maybe suicidal. I was sure of it. Everything I'd been through... was it worth it? My foot inched back, pulling my weight with it.

"Please tell me you've got more balls than that," she hissed.

There was something about the little temptress, foolishly dancing on the car. I jumped on the tree planter and held my arms out to the side, balancing myself, karate-kid-style. My foot hovered near hers. Finally, I closed my eyes and felt the metal beneath my shoe. I stopped, unsure if I trusted the roof to hold my full weight.

"I'm pretty sure this kind of thing isn't tested in the collision inspections," I said, trying to smile.

"Life isn't tested. Keep going. One foot doesn't count."

I closed my eyes. My weight shifted and my foot followed, finally coming to a rest. No alarms, no cave-ins.

"Holy Shit! That's incredible!"

Piper waited with a fiendish look of excitement. "Step three."

"Really? I passed your little test. What else could you possibly want?"

She held each glass up, looking out of the corner of her eye, from left to right. With a wild motion, the glasses flew to the ground, exploding into pieces.

"Step three." She jumped down, grabbing two slivers of the broken glass.

I cocked my head to the side and jumped off the car. "What are you going to do with those?"

The smaller of the two fit perfectly in her hand, which concerned me. Another sinister spark flashed across her face as she skipped back and forth in front of the car.

I looked down at the glass, then traced it up to the tiny cut on her palm where she gripped the shard too tight.

"What are you doing?"

"Establishing a line." She winked and slid to the side, revealing a navy, police jacket in the back window. The jacket wasn't the cause for my heart to skip a beat. The name stitched above the crest was another matter altogether.

"Detective R. Boudreaux," I read aloud.

"You... you knew this was his car. You knew he'd be here. This wasn't random. It couldn't have been."

"I never said it was."

"Do you have some kind of death wish?"

"I sat in that cell for Fifteen hours, thirty-three minutes, and twenty-four seconds! I'm a seventeen-year-old girl that was attacked by a drug dealer. I don't have a badge! I don't own a gun! But, I do have a voice!"

With a wild stab, the glass knife ripped into the tire, creating an explosion of air. It sank down and to the left as she yanked the glass from the rubber. She giggled with excitement. "And he's going to hear it."

She handed me the second shard. "Go ahead."

I shook my head in disbelief.

"What have they ever done for you? Have they caught Jericho? Did they find your dad? No, they locked you up for helping a girl in trouble. Are you okay with that?"

Then, for some reason, I stopped asking questions. I didn't know the answers, and for once, I realized that I just didn't care. I grabbed the glass because I wanted to. There was no driving force, no reason, and no end goal. I just wanted to, and that was enough. Screw the reasons. Screw right and wrong, good, evil, heaven, hell, and everything in between. Screw trying to live up to Joss' expectations. Because it would feel good to piss them all off... Because it would send a message... Because I was free... And because, well, just because.

I slashed Boudreaux's other tire and the car sunk completely on its side. Piper jumped back on the tree planter, screaming with glee.

"Now what?" I asked.

"Now, we dance," she said.

We danced, or pranced, whatever you'd call it, when someone skips around to music they can't hear, slashing tires of every car in a lot. It was reckless, and a little insane, but I guess that can keep you sane. As the last car dropped to its knees, she jumped up, latching to my waist. She squealed and hugged me as she tossed her weapon in the air. She was raving mad, and for some reason, it worked for her. I held her little body tight, getting lost in the powdery blue flecks in her eyes.

A moment of confusion swept over me. What was I doing? I hated this girl. Ever since I met her, nothing but bad things have happened. What about Joss? What was I doing?

As if she could sense my confusion, she jumped down and headed back the way we came. "Come on!" she pulled me along.

I glanced around at the wreckage. Tens of thousands in damage, not a single car was missed.

"Where are we going?" I yelled after her.

"That's all three steps. Time to go!" she yelled back, cackling as she sprinted ahead.

The jog was much shorter than what I remembered on the way in. Maybe it was just that I knew where I was going. Maybe it was the fear of getting caught. Maybe it was the tequila. Either way, the car was a welcome site. I could see it peeking out from behind the trees surrounding the green.

Piper was, of course, not in a huge hurry to make our clean escape. She jumped in the sand trap, kicking up waves of brown as she laughed hysterically.

"Come on, we've gotta get out of here. I don't want to see the wrath of a hundred cops."

"It's not like they could catch us anyway. You know," she said, tapping her finger on her lips, "if I could introduce you today, I would say, hello, this is my bad influence."

"Yeah, because I'm the influencer here..."

"I think sand traps should have quick sand."

I shook my head and stared at my feet, trying to avoid asking why. The dew on the fringe was soaking through my shoes and sending a chill through my toes. I kept watching the blades of grass as they got longer, eventually leading up to the small gravel on the side of the road.

I looked back at Piper, lying in the sand, smiling. Like magic, she had a way of erasing the pain. Maybe she had it all figured out. She seemed happy. She wasn't worried about picking fights with an entire police force. Why should I care about a drug dealer, or Jackson, for that matter? Why would I worry about Darren's death? He made the choice, not me. As long as I made my father pay, what did I care who got pissed off along the way?

I finally reached the car and wrapped my fingers around the door handle. I heard a click, but it had nothing to do with the car.

"Hold it right there, son!"

It wasn't the over-confident voice I expected from a cop, but the sound of a weapon sliding from a leather holster was enough to get my attention. The black berretta, standard issue, did all the talking. His hand shook violently like the handle was burning hot, but even he wouldn't miss from that distance. With each wave of the gun, his finger slid further away from the trigger. I was quite certain he'd never come close to firing it.

"Put your hands on your head!" He had to be near retirement. He looked like he could barely hold up his own weight, yet alone chase bad guys.

"Shouldn't you be playing golf with the rest of them?"

"I said, put your hands on your head!" His voice grew louder, but his tone wasn't any less shaky.

Slowly, and steadily, I raised my open palms and placed them on top of my head as instructed. Piper was behind me. I hadn't realized it until then, but she did the same, rolling her eyes. "Are you serious?" She hissed at me. "You're going to let this goof arrest you?"

"Now, get down on your knees. Keep your hands where they are. Make sure I can see them."

"What do you want me to do? I'm not wearing teflon," I sarcastically whispered.

"Here we go again," she whispered. "Is this how you want to go down? On some bum trespassing charge because a glorified mall cop pointed his trembling hand at you?" She shook her head as she got to her knees.

The old man crept closer. He had cuffs in one hand, barely able to stop them from rattling together. "Put your hands out!"

I did as he asked, but never took my eyes off Piper. She was trying to hold something back. I could see it running wild under her skin. Her bottom lip hung open, waiting to say something. I squinted, trying to read her facial expression

We kneeled motionless as he approached, but when he got within arm's reach, she snapped.

"Is this how you're going to punish your father?"

As much as I wanted to lash out at Piper, I couldn't. Her words felt like bait, but they tasted like freedom. I didn't hear them once, but repeatedly.

Any piece of humanity dissolved. Complex, conscience-laden choices, like attacking police officers, became beautifully simple.

I didn't fight through purgatory so I could return to my pathetic excuse for a life. I didn't even come back to hang out with a girl. I came back because my father killed her. He killed my mother the same way he killed so many other addicts: slowly, milking them for their money while he fed their addiction. I couldn't let him get away with that. He stole her, and my childhood. Since the cops weren't going to do anything, I was, and this old man wasn't going to stand in my way.

I opened my eyes to the sound of rubber soles on gravel, and the smell of bad aftershave. A thin, bony hand grabbed my wrist and I could feel the steel rings slide around my wrist. She was right. I couldn't let this happen. I wasn't going back to foster care. I'd come too far for that.

Before he could react, I threw my shoulder into his chest and knocked the gun out of his hands. We both fell to the ground, rolling into the grass. I scrambled to my feet, spinning to find the gun. It was by the tire, nestled into the gravel.

Piper made a break for the car, starting up the engine. I used my sleeve to pick up the gun and point it at the old man, careful not to leave any fingerprints.

"What are you waiting for?" Piper asked. Her sick little smile was full of excitement.

"Hold on! Let me think!"

The old man rolled over in the ditch, looking up at me. "Don't do this son. You don't want to do this."

"Cuff yourself," I said waving the gun. I'd gone too far to turn back.

He shook his head and obeyed. When I heard the click, I breathed a sigh of relief.

I couldn't even finish my thought. Screw it. I tossed the gun. His keys were still in the ignition, so I yanked them out. I also ripped the radio handset from the dashboard.

"Are you done yet?" Piper asked.

"Yeah, I'm done." In more ways than one, I thought to myself as we sped away.

Chapter 8
CROSSING THE LINE

Last night's thrill of excitement wore off quickly. I was glad to be back in the bank, but I didn't like what I was seeing in the money drawer. Two lonely bills hid in the back, beneath the St. Louis Blues schedule. Shifting them around didn't make a difference. I couldn't force them to make baby twenties.

I'd been so focused on my dad and the book that I forgot Piper stole my money. Starvation quickly moved to the top of my growing list of concerns. At least there was a solution to that problem. I flipped through the schedule until I found today's game. I would use my last forty bucks as seed money.

That slight glimmer of hope couldn't mask what was really going on though. My gut wasn't churning because I was hungry. I was used to that feeling. This new strangeness didn't have anything to do with food.

I couldn't get Piper out of my head. I kept thinking about last night and, for a split second, how I almost kissed her. I still didn't quite understand how that happened. She was evil. I knew she was, but there was something about her that drove me crazy. More than crazy, it made me want to be with her. I was free with Piper, free to do whatever I wanted. I didn't have to live up to some stereotype or angelic mold of how Joss thought I should be.

Maybe I really was crazy. Or maybe I was just trying to get back at Joss for lying. I didn't think it was that simple. Part of me, a deep hidden pocket I didn't want to think about, actually wished it would've happened. I wondered what it would've been like, what her lips felt like. Was I really into her?

The rumble in my stomach grew at the thought of kissing anyone but Joss. How could I? Even in my current anger, she was it. She was the girl for me. Her face was etched in my mind when I closed my eyes at night. She was the first thought when I woke up. She was kind, and selfless and even after all the lying about DCFS, I trusted her. I trusted her more than I'd trusted anyone, definitely more than Piper. I could picture us together, even if my future was doomed. She wanted me to be a better person and for some reason, that mattered to me. I wanted to be a better person. Somehow, I had to show her that.

Aside from my girl troubles, I was starting to realize that I was in a lot of trouble. Why did I slash those tires? Why did I knock out that cop? How stupid could I have been?

A loud thud rattled the front door. Instinctively, I reached down and grabbed the money and my jacket. I was half way to the door when curiosity grabbed hold of me. Was it Boudreaux or Jericho? Could it be Jackson? For some reason I was convinced it would be Boudreaux. I ducked down, leaning around a structural pole to peek through the window.

I was wrong. It was none of them. I breathed a sigh of relief, but I couldn't fully relax.

Joss was standing at the door, looking rather cold and angry in a thick ivory hoodie. I moved closer to the wall, slinking up to the window to get a better look. Beneath that fuzzy hood was white-blond hair, draped over and around a disheveled scowl.

She hit the door with the back of her fist twice more, exhaling fire into the cold air.

The back exit looked awfully inviting, but I eventually gave in and trudged to the door. It was an odd feeling to not want to see Joss. Billie must've told her what happened last night. She'd probably be disgusted with my actions.

"Did you have a late night?" she asked as the door swung open.

Like always, her beauty nearly knocked me over. It was hard not to stare. "Yeah, something like that."

Maybe if I played dumb.

I watched her fling her purse into the chair and stomp into the bathroom. She put a handful of water bottles on top of the old cabinet for me. Maybe she wasn't that mad. No, the fire escape still looked tempting. Hell, so did the front door as she stomped into the lobby.

"Okay, let's get this straight. You can be mad at me for hiding the truth about my job, but that's nothing compared to this." Her arms crossed over her curvy chest as she waited for me to say something.

It took me about thirty seconds, but I finally strung a few words together. "I can explain."

"Oh, please do. This should be good. Which part first? The part where some poor guy got stabbed? Or maybe the part where you ditched your friends? Or even better-how about the part where you picked a fight with an entire police department?"

Again, she held her ground, eyes drawn to a squint. Her twang couldn't cover up the viciousness in her voice.

"Sounds like you got the whole play-by-play. Let me guess... Billie?"

"Well, yeah, she called me last night. But I didn't need to hear about the golf course from her. I could've just picked up a newspaper."

"What did you say?"

She stomped across the room. "Do you have any idea how much trouble you're in? Half the town is looking for you!"

I looked across the room at nothing in particular. An image of that parking lot, full of police cruisers, flashed in my head. She was right. Every single one of them now had a reason to hunt me down.

Last night it seemed so free, so liberating to lash out. The weight was lifted from my shoulders. I wasn't thinking about Darren's death, my father or finding that book. As Joss explained the consequences though, that freedom was sucked dry. The weight came crashing back, only ten times heavier.

For the first time, a thought crossed my mind. What if Joss knew about Piper? How would she react? It actually felt better to imagine that she'd be hurt. It meant that she cared. What if I had just ruined my already slim chances?

"What are you going to do?" she asked.

I didn't have to play out too many scenarios to determine that there was only one option.

"Where are you going?" Joss asked as I stuffed the cash in my pocket and grabbed my jacket.

"Work," I replied, brushing past her.

"You're just going to leave? How can you think about scalping tickets right now? Did you not hear what I just told you?"

"I'm out of money and food. It won't do me any good to starve to death before I leave."

"Leave? You're leaving?" she asked.

"I thought that's what you wanted me to do in the first place. Do you expect me to stick around and let Boudreaux cart me off to jail?"

She didn't have an answer, so I kept moving.

"You can't leave!" Her footsteps rattled the fire escape behind me.

"Really? Why is that?" I asked. "Because the other day in Wood River you were practically begging me to leave." The anger in my response surprised me, but once I started, I couldn't stop.

"How are you going to find your dad if you just run away?"

I stopped at the doorway. "I'm not. Again, why does that matter to you now? It didn't before."

Silence was her answer. That's all I ever got from her. Any time she actually had to open up, she'd shut down, like she hadn't quite convinced herself that I was good enough. I wasn't, so I kept walking.

"No!" she yelled, causing me to stop again.

"No?"

Her hair always got in her face when she was mad. She brushed it back into the hoodie. "Don't you dare! Don't try to push me away!"

"I'm not pushing you away. Maybe I'm just sick of trying to find someone that doesn't want to be found. I'm not a fucking bloodhound."

She shoved me up against the brick building, gripping my arm tight. I didn't know where her sudden aggression came from but I liked it.

"You're going through something right now. I get that. But I'm not going to let you throw everything away and take the easy way out." She shoved me again as I rolled my eyes. "I've seen this before. All that time in the shelter... Believe me, I've seen what happens when people quit caring."

I hated it when she compared me to them. "What exactly do you think I'm throwing away? If you haven't noticed, I don't have a lot to lose."

"Nothing to lose? What about your friends? What about me?"

"That's not good enough," I said. "They'll be relieved when I'm gone-one less homeless kid to worry about. So will you."

"How can you say that?" She sniffled in the cold air.

"Why do you care what happens to me?" I demanded, leaning over her.

"Because you're my friend," she said. Tears gathered in the corners of her eyes.

She shoved me again, this time my head bounced hard off the brick. Her face was only inches away from mine. I caught some people watching from across the street.

"Last night, when you were getting the story from Billie, I know she told you that I wasn't alone."

She nodded her head. "Yeah, she told me about the girl."

"Her name's Piper," I said, unsure why. "Why didn't you ask me about her?"

"It's none of my business."

"It is if you want it to be. It always has been." I stopped to breathe and stretch my fingers. My hand was pulsing with cold bursts. "Why do you care?" I yelled, spinning so her back was against the bricks. "Why?"

"Because-" Her bottom lip quivered. "Because I didn't want to know!"

"Why?"

Her response was the one I'd been wanting since that first night in the shelter. Her lips were soft like a pillow, but wet from the tears. Heaven tasted like caramel. My mind, my thoughts, everything went snow white. I wrapped my arms around her as she rested her hand against my chest. I wasn't sure if it was because I was taller, or if she was ensuring I wouldn't leave. There was no threat of that.

When we finally parted, her eyes grew wide and her cheeks flushed a carmine hue. She took a deep breath and looked up at me with an embarrassed gaze. My chest was exploding into a repercussion of heartbeats. My breath was completely gone and both of my hands were numb, but I'd never felt better in all my life.

"I would've yelled at you a long time ago had I known that's what it would take," I said, my legs still shaking.

"Yes, apparently I like it when you act like an ass." She leaned in again, this time much shorter as she was out of breath too.

"Luckily, that's one of my specialties."

"Look, I'm not going to pretend I know what you're going through, but I can't imagine you giving up." She leaned in, close enough to whisper. Her breath washed over me, luring me in for another kiss.

"What do you want me to do?" I finally asked.

"I want to help you find your dad. If there's even a small chance..."

"I need the book too," I said.

"It's really that important?"

"The book is everything. Without it, there's no proof of the things he did."

"It's more than that," she tilted her head to meet my eyes. "You look so desperate when you talk about it. What's so special about that book?"

I leaned back and sighed, knowing she wouldn't let it go. "It's the only connection I have to my mother. She gave up her life trying to protect me and I refuse to let it mean nothing."

I still wasn't thrilled about continuing the search, but maybe she had a point. Maybe I could find him first. I didn't have any leads and I felt further away from finding the book than ever, but what the hell.

"Fine, but I want you to remember that this was your idea."

She gave me a peck on the lips, reminding me why I was suddenly agreeable. "Fine, but you need to remember I kissed you first, sugar."

"I won't forget."

I wanted to stay in that spot forever, but my head was starting to hurt from hunger. I looked down the street toward the Metrolink station, then back at the bank.

"Do you want to wait at the bank?" I asked.

She covered her mouth as she laughed. "Seven, I can buy some food."

"No. I can take care of myself," I said firmly.

"If you're going out, someone may recognize you."

"I'll be fine." The thought of being a celebrity seemed absurd.

I could see that she wanted to argue, but I wasn't going to change my mind.

"Fine, but I'm coming with you," she said. "I'm going to help."

"I didn't ask for help."

"And I didn't give you a choice." She walked past me, heading for the station.

* * *

My mind wandered as the Metrolink rambled down the horizontal dividing line of St. Louis. The northern half of the city was run down, rough and dangerous. The southern half had all the money, huge buildings, nice houses, and a beautiful landscape.

I was happy to have Joss with me. Just having her near seemed to defuse my worries. But part of me wondered where Piper was. How was she going to deal with the fallout from last night? She probably ran. It was the smart move. I couldn't picture her sticking around and risking jail. I hoped she was safe.

Joss slid in beside me after reading the map. "Mind if I sit here?"

Just having her near me changed my entire demeanor. No matter how hard I tried, I couldn't stop smiling. "Where's your ticket, young lady?" I asked.

"Same place as yours."

We looked up in unison to a sign warning that riding with a ticket would result in a $250 fine plus a night in jail.

"See, that's how it starts. Before long, you're going to be lifting expensive underwear from Victoria's Secret."

My mind played with the imagery. I forced myself to stop before I got too excited.

"I worked for DCFS. I couldn't afford nice things like that." She smiled beneath her blond locks, freezing me in place. "Does it make you feel better to joke about it?"

"What's that?" I asked, still frazzled from the underwear talk.

"Stealing."

"Oh, I don't know. Maybe a little."

She frowned. "There are other ways to live. You have so much potential."

"Quit it," I groaned. "I'm not one of your shelter kids. I choose to live this way." Something she said just hit me. "Shelter... You said worked, as in you don't work there anymore. Did you quit?"

"I had to," she said. "They were going to find out that I broke you out eventually."

I looked at my shoes, wishing I felt worse about her losing her job. I didn't though. It meant that she wasn't part of DCFS anymore and I didn't have to compete for her time.

She bit her tongue and smiled, avoiding eye contact.

It was too early for the hockey rush so the train was nearly empty, but the people that were on-board kept staring. I didn't blame them. Joss was worth the second look, or a fifth one.

I tried to ignore it, but the sideways glances were constant. "This is our stop," I said, standing up and heading for the front. I made eye contact with the conductor, who stared just a little bit longer than he should of. I turned around to find Joss hovering behind my shoulder.

"Okay, I give."

She looked confused.

"I'm watching every guy in sniffing distance perk up as you walk by. It's annoying. As happy as I am that you're here, I can't figure out why you're here with me."

She leaned around my shoulder, softly touching my arm. "Are you sure they're staring at me? They seem to be looking at you."

"Don't give me that. You're the stereotype of a seventeen-year-old's wet dream." Her eyes immediately hit the floor. "Look, I couldn't tell you the last time I cut my hair. I badly need a shave because I'm starting to resemble a muskrat. I wear the same clothes all the time because it's all I have, and I smell a little funny because I have to sneak showers out of any public bathroom I can find."

"You're also kind--when you want to be--intelligent, witty, determined, tall, dark, and handsome. Where is this coming from? You should be comfortable in your own skin. I like you, and if I didn't want to be with you, I wouldn't be here. "

I stopped, but the door flung open, slapping me in the face. Joss burst out laughing.

"Oh, and you're graceful. Did I mention that?"

I recovered, physically, and hopped onto the platform before the doors shut again. "Sorry, I guess I never noticed all the staring before."

"Don't be sorry. But I wasn't kidding. I really think they're staring at you."

I looked up, catching a few more eyes. She was right. I just assumed everyone was looking at her.

"Where do we go to do our ticket thing?" she asked. "This place is starting to give me the heebie-jeebies."

"Heebie-jeebies?" I smirked.

"Be nice."

I twisted at the waist, surveying the surroundings again. We were the focus of the otherwise mundane, concrete scenery. Random people glanced our way like we were standing on a red carpet. A couple in loud blue and gold jackets stared from across the platform. They were looking at the map, but every few seconds their eyes shifted our way. An old man, getting a soda from the vending machine, fumbled with a quarter because his eyes were on us.

"What is going on? First the people on the Metrolink, now this?" She asked.

"They must be thrown off by my tall, dark, and handsome presence," I said, cocking my head to the side.

"Maybe we don't have to worry about you being arrested. I'm not sure they'd have a cell big enough for your head." Her lips curled, but the strain never left her face.

"Come on, let's get out of here." I grabbed her hand tight and moved down the stairs, but the creepy feeling only got worse.

The street was empty, with all the warmth of a coffin. It was still hours until the puck dropped, but usually there'd be people hanging out, looking for tickets. Nothing. Cemeteries had more movement.

"Was it canceled or something? Where are all the people? Where are the scalpers?"

We circled the building, twice. After about thirty minutes, and blue fingers, we finally found someone. An overweight arena worker stumbled out of the entrance. His navy uniform was sloppy, barely tucked in, with stains on his stomach.

"Hey!"

He didn't turn.

"Hey!" I shouted loud enough to startle Joss. That finally got his attention. He pulled earbuds out and scratched his scruffy jowls.

"What?" He asked grouchily.

"Is there still a game tonight?"

He looked around like I was crazy. "Yeah, why?"

"Where's the crowd? I need tickets."

"The box office is just in through those doors, but they ain't open yet."

"Not those tickets. I want good ones. Where are the scalpers?"

"You from 'round here?"

"No, I'm from down south, near Little Rock."

"That's funny... You look like that kid from the news. Anyway, I guess no one told you. The scalpers aren't working anymore. After that last one went missing, the rest of 'em quit showing up. It's not worth the risk, ya know?"

"What are you talking about?" I asked.

"My buddy John says some lunatic's keeping them in a basement. My money says they're dead."

"Hold up there, Grizzly Adams. How many scalpers are missing?"

"I think they're saying three."

I felt the air jump from my lungs. "Three?"

I was sure Joss was thinking about Jericho, but I knew in my gut that it wasn't him.

It was Jackson.

My gut stirred, scrambling into a mush of guilt. It was hard enough to think about Darren, to picture his face as Jackson ripped the life out of him. Now there were three deaths, all on my hands.

My mind was racing, wondering what he'd do next. What would he do when there weren't any more scalpers to kill? Could I sit back and let him hurt more people?

A sickening thought hit me. What if he wasn't going to hurt more scalpers? What if he shifted gears and went after my friends? I'd been so selfish, worrying about Jericho and the cops, but I never contemplated how much danger I'd put everyone else in. How could I be so stupid? Their faces flipped through my head: Gabe, Billie, Piper, one by one until I stopped on Joss. I imagined her face, all leathery and cold like Darren's. Sweat beaded up on my brow. My throat was dessert dry and I felt shaky like I might black out. If he got his hands on her I'd never forgive myself. I couldn't.

"Um, thanks for your help. We'll have to come back later when the box office opens."

"So, you're not him, huh? That Six kid. You look just like him."

"Got no idea who you're talking about," I shouted over my shoulder. Our feet couldn't shuffle fast enough, making our way back.

"Three people?" Her voice was faint.

"We need to get out of here," I said, pulling her around the metal railing.

"What kind of monster would do something like this?" she asked.

A loud screech interrupted our escape. We jumped back to the curb, barely avoiding a set of old tires. Melted rubber filled my nostrils.

"What in the world are you doing?" Gabe's voice overpowered his beat-up Corsica. "Are you insane? If anyone spots you..." He reached back and unlocked the door. "Get in!"

Before we could climb inside, I caught something in the corner of my eye. A huge figure appeared on the opposite side of the car, towering over us. My head flipped back to Joss. Her eyes were frozen in place. Her bony fingers latched deep into my arm. The street seemed to fade into a dark cloud. It fell over the top of us and all I could smell was rot, growing into a mildew that pinched my senses. Jackson stood with his arms crossed. A wide grin was plastered across his face.

"Are you looking for tickets?" he asked. "I've got one with your name on it."

Joss let out a sharp gasp. "Seven, who is he?" she whispered.

He looked down and raised an eyebrow, studying her face.

"Get behind me," I yelled to Joss. But it was too late. He already caught the fear in her eye.

He swung around to get a better look. I was dying inside, watching his mind work, imagining all the things he could do to her. This was my worst nightmare, coming true right before my eyes.

"And who are you supposed to be?" Jackson leaned on the rusted hood. "His girlfriend?" The engine sizzled and died at his touch. Green smoke billowed from underneath the chassis. Gabe jumped out of the car, backed away and stumbled to my side.

"Wow Seven, she's a looker. How'd you pull that off?" he asked.

"Stay away from her!" I demanded, drawing back.

There was a staircase just a few feet away that led underground to a MetroLink station.

"Do you really think I'd hurt a beautiful little thing like that?" he asked, grinning.

"I won't let you," I said, my right hand burning.

"Oh, that's not fair," he said. "Now she's like forbidden fruit. Maybe I will hurt her. After all, I can't be blamed for what happens. That's on your shoulders," he said, sliding closer. "Let me explain what happens next. I'll do it slowly. I'll drain the life from her until she's within an inch of death." He extended his hand, spreading a chill through the air. "Then I'll stop and watch while she begs you to kill her." He tapped his finger against his head. "Yeah, I like that plan. You'll have to put her out of her misery, or watch her suffer."

I pushed her back even further, sneaking a glance at Gabe.

"All you have to do is come with me," Jackson said. "And I'll promise not to hurt her."

"You won't lay a finger on her!"

"Oh, I will. That I promise."

"Holy crap! You were telling the truth?" Gabe asked. "This guy is real?"

I took another step back, trying to put some distance between us. "I'm not going back. Not until my dad's behind bars."

"I don't think you understand how this works. You died. Whether it was your time or not makes no difference, not anymore. You put up a good fight, catching me off guard like you did, but the rules are clear." He slowly marched forward. "You have to die."

I slid back another step and grabbed the railing to the stairs. Joss clung tight but I forced her down the first few steps. Jackson took his time, methodically closing in.

"When someone dies, they stay in the afterlife. They don't get a mulligan," he said.

"Who are you to talk about rules? You've killed three people trying to catch me. It wasn't there time," I replied. I was trying to come up with an escape but I needed time.

"Don't you worry about that. Trust me, I was doing the world a favor by taking those three."

"They were my friends!"

Gabe grabbed Joss by the wrist and pulled her down the stairs.

"Since when do you get to play god? Who gave you the right to decide someone's fate?"

I motioned for Gabe to keep moving behind my back.

Jackson chuckled. "It's like Power of Attorney from above. My job is to bring you back, at all costs. Sometimes there's collateral damage."

"You're a murderer, no better than my father," I said through gritted teeth.

There was small newspaper dispenser next to the railing. I grabbed the rusty base and flung it in Jackson's direction. It wasn't the best of throws, but it caught his knee with a loud pop.

He groaned in pain and grabbed his leg. I flew down the stairs, taking them six at a time with the help of the railing. When I reached the bottom, I ran into an older couple. The woman fell into her husband, who scowled at me.

"Sorry!"

The platform was packed with people, unloading the train for the game. I scanned left to right, but there were too many people. I couldn't see where they went.

"Seven!" Joss yelled. "Seven!"

I followed her voice to the far corner, behind a woman with a stroller. Her blonde curls bounced above the crowd as she waved for me. I had to reach them before the train pulled away.

Pushing my way to the right, I reached the yellow warning stripe near the edge of the platform. It was only a few inches wide, but it was a clear shot to the front of the train where Joss was.

My feet were all over the place, stepping on feet, tripping into people. Piper would've done this easily, I thought. She'd be laughing at me.

My time was running out. I was the only idiot going against the grain but I had to reach Joss and Gabe before the doors closed. As I slid around a couple hugging the yellow line, a hand sprung out and clamped down on my arm.

"What the hell?" I exclaimed.

"Son, you need to get behind the yellow line!" A cop stood behind me. He was a few inches shorter, with a stern voice and an intense scowl. I couldn't shake free from his meaty hand.

"Alright! Alight! I'll get behind the yellow line, just let me go!" I yelled.

"I've heard that one before. You can wait to board, just like everyone else," he replied.

"Behind who? All of these people are getting off! I'm trying to get on!"

My eyes went to the staircase, wondering where Jackson was. Could I hit another cop? Could I break free?

Before I could decide, his grip loosened up. His fingers went limp and cold. His facial expression went blank. His body fell to the floor, revealing Jackson behind him. The reaper let go of his collarbone and stepped over the body.

I spun in place and shoved my way through the crowd. I tossed someone's bag behind me and caught a glimpse of the train's closing door. Gabe was in the window, screaming for me to get in. Joss was trying to force her foot across the threshold but some passengers were pulling her back. She couldn't hold it open any longer. I leapt on top of a bench and dove for the train. My shoulder slammed into the door but I twisted inward and fell to the floor.

Jackson watched from the other side of the door, scowling in.

"Looks like you're going to have to wait a little longer!" I yelled.

"Seven!" Gabe yelled. "He's not done yet!"

Gabe was right. Jackson placed his open palm against the plexiglass window. Frost formed all around it, cracking under the frozen pressure. He reared back and slammed his foot through the opening, splintering the window in four long pieces. Alarms howled in our ears. Red lights flashed through the cabin. The few people on the train began to panic.

I couldn't let it end this way. Not here. Not with Joss and Gabe in the line of fire. I jumped up to the opposite side of the car and pulled the emergency door open. "Come on!" I yelled, motioning Joss and Gabe through.

More screams came from inside the train. Jackson had climbed through and was pushing through the door. I heard someone gasp. I couldn't turn around but the sound ripped through my chest. Did he just kill someone else?

"Go! Don't look back!" I shouted. We tore up the stairs, back to street level.

"Who is that guy?" Joss cried.

I swiveled back and forth, franticly trying to come up with an escape.

"Seven, he'll be here any minute. Where do we run?"

I laughed at the suggestion. "We can't outrun him..."

A thought hit me as I stared across the street at the arena's side entrance. There was a catering truck parked along the street. The trailer door was cracked open at the bottom.

"We can't outrun him, but we can hide!" I jogged over to the back of the truck. The engine was still running but there wasn't anyone in the cab.

"Climb in!" I exclaimed.

"Are you sure about this?" Gabe asked.

"It's either this or you can stay here and deal with the Grim Reaper."

He closed his eyes and nodded. We squeezed through the opening and pulled the door down behind us. Shuffling to the back, we felt our way to the corner, hiding behind some kind of plastic-wrapped package.

"Will you get off me?" I whispered to Gabe.

"It's not my fault. I can't see a thing."

I felt a hand push down into my front pocket. "Hey!" I said.

"Relax, I'm just trying to find something," Joss said.

Gabe snickered. "Is this really the best time for that?"

She pulled her hand out and I heard her flick my No. 7 lighter open. A tiny flame filled the black trailer. Her big blue eyes sparkled in the amber light.

"Man, this was a good gift," she beamed.

I breathed a sigh of relief and caught Gabe's eyes. "How'd you know where we were?"

"I didn't, but you're an idiot, and only an idiot tries to scalp tickets after pissing off every cop in the greater St. Louis area."

"Yeah, that wasn't my best decision," I admitted.

"I was thinking you could strike a deal. If you could draw out Jericho, the police would have to take it easy on you for the cars. Maybe they'd just put you back in foster care," he said.

"That plan won't help much if I'm dead," I said. "You really didn't believe me about Jackson, did you?"

"No," Gabe said.

"Why do I even tell you stuff? Go back to the convent, dad."

"Nuns go to the convent, Seven."

Two gentle fingertips found my wrist. "Why do you always call him dad?"

I shot a glance to Gabe.

Clearing his throat, he explained, "Seven doesn't think I should become a priest so he calls me dad, instead of father."

"He's a sweetheart like that," Joss said.

"It's just his way."

"Now will you explain who that was? Who's Jackson and why was he trying to kill us?" Joss asked through a yawn.

I was too tired to come up with a story that would make sense. "This will sound crazy, but I don't want to lie. The truth is that I saved a couple of girls from getting hit by a car."

"Oh my gosh. Are you all right?" she asked.

"Well, I wasn't so lucky to avoid the car. It hit me and... I died." Surprisingly, she didn't respond, so I continued. "I was able to escape purgatory and return to life, but Jackson is determined to take me back."

"And Jackson is?" she asked.

"He's Seven's grim reaper," Gabe answered. "He took on the form of an old friend from Vegas."

"Oh," she said, trailing off. "That's a lot to take in."

"It's okay if you think I'm crazy."

"It would be hard to think you're crazy based on what I just saw. Did you see when he touched the window?" She paused. "However, you're going to have to give me some time to process all that." She yawned again.

"Where's Billie?" I asked, attempting to avoid the awkward silence. "Is she still pissed about the other night?"

"No, I don't think so. She's probably waiting for us at the bank." The truck's engine started up and someone climbed into the cab. After a brief second, it jolted forward and we exhaled.

My neck stiffened, followed by a shudder. I recalled Piper's questions about Billie. Something didn't sit right as I thought about her, alone in the bank. What would she do? Billie didn't do anything without a reason. Why would she want to wait there?

I wrapped my arm around Joss, feeling slightly awkward about it. I wasn't sure what to expect, but she didn't shutter away. She pulled me in tighter, and locked my left arm against her stomach like she sensed my hesitation. Her body curled in and spooned into me. Her hair draped over my chest, swarming me with caramel aroma. I didn't want to move.

My heart was pumping so fast it was distracting. I didn't want to close my eyes in fear that I would wake up from a dream.

"I don't know what Billie's doing. She said she'd wait for us there. I wonder where we're headed," he said.

The truck rattled along the way, slow, bumpy, but steady. We sat in near silence, almost in a trance from the rhythm. Joss stretched out and then curled back in. Every yawn was a little sexier than the last. Her tiny hands were swallowed, like the rest of her body, by that fuzzy shirt. It was the kind of beautiful that didn't even have to try.

Gabe hung up his phone, looking a little flustered.

"Well?" I asked.

"She's not answering. It's strange. That's really not like her." I imagined more wrinkles growing on his forehead. "I'm sure it's nothing. This whole thing has me worked up. I'm sure she'll call back."

I could feel Joss slip into deep sleep, lightly breathing through her mouth.

"I'm sorry you were dragged into this," I said to Gabe.

His face drew to a scowl. "I'm your friend and I should've believed you. I didn't realize how big this thing was before. I do now. I get it. Whatever it takes, I'm with you."

I leaned against the trailer wall, glad to have him there.

"I really made a mess of things, didn't I?"

"Yes, you did," he said, leaning against the counter. "It probably would've been better if you hadn't picked a fight with the cops."

"Yeah, not my wisest move."

"For that matter, it would've been easier if you hadn't saved those girls and pissed off Jackson. Maybe if you wouldn't have been born into a shitty family. Oh, and if you wouldn't have saved Piper from Jericho's goon. That would've been good."

"Okay, I get it. You can stop now."

"You're not getting my point. Look, everyone makes mistakes. With the exception of the golf course, I think you've been, well, admirable. You've saved three people from danger. You didn't have to do that. You could've looked the other way. That's what most people would've done."

I shrugged him off and rubbed my forehead.

"I'm serious dude. The only thing necessary for the triumph of evil is for good men to do nothing."

"Okay, scholar Joe."

"Yes, I ripped off Edmund Burke, but you get my point."

He was better at this than I wanted to give him credit for. But I wasn't going to give him the satisfaction or further incentive to go to Seminary.

"So, Jackson killed the scalpers?" he asked.

"Apparently. But something doesn't add up though. Do you remember Mardi Gras?"

He looked at me with a crooked face. "Yeah."

"Jackson wasn't the only one who knew I was a scalper," I said.

"Who are you talking about?" he asked.

"Piper-she knew I was a scalper. She asked me if ticket scalping was an honorable profession. Remember?"

"Oh yeah, right before she stole your money." He chuckled. "Wait, are you saying that Piper's been helping Jericho?"

The thought made me squirm. "Maybe." My heart was screaming at my brain, refusing to believe that Piper would help Jericho.

"Okay, I'm with you, but why would she help you slash those tires at the golf course? It seems like that would be counter-productive to helping Jericho. The last place he'd want you is with the police."

"You're right. That doesn't make sense."

"Something else seems funny to me," Gabe said. "Jackson's after you so he can get into heaven, right?"

"According to him, yes," I replied.

"How is killing innocent people going to help him get to heaven?"

"Jackson never was a model of self-control. Neither was I. My guess is he's a little drunk with power. He is Death, after all. Reapers kill," I said, looking down.

"I just don't want to believe it. How would God be alright with that?"

"Maybe he's lying about that part," I said. "Maybe he's off the reservation, angry that I embarrassed him."

"Maybe," he said, nodding in the light. "So, what's the plan? What are we going to do?"

"That part's easy. I leave town."

He looked up at the ceiling and groaned.

"She doesn't want me to leave either," I nodded at Joss, "but I don't see another option. If I stay, either the cops or Jackson will eventually find me."

"What about your dad?"

"I don't know what to do about that right now."

"Okay. I just wish there was another option. You know, one where you didn't have to leave."

I looked down at the blonde halo against my chest. "Yeah, me too."

Chapter 9
ANIMALS

"Why isn't she answering?" Gabe asked, staring into his phone.

"She wouldn't avoid you because she's mad at me, would she?" I asked.

He banged wildly on the redial button. "Of course she would. It's Billie. When have you known her to not hold a grudge?"

There was a snap to his voice as he huffed and puffed into the receiver. I didn't know what to make of it. I'd never seen Gabe lose control.

"Are you sure this is about Seven?" Joss sat up and rubbed her eyes, stretching out with a heavenly yawn. Confusion swept across our faces as we sat in the trailer. "Think about it. If she was mad at Seven, why wouldn't she answer your call?"

Another wrinkle sprouted on Gabe's forehead.

"Did you do something to piss her off?" I asked.

His hands ran over his skull as he groaned. "I don't think so."

I stared into the darkness, wondering where the truck was headed. Concern sunk in as I pondered the situation when we came to a stop. Could Jackson have followed us? Would he be waiting for us when the door opened?

"Seminary," Joss muttered.

He torqued his head to face her. "Yes, what about it?"

"Have you made a decision yet? Are you going to priest school?"

He chuckled lightly and looked up. "No, I haven't. Why? What'd she say to you?"

"Nothing in particular, but she was pretty worked up about it the other day," Joss said.

"Yeah," I jumped in, "she was at the bank and asked me about it too. It's really starting to get to her."

"Billie came by the bank?" Joss asked. I was thrown off by her tone.

"When did she come by the bank?" Gabe asked.

"The morning of the musical. You knew that. She came and picked me up."

"Yeah, she told me she was giving you a ride. She never mentioned anything about hanging out beforehand." His brows drew to a point.

"What was she doing there?" Joss wasn't letting it go. It didn't make any sense that she'd be jealous of Billie. She didn't even react that strongly when she found out about Piper, although I still wasn't clear what she knew.

"She was cleaning." The absurdity of that answer made me laugh as I thought about it. I could only imagine what was going through their heads.

Silence filled the trailer.

"Seven, she hasn't been around much since that night. The few times we were together, she was distant, barely there at all."

"So, you're blaming me for that? Look, I really don't know what you're saying, but there's nothing going on between me and Billie. Think about it." I looked over at Joss. "That's ridiculous."

Gabe wasn't an idiot. I could see a bit of resolve creep in as he took a deep breath. "Then can you please explain what heck's going on? Where is my girlfriend?"

"I don't know." I suddenly felt surrounded. Gabe's glare burned my forehead as I looked down at the floor.

"Alright, we'll just have to find her," Joss said.

The truck jerked to a stop as the words came out of her mouth. We braced for a moment, looking nervously at each other.

"What do we do?" Gabe asked.

"I think we have to get out before the driver opens the gate," I said. "The last thing we need is for him to call the cops."

I shuffled to the back and unlocked the hatch. Holding my breath, I pulled up on the door. An image of Jackson standing on the other side flicked into my head. If he was there, we'd be trapped. Joss and Gabe would be killed and I'd be to blame; me and my stupid escape plan.

"What are you waiting for?" Gabe asked.

He ripped the door open and to my relief, Jackson was nowhere to be seen. Dusk had set in and I didn't recognize where we were. We jumped down onto a concrete path. It looped around a cluster of bamboo, still brown from the cold weather. There were trees everywhere and I could hear water in the distance. I guessed that it was some kind of park.

"Where are we?" Gabe asked.

Joss looked up at him. "The zoo." She was pointing at a sign labeled 'The Wild' with a picture of a bear next to it.

The truck door slammed shut and footsteps were behind us. I pulled Joss and Gabe around the corner and hushed them quiet.

The driver was a round Italian man with a pin-striped uniform. He slid open the back and pulled out a case of red wine. I looked down at Joss but she looked as confused as I did.

"Why are cases of wine being delivered to a zoo?" I asked.

Gabe snickered. "Maybe the giraffes like a night cap."

"Hilarious, dude."

A group of people walked by, too busy to notice three kids kneeling in the bushes. They wore tuxes, high-heels, and dresses that cost more than I'd seen in my lifetime. Everyone smelled like dry-cleaning and perfume. Just a few paces behind, a tall couple followed. They resembled peacocks strutting their feathers. His nose was in a phone and hers in a compact, both still managing to sniff the clouds. Neither one of them were paying attention to their son, who was buried in a video game. With their attention drawn to more important things, I quickly relieved her purse of three invites sticking out of the side pocket.

It seemed harmless, but I could feel the anger emanating from Joss as I fanned them out.

"I'm just trying to figure out what's going on," I said, refusing to look up. "Why are they dressed like that at the zoo?"

Her face grew sharp. "You could've just asked."

"I'm sure we could, but as luck would have it, we don't need to," I said, handing them each an invite. She took it grudgingly and stuck her hand in my jacket pocket. The ticket was made of thick paper with gold lettering at the top.

"Zootini's?" she read aloud. "It looks like it's some kind of fundraiser."

Gabe ripped all three tickets back and gave them to the husband. "Sir, you dropped these."

"Oh, thank you son," he said, taking them back.

I stood back with a scowl as Gabe walked ahead where the concrete path turned into red carpet. I exchanged glances at Joss as he stopped at a ticket booth with purple drapes. I couldn't hear what he said, but after some questionable looks, he paid for three tickets. When the smug bastard motioned for the gate, I nearly decked him.

"Couldn't let that one go, could you?" I asked.

Brushing it off, he waved us on. "Come on, it'll be fun."

"How is hobnobbing with rich people going to be fun?" I asked. "Don't you want to find Billie?"

"No. Well, I'm sure she'll call me when she's ready," he stuttered.

Joss smiled and squinted her eyes. "So, you're scared that she's mad at you."

The corners of his mouth twitched before he turned around to hide his guilt.

I shrugged at Joss and followed behind. "How bad could it be?" I whispered.

Before she could respond, a hand shot out from the portable entrance to our right. A boy band wannabe leaned over, taking a long look at my disheveled outfit. "Are you in the right place?"

I twisted back over the counter, looking down at his zooniform. "You're wearing Dickies. Do you really want to ask me that question?"

"Be nice!" Joss said.

"Sorry. What I meant was, if you don't take my damn ticket, I'm going to drag your fohawk across the park and feed you to the polar bears."

A fierce pinch dug into my side, but I wouldn't acknowledge the pain. He took our tickets, smiling politely as he did.

"You really don't have to be a jerk," Joss grumbled.

We followed the red carpet around a pond with all sorts of ducks milling about. The sun tucked beneath the horizon, leaving only a bitter wind, cutting across the water. I was actually thankful for the chill. Joss lasted about five steps before she wrapped her arms around my waist and buried her head into my jacket. Her sniffles were leaving stains on one of the five shirts that I owned.

White Christmas lights speckled along a large wooden deck in the middle of the pond. It was lined with fake vines and purple tulips. Skinny metal cylinders radiated heat through the sea of black and white formalwear.

When we stepped down to the main platform, the music practically stopped. Staring would have put it kindly. We were the three-person leaper colony in the sea of skin models. I couldn't help but laugh at some of the glares.

Brushing off the frigid welcome, we cruised around the pedestal tables, making ourselves at home with hors d'oeuvres and champagne. I didn't know what Gabe paid for the tickets, but I was determined to eat his money's worth. I felt the last couple of twenty dollar bills in my pocket and recalled that scalping was no longer an option. Concern for my next meal drove me to gluttonous measures.

I piled on the shrimp, snagging every prong I could get my fingers on. My stomach started gurgling from the strange presence of food, but it felt good to not be hungry. Eventually, after the free-for-fall, we huddled next to a space heater and scanned the crowd.

I looked down at Joss. "Are you warm enough?"

She was distracted by something on the far side of the deck. It wasn't Gabe. He was a few feet away, talking to one of the waiters. I leaned over, but I couldn't see what she was staring at.

She rested her hand on my forearm and took a step forward, ducking down a few inches and tilting her head to the side.

"What are you looking at?" I asked.

"Where's Gabe?" she replied, never breaking her stare.

"He's right over there. Why? What do you see?"

Just then, I saw a hint of what she'd been looking at. Stepping off the deck and turning into the park, was a skinny figure with a dark ponytail bobbing in the moonlight. I moved closer and leaned around one of the cylinder space heaters. It was so close that the heat singed the hairs on my neck but I didn't care. I couldn't believe it was her. What was Billie doing at the zoo?

"Why would she be here?" Joss asked.

"Why would who be here?" Gabe said, sliding in behind us. "Who are you looking at?"

I felt the snap as he caught a better glimpse. He took off across the deck, wildly plowing through partygoers. Joss and I slammed our drinks down and ran after him. We sprinted off the deck and around the water, past the apes. He was much faster than I gave him credit for. We could barely keep up.

He finally stopped when we reached a sign for The River's Edge, leaning on some red boulders. I wanted to be in his head and understand what he was thinking. I felt bad watching him come to grips with the fact that Billie had been lying. His hand hovered out to the side as we caught up behind him.

"It's not just me, right?" he asked. "Why would she lie about being here?"

I shrugged behind him and looked at Joss, hoping she'd know what to say.

Before either of us could muster a response, Billie was on the move again, walking further into the exhibit. Every few steps she'd check over her shoulder, making it hard to follow without being noticed. Why is she so worried about being followed?

The temperature was dropping fast. Even Gabe, with his thick jacket, started shivering. Joss' grip tightened. Her breath grew short and her cheek became permanently attached to my arm.

Billie stopped near the western fence and twisted to face us. We jerked to a stop and ducked around a tree. I squinted to make sure it was her. I loved Billie like a sister, but I couldn't imagine what she was doing there. Why would she be at the zoo of all places? And why would she be ducking Gabe's calls?

"Wait!" I stuck my arm out, holding Gabe back. He didn't look happy.

"What am I waiting for?"

Piper's warning about Billie rang in my head. Was this what she was talking about? What exactly is this?

"I want to see what she's doing," I whispered.

"Me too," Gabe said, jaw clenched.

"Think about it for a second. Look how secretive she's being. If you walk up to her, you'll never get the truth," I said.

"What do you propose then?" he asked. "I feel like a creep following her around like this."

"I know, but she's up to something. Just keep your head down and follow me." Joss nodded and Gabe exhaled a long breath that I took as an agreement.

Billie's brunette ponytail bobbed slowly as she talked to one of the staff, who pointed her west. She looked even more nervous as we drew closer, scared even.

We crept around the winding path and came up behind her. We stood only twenty feet away, but I'd never felt further from my friend. Her face was cold and withdrawn. Her hands clenched into tight balls. She picked up the pace with short, rigid strides. Her stiff motions didn't resemble the athlete I knew she was. Was she scared to be there, or was she running away from something?

We snuck to an unmarked brick building, surrounded by trees. I checked for the fence line. We still appeared to be on zoo grounds, but I was sure this place wasn't on the visitor's map. The path split two plots of mud, completely overrun by weeds and branches. Random garbage piled up like a redneck's trailer, hardly what I expected at the zoo.

Our steps came to a crawl as Billie moved slowly for the entrance. She didn't want to go in the building.

"Do you hear animals?" Joss asked.

I looked down at her with a sarcastic grimace. "Yeah..." I said, motioning all around us.

"No, I mean from inside," she said, rolling her eyes.

"She's right," Gabe whispered.

A deep growl resonated from the building when Billie opened the door. The repercussion was steady, with little break for air. I wondered if it was some kind of recording at first, but as we crept closer, it exploded, pounding my ears. Whatever they were, they were large and unhappy.

"What is this place?" I whispered.

"We could just wait for her to come out," Joss suggested.

I shook my head and walked to the entrance. Slowly, I swung open the iron door to the brick tomb. I hadn't come that far to chicken out. The smell of formaldehyde and mold greeted us with welcome arms as we stepped into a dingy hallway. Stale air clung to the inside of my lungs, leaving a depressing aftertaste in my throat.

Industrial light fixtures hung from the ceiling with yellow bulbs covered in dead flies. The mortar had stained seven different shades of grey over the years and dust created a thick, furry layer on the concrete. Our echoes grew louder as the hallway sloped down, leading deeper underground.

An open office on the right had a white label at eye level, reading Dr. Schimsel in small black letters.

"Dr.?" Joss asked.

Confusion etched my face as I pulled her into the small room, complete with a desk, more books than I could count, and plenty of locked cabinets. Joss hesitated, hovering near the doorway as I scavenged through the messy stacks of paper on the desk. Most of the pages were on zoo letterhead. They had something to do with animal exchange.

"Get down!" Gabe whispered.

Two thugs, very serious looking, stomped down the hallway and left through the iron door. When they cleared earshot, I went back to the hallway, avoiding the tarantula sitting in a small aquarium on the edge of the cabinet.

"What is this place?" Gabe asked.

"I think this is the quarantine," I replied, looking down the hall. "I bet they keep animals here for a while before putting them in the main population."

Gabe looked around at the dirty hallway. "Yeah, I bet this is a great place to get rid of germs."

As if affirming my guess, another outburst tore through the hallway. The frantic roar echoed through the building. Joss nearly jumped out of her skin, clinging to my sleeve again.

"Why don't you wait outside? You can keep watch," I said.

She looked up at me with big, ocean blue eyes. "Nice try."

I couldn't blame her. The echoes made it feel like the angry animal was right behind you.

A group of voices finally became audible as we peaked around the corner. They were mumbled at first, but Billie's angry tone was easy to pick out. It was a significant pitch higher than the person she was talking to.

As we walked up a short incline, the ceiling opened up, creating a cavernous effect in what appeared to be some sort of makeshift break-room. A table and chairs sat off to the side. Animal posters lined the walls.

"What's the plan?" Joss asked.

Gabe didn't wait for one. He broke for the door when he heard her voice climb higher. As he reached the threshold, short quick steps came rushing toward us.

"Crap!" he yelled, diving behind a trash can.

I grabbed Joss and slammed her on her back, a little harder than I expected. I landed next to her, our hips overlapping against the concrete floor.

An older guy with short, pudgy legs led Billie through the room. Underneath his tux jacket, a purple sash wrapped across his chest. What were those sashes? Where were they coming from?

I mouthed to Joss, "Purple sash."

"Right this way," he said. Billie followed close behind, but her face spoke volumes for how she felt about Mr. Crew-cut.

Gabe slunk away from the corner and gave us a nod.

He disappeared around the corner, leaving us alone on the floor, which could no longer go unnoticed. Joss turned her focus back to me, inches from my face, her lips breathing a sigh of relief. I could have relived that insignificant moment for hours, but the rest of my body was putting me in a compromising position. I had to either move my leg, or Joss might've done it for me.

"So, you're not turned on by the zoo quarantine?" I asked, rolling away.

"No, but it feels like you are," she replied.

"Has nothing to do with the location. We could be in a church for all I care." I thought about that for a second.

"Don't even go there." She stood up, brushing off her back. I took a couple of seconds but eventually made it to my feet. "Boys are shameless."

"Guilty."

Another growl pierced the air. It didn't sound too happy to be cooped up in this dungeon.

"Should we follow them?" she asked, looking a little flustered by the roar.

I shook my head. "Gabe will find her. I want to know what she was doing here and what it has to do with the purple sashes."

"Are you sure?" she asked. "Billie may be sneaking around, but she's still your friend. Does she deserve a little trust? Or at least to be heard out?"

I wanted to sneer back at her with a snide comment about her DCFS lies but I was interrupted.

"Trust is a funny thing, Ms. Gordon. Isn't it?" That crusty voice was worse than the growling animals. My fists immediately balled up as I glared at Detective Remy Boudreaux, standing in the doorway with a fiery scowl.

"For instance, I trusted you to take this young man back to foster care. And with that trust, you decided to make me look like a fool." A cigarette danced in his mouth with each word. The rings under his eyes were deep with a faint, yellow tint.

"Mr. Murphy-Collins, it's nice to see you again." He waved his gun to the doorway. "Both of you come with me."

Joss went first, avoiding eye contact as she walked in the other room. I followed suit, trying to take notice of our surroundings. I looked for any kind of exit, or distraction, anything to get us out of the building.

He led us into a much bigger room. Chairs were scattered randomly in front of a large, metal cage with multiple latches and a sliding door, reaching floor to ceiling. Inside the cell was the source of all the noise. Two lions were at the edge of the cage, furiously itching to get out. The grey metal was scratched to hell and despite the very clear danger we were in, I couldn't look away from their sandy eyes. I could see their hunger to be free, their desperation to break out from their prison.

Joss sat down in one of the chairs. I could read the fear on her face, although I couldn't tell if it was from Boudreaux or the man-eaters behind her.

"Go ahead," he shoved me next to her.

As he hovered, curiously staring at us, I should have been worried. At the very least, I was about to go to juvee. Strangely though, I couldn't stop thinking about Piper. My hand was on fire, burning with an itch that climbed up my arm. If she knew that Billie was up to no good, did that mean she was right about my hand too? Was it some kind of weapon? If she wasn't crazy, then all I had to do was reach out and grab him, as long as he didn't shoot me first.

That seemed like a pretty big gamble.

"I have to say that I'm surprised to see you again. Most people would've skipped town after that stunt you pulled. Don't get me wrong, I'm glad you didn't. It saves me the mess of having to track you down. But I have to ask, what's keeping you here that you'd risk jail?"

Standing on the balls of my feet, I looked down at him, trying to figure out how to respond.

"Sit down son. There's no reason to be a hero." He stood chest to chest with me, gun at his side, "Don't make me shoot you." His fingers dug into my collarbone, clamping down and forcing me to crumble in pain.

Damn old man strength.

As I knelt crookedly under the pressure, my fingers shot to his leg. They hovered an inch from his knee.

I wanted to grab him. I wanted to hurt him like I did Jericho's men, but I was nervous. Nerves were exploding in my fingertips, prickling with anticipation. What if I was wrong? What if I was imagining the whole hand thing? I really didn't want to get shot.

I slipped a glance at Joss. I already knew what was going through her head. She'd rather go to jail than watch me do something stupid. I dropped my right hand, but swiped his keys with my left.

"Okay, okay! Enough. I'll sit down," I said.

"What brings you here, Seven?"

"Just trying to save the animals."

"Fine, let's try a different approach." He kept the gun pointed at me, but pulled some cuffs out and moved toward Joss. My chest sunk into a black hole. I could feel the blood rush to my eyes, tearing my sanity apart. I could deal with death, but Joss was better than this.

"Were you at the golf course the other night?" he demanded, holding the cuffs behind her.

"What are you going to do? Arrest her? She hasn't done anything wrong."

He smiled. "I know she wasn't with you. Deputy Peterson said the girl had dark hair." Joss' eyes slid up to mine, a quiet rage within. "Either way, Ms. Gordon's hardly innocent: aiding and abetting, breaking someone out of police custody, misuse of government resources. Shall I go on?"

He cocked the gun and watched me squirm. I couldn't hide the anger. I wanted to rip his heart out. I clenched my hand tight, trying to suppress the avidity exploding from my skin.

"Enough with the games. What are you doing here?" he asked.

An idea popped in my head, but it seemed crazy, even for me. "We were following my friend," I said. "What are you doing here?"

He tilted his head to the side. "My guess is that your friend has been running errands for Jericho Splitzer."

I didn't want to believe what he was saying. I knew Billie was hiding something but she couldn't be double crossing me. She wouldn't do that. Why would she? That made less sense than Piper helping Jericho.

"You're lying," I said.

He shook his head. "We planted a message about a fake meeting. We wanted to see who'd show up. She did," he said, trailing off. "And you did. But you working for Jericho doesn't make a lot of sense."

I tilted my head to the side, unsure how to respond. How could she do it? How could she lie to our face?

He reached down and grabbed a cell phone from his hip. "Hey John, bring that girl back here."

He paused to listen.

"Do you know which direction she was headed?"

He flipped the phone closed. "Damn."

"Alright, back to you. Where's your father?" he asked.

That was the million dollar question, I thought to myself.

"Where is Billie?" I asked again, a bit frantic in my response.

"I'll be asking the questions. Now talk or I'll just cart you both off to jail."

"I don't know where he is." I slowly reached behind my back and slid the lowest metal bar down, coughing loudly to mask the sound.

"He must have something really good on him."

"Jericho said he owed him money," I said.

He chuckled. "A guy like Jericho doesn't poke his head out of the desert and come all the way to St. Louis for a couple of bucks. Whatever your dad knows must be extremely important."

"What does it matter? Just arrest Jericho and be done with it."

"I can't just arrest people for fun. I need proof. How is Jericho moving the drugs?"

"What makes you think I would know?" I asked.

"I think your dad told you," he replied.

"Obviously you don't know my dad. He's a coward. He'd never tell me anything important like that."

He shook his head slowly. "I'm going to get the truth out of you, kid."

Boudreaux looked up at the ceiling. I needed to pick my spot while he was distracted.

"What are we going to do with you? Of course, I should lock you up for your tire stunt, but I might have a better idea. How would you like to not go to jail?"

"What are you proposing?" I asked, staring intently at Joss. I wasn't sure if she saw what I was up to.

"If you tell me where your dad is, I'll make the rest of your problems disappear."

If he only knew what that would entail... "Sure, let me pull him out of my back pocket." I wrapped my fingers around the top latch, twisting my arm awkwardly as I leaned back.

"It would be wise to cooperate with me." He looked down at Joss, then back at me. "Ms. Gordon isn't a minor. I can make sure she spends a long time in big girl jail. You wouldn't want that, would you?"

"It will be okay, Seven. It will be okay," Joss said in a low tone. She was trying to mask her fear, poorly. I imagined her alone in a cell, desperately clawing at metal bars like the cats behind me. I couldn't let that happen.

"Now!"

I ripped the top latch open and lunged at Boudreaux. He hip-tossed me into the wall but his gun flew through the air. Joss threw her chair at his legs, knocking him off balance. The scary part of my plan came into fruition as the door to the cage popped open.

"Augghhhh!" Boudreaux screamed as the angry beasts worked through the open door.

I didn't wait around to see if he was going to get away. I grabbed Joss' hand and tore back into the darkness of the hallway.

"Are you just going to leave him back there?" Joss asked.

"Do you have a better idea?"

We ran down the hallway, ignoring the sound of our footsteps. They were loud and sloppy, like a wounded animal trying to escape. I reached for the handle, but the door didn't budge. I fell back and landed in the same sticky puddle we passed earlier.

"They must lock the doors from the outside, in case the animals get loose," she said, exhaling frantically.

"That's great. I mean, we wouldn't want man-eating lions getting free, would we?" An angry scream echoed through the hall. Two more shots followed. I got up, running back the way we came, but turning right at the end of the hallway. There had to be another exit.

A third set of footsteps came into earshot, light and muffled at first, but growing quieter as they crept closer. We ducked into a dark classroom and jumped blindly down the steps. I thought I heard the door whine behind us, a soft nudge pushing it open. I grabbed Joss and we slid behind the podium. My chest heaved in and out as I tried to come up with a plan.

"We're going to be eaten by a Lion." Her voice quivered with her bottom lip.

"No were not!" I said, searching for some courage. "You don't think I'd unleash some lions without having a plan, do you?"

She didn't have time to respond. That was good, because, I definitely didn't have a plan. I started counting steps in sequence.

One, two... three, four. Each thump was followed by a series of clicks, like someone tapping their fingernail on a hard surface. My finger went to my mouth, warning Joss not to make a noise. I'm sure she loved that. What did I think she was going to do, jump up and say here kitty, kitty?

"Maybe we can trap it in here," I whispered.

"If it means not getting eaten, I'm all for it."

A purr hung in the air as Simba stalked through the aisles. Chairs toppled down the steps, crashing loudly at the podium, by our feet. I looked at Joss for ideas, but she was sporting the same clueless expression I had. The angry animal was getting closer and it wouldn't be long until we were officially on the menu. I could hear the hunger rippling through his teeth. He was stalking, waiting for his dinner to do something stupid. We were trapped against the back wall.

Like a prayer answered, more shots rang through hall, breaking Simba's attention. I grabbed a pen from the top of the podium and looked across the room. Grabbing Joss by the forearm, I tossed the pen in the far corner. No sooner did the tiny sound of plastic meet concrete, than did the explosion of chairs and a snarl that curled the hairs on the back of my neck. We blindly ran through the room, banging into unknown obstacles. I could hear him shift as more chairs rumbled. A sleek, feline figure leapt across the tables in a single bound, landing on the long desktop. Gold eyes cut through the black room, staring into my soul. His head was bigger than my entire torso. The cat sunk to the Formica surface, his tail hovering like a cobra.

I swung the door open and shoved Joss into the hallway. I tried but I couldn't shut the door behind me. It slammed into my ankle and dropped me to one knee. I ripped my foot through, not sure if it had been broken. I wanted to breathe a sigh of relief, but the only thing I could hear was short, heavy breaths. Two more gold eyes stood three feet from us, leaping into the air as I stared down the mouth of the second lion.

My hand instinctively shot up and caught his furry chest, striking a cold surge through my fingers. It was enough of a shock to stand him up on his hind legs, leaning into me. His head snapped forward. I jerked back in the deadly tango and shut my eyes. I could feel his teeth up against my neck. He let out a sharp roar and a flurry of rank breath brushed over me.

This was it. This was how my second life would end: at the hands of my own idiocy.

I had a grip on his chest as I tried to fight back the inevitable death blow. I could feel the furious engine within, pumping wildly. I felt the rhythm.

I could do more than feel it though. I could control it. I could stop it.

I dug in deeper, piercing his skin and matting the hair with cold, bloody fingers. Remembering last time, I focused on his heart.

It grew weak, but as it did, a fire grew within my own. It torched my soul, begging me to push harder, begging me not only to slow his heart, but to stop it completely. I didn't want to kill him, but the urge, the drive to finish the beast off, felt raw, almost animalistic; I didn't have a choice. It consumed me.

Bang!

My eardrums burst into pain and smoke filled the hallway. A vicious cry severed our connection as the lion spewed blood on my shirt. He fell to the floor in a heap, scraping his claw along my chest, tearing into my skin as he went. I was lucky there wasn't any force left in his dead muscles, or I would've been split open. It was too dark to see where the bullet entered his body, but warm liquid pooled beneath him.

Joss and I turned to Boudreaux, silently standing at the end of the short hall. His gun hovered, smoke billowing around him. He stood beneath the red exit light. I waited for him to say something, to make a move, but he didn't. He stood silently, grinding his teeth.

I looked down at my hand, in awe of its power. There was a mix of fear and excitement brewing. I could take down a lion? All I had to do was touch someone and they felt cold. But when I got angry or scared, that's when they truly felt it. That's when I could grasp their heart; grip their life. I could kill someone with a touch.

Before Boudreaux could react, the door swung open and cracked him on the side of the head, sending him into crumbled mess on the floor. The gun slid across the floor, skidding to a stop at Joss' feet.

"What are you waiting for?" Billie yelled from the other side of the door. She swung into Boudreaux's head again, making sure he was unconscious.

Gabe peeked into the doorway. "Come on. We can climb the fence behind the building."

Chapter 10
LESSONS

I slammed Gabe's phone down and stared into his passenger side mirror, running my hand along four parallel lines of raised skin. The dead lion's signature ran from the edge of my neck to my midsection. I was already built like a scratching post, now I looked like one too. As scars went though, it was the super bowl trophy. It made me want to walk around with my shirt off... classy.

A few weeks had passed since that crazy night at the zoo but I hadn't seen Joss since we escaped. I wondered if I'd ever see her again. I didn't blame her for not wanting to deal with my crazy world, but I didn't understand either. She was the one who insisted that I stay. I guess it could have been watching me almost kill a lion with my dead hand that drove her away.

She seemed relieved when we got back to the bank but when I woke up the next day, she was gone. No note. She didn't even say goodbye, just took my heart with her. She had disappeared for periods before, but not like this. She kissed me. She admitted her feelings. That was supposed to fix everything.

I'd called about a hundred times from Gabe's phone, but it always went to voicemail. Every time I hung up, a blend of anger and emptiness coursed through me. How could she do this? And why didn't I expect it? Who was I kidding? I might be able to trick a girl like that for a while, but eventually she'd realize that I didn't bring anything to the table. "Tall, dark, and handsome," I muttered to myself.

It probably didn't help that Boudreaux put a warrant out for her arrest. I got sick to my stomach at the thought. Maybe a good night's sleep was all she needed to realize that I wasn't worth the trouble. I was surprised it took her that long.

I lost a lot of things that night. Along with losing Joss, Jackson had seen to it that I couldn't scalp tickets anymore. I'd gone downtown a couple of times to scout it out, figuring the fear might wear off, but it was always the same-a ghost town right up until when the puck dropped. People must really be scared.

Admittedly, losing my source of income hurt more than I had expected. I was good at living on next to nothing, but even I needed a little money. Getting a job wasn't an option. That's what I told myself anyway. Instead, I reverted back to old survival techniques. Rusty and I had to eat, so I'd been thieving from various grocery stores, little bit at a time.

"What's the plan now?" Gabe asked as he pulled into a gas station near the bank.

I laughed out of frustration. "There is no plan."

"So, you're just giving up?"

"My dad's trail has gone cold and I don't have a clue what he did with the book. I have a grim reaper and a police department hunting me. What do you want me to do? Where do I even start?"

"I don't know. It's just that I've never seen you give up before. Hell, you chased him across the country with barely a dollar to your name. You didn't let that stop you."

I continued to laugh, looking up at his dome light. "Do me a favor and don't give me any advice on perseverance."

"What is that supposed to mean?"

"It means you should look in the mirror. You've been hanging out with me for the past couple weeks and not once have you brought up Billie. Have you even tried to talk to her since the zoo?"

I wasn't sure why I was picking a fight. Maybe I was trying to mask my own pain for a while.

"This is about you and Joss!" he yelled. "Quit projecting your problems on me."

"Okay, tell me then, what was she doing there that night? Detective Boudreaux said she's running errands for Jericho. Tell me, is she working for drug dealers now? Is she telling him how to find me?"

"I don't know. She won't talk to me," he mumbled.

"Think about it! Why else would she be at the zoo? She fell for Boudreaux's note and showed up to meet Jericho." I felt like I was channeling Piper all of a sudden.

"You don't think I've thought about that?" he asked. "I know how it looks, but I believe in her. There has to be a good explanation."

"You have to face it. She stabbed us in the back," I said, meeting his eyes. "Piper told me not to trust her. She was right. Somehow, she'd been right all along." I looked down at my hand and wondered what else she'd been right about.

"If I call her a liar, she'll never speak to me again."

"How in the world are you going to be a priest?" I asked, wiping my mouth as I spat. "You can't even straighten your own life out!"

"Go to hell Seven." He slammed his door shut and headed for the gas station entrance.

I climbed out of the car and grabbed him by the arm. "Don't whine to me about Billie. You're the one who's been pushing her away."

"What are you talking about?" he demanded.

"Every day that you hem and haw about Seminary... You're making a choice, whether you realize it or not." His eyes darted around like he was going hit me. "It serves you right that she's been lying."

I wanted him to hit me. It would make us both feel better.

"Find your own way home," he said, "before I call Boudreaux myself."

That was much worse than getting punched in the jaw. Gabe was my friend. How could he even think that?

As he walked through the door, I thought about stealing his car. It would've served him right. I knew the truth though. He wasn't going to call anyone, even if he wanted to.

As I walked home, I thought about what Gabe said, and I thought about Boudreaux. Why did he save me from that lion? He could've just let it go and he'd never have to worry about me again. Was my dad really that important?

Stepping onto Third Street, I couldn't help notice how much warmer it had gotten. It was nice, but it wouldn't last long. The brutal summer waited, and it was especially tough when you didn't have air conditioning, or a refrigerator, or food. I missed Joss. And I was hungry. I thought about doubling back and asking Gabe for some money, but I couldn't. I refused to become a beggar.

The corner house on the third block was my landmark for getting close to the bank. It was long and narrow, trying to look Roman with columns supporting a wide arch across the front. It wasn't made of concrete or stucco. That would've made a little more sense. It was wood, and my favorite part: it was yellow. Not soft yellow, or faded yellow... puke yellow. When the power went out, that house still shined brightly.

Tonight, as I reached the banana house, a figure caught my attention. Walking slowly, it crossed the street, heading downhill toward the river. I wasn't sure at first, but as I drew closer, the overwhelming size became clear. I stopped behind a tree, leaning casually against it like I hadn't noticed the gigantic person. He continued to the other curb, and disappeared behind the corner house. Immediately, I turned and sprinted through the nearest yard, hurdling the fence and ducking behind a firewood stack. The motion sensor kicked on from the back porch but I held put as I knew he couldn't see me. I could see him though. The streetlights kicked off his face as he drifted between the shadows.

I crept closer, and pressed my face up against the chain link fence to get a better look. I couldn't, or didn't want to believe it, but I knew that face. How had Jackson found me? Or had he found me? He was only blocks from the bank, but he wasn't headed in the right direction.

I crept through the yard, cutting behind another fence and around a giant maple. He was moving slowly, so I could shoot down to the end of the block and turn the corner before he made it very far. If not to find me, why would he be there?

I tried not to get lost in that question as I silently shuffled through the shadows. My hand started burning again as I pictured him killing Darren. I wanted to rip his head off, but I'm pretty sure I knew how that would go. Maybe I could at least find out what he was up to.

When I turned the corner, I expected to see him, halfway to the end of the block. He wasn't there. I scanned the entire street. I even checked behind me in case he doubled around. There was no sign of him. He couldn't have gone inside. I would've heard something, a gate, a door, something. I began to walk faster, paying less attention to my own noise level. Six houses passed, but still no sign of death.

Mentally, I was losing it. I knew I'd seen him. I wasn't crazy. He was there. Maybe he had some mystical voodoo thing where he could evaporate into thin air. A growl ripped through my insides, reminding me how long it'd been since I ate. I felt the rings under my eyes. It's bad when you can feel them. Maybe I was just so hungry that I was hallucinating. I'm not sure why that made me feel better, but it did.

The street was empty in both directions. The only sound I could make out was the occasional car on Main Street and a tiny whistle from the breeze.

"You keep saying that you're not stalking me, but every time I turn around, you're staring at my ass."

I'd thought a lot about Piper since I last saw her. I actually wondered if I'd ever see her again, but I should've known she'd sneak up when I least expected it.

"I wasn't staring at your ass, but could you blame me if I was?" I turned to face the little minx. She was leaning against a tree that decided to grow through the sidewalk. The moon was playing games with her skinny little silhouette.

"While you were following me," I began, "did you happen to see an elephant-sized guy stroll through here?"

She scrunched her nose. "No, but he sounds hot. I wasn't following you."

"Then, what are you doing here?"

"I," she quickly glanced at the house she was standing in front of, "have been house-sitting."

"Really? Who do you know--" I stopped because I already knew the answer to that question.

"They're on vacation. Somewhere in the Balkans, I think."

"I'm sure you're doing a great job, keeping an eye on things, feeding the dog, watering the plants..."

She looked down at the sidewalk with an angry grin, then quietly turned and walked back in the yard, toward the front porch.

I sped up behind her. "Hold up!"

She spun in place, planting her finger in my sternum. "Don't you dare judge me! I don't have a fucking bank to hide in." Tequila perfumed the air as she yelled.

"I wasn't judging."

She eyed me closely and then checked left and right. "Great, then why don't you come in and prove it. Or are you being uptight again?"

I snickered as I recalled her stupid little dare. She blew me away that night.

"Well?" she asked.

I looked over her shoulder at the red brick house. Stealing from grocery stores and lifting wallets felt different than B&E. However, my perspective had changed dramatically in the past few weeks as things didn't seem quite as easy as they once did.

She didn't wait for my excuse and stomped up the wooden stairs in her skippy steps, happy to be up to no good. The front door swung open like it was nearly off the hinges. I wondered what she did to get in.

Looking back at the street, there was still no sign of Jackson, but my stomach had begun to eat itself. It made my decision a little easier. Picturing a stocked fridge made my mouth water with anticipation.

Once inside, I questioned how long she'd been squatting. The lights were all off and it didn't look like anything was out of place. Somehow, I couldn't picture her as a considerate thief.

"What's going through your head right now?" She asked, fumbling through the dark.

"I'm concerned that you might be setting me up."

"You really don't trust me, do you?" she asked, flipping on a lamp, revealing a living room straight from the early 80's.

"Does that really surprise you? I mean, so far in the brief time we've known each other, I went to jail after you picked a fight with a drug dealer, stole a car, slashed an entire police department's tires, and nearly shot a cop."

"Are you forgetting half of that equation? I believe you were there for all those events, and if I remember correctly, no one had a gun to your head. Personally, I think you might be the bad influence."

I laughed because it was the only way I could convey how ridiculous that was.

"Come on, get some food. I know you're hungry."

She didn't have to tell me twice. I moved through the house and found the black fridge tucked in the corner of the outdated kitchen. When I reached for the handle, I was distracted by the pictures stuck to the freezer. It was a family of five, all happy, all healthy. Some of the pictures were posed for, some were action shots, but they consistently showed all five faces. I was particularly struck by the mom. She wore a smile mixed with stern laugh lines. I wouldn't want to mess with her.

"It's easier if you don't look at their faces," Piper said from the doorway.

"So, that's the secret? If I don't look at them, I don't have to care?"

"Yeah."

"How often do you do this?" I asked.

"How often do you get hungry?"

My mouth dropped a little.

"There are other tricks too. For instance, it's always better to go for the nice subdivisions, but not too nice. Typically the real nice places have alarms."

I shook my head, still amazed.

"Let's see, what else... Only steal stuff you need to survive. That's a big one. Food, clothes, windsocks... stuff like that. People tend to be more forgiving if they think you're desperate, not greedy."

I tilted my head to the side. "Did you say windsocks?"

"Yeah, windsocks."

"You need those to survive?"

"Of course. You never know when you're going to need a windsock."

The girl was flippin' crazy, but she made me laugh.

"Never steal a car from the house you're picking clean. That opens a whole other can of worms."

"What about fingerprints?"

"Yeah, you have to be careful about that. Only touch stuff with your sleeve, or something like that. Oh, and don't turn on too many lights. That one's kind of obvious though."

"Thanks, those are some good tips." I hoped that I'd never have to use them, I thought.

She nodded and spun, heading back outside. "We can eat on the front porch," she called over her shoulder, turning on the radio as she went. That seemed like it would be against one of her rules, but I didn't ask.

Suddenly we were an old, retired couple. I wasn't going to complain though. My stomach was twisted into knots. After raiding the fridge, I had BBQ ribs, pancakes, leftover french fries, and peanut butter, lots of peanut butter. While I ate, she sang along quietly to Ray Charles and stared out at the street. I couldn't figure the girl out, but I was so hungry I didn't try.

When I finally stopped shoveling in food, I leaned back and stared right along with her. I could've sworn Jackson walked on that sidewalk just a short while ago. It was a quiet block. I couldn't hear much, other than the occasional dog.

"If I could introduce you today, I would say, hello, this is Pac-Man," she said.

I smiled at my shoes. "You know, we don't have to do stuff like this. We could just get jobs." I think I just wanted to see her reaction.

"I don't know about you, but my life's too short to worry about clocking in and out for someone else."

"So, it's better to steal from someone who does?"

"That's how the system works. Those who choose not to work, steal from those that do."

She sounded like I did when I talked about DCFS. I wondered what her story was.

"What's got you so damn angry? I thought it was just because you're hungry but you keep trying to piss me off. Why?" she asked.

I shook my head, knowing she was right. "Nothing. Just been a tough few weeks."

"So barbie ditched ya, huh?" she asked, leaning back in her chair.

"How'd you... never mind."

"Serves you right," she said.

My forehead scrunched into eight different layers. "What did you say?"

"You heard me. Why do you keep chasing after little-miss-saintly? If she really cared about you, she'd be here. Seems like you're always looking for her. Maybe she doesn't want to be found."

That sounded familiar. "Yeah, I think we're done talking about Joss."

I felt her eyes on me so I kept my head down, focusing on my feet. "So, what about you? You dating anyone?"

"Got 'em lined up around the block," she joked. "Actually, seems like I keep chasing after guys that don't care too."

There was a moment of silence while I felt blood rush to my head.

"Where have you been? I haven't seen or heard from you since the golf course."

"Don't worry about me. I'm around," she said with a wink. "So, are you going to tell me how you dropped that guy at Mardi Gras?"

"Still on that, are ya? What if I told you that I punched the grim reaper in the face? And that ever since then, my hand's been cold, almost like it was dead." Of all people, she couldn't think I was crazy. Besides, who could possibly believe that story?

"Sweet! Does that mean you're slowly dying? Or that you're becoming like him?" Her frosty eyes were wide with excitement, but her seemingly harmless joke struck a chord. It pained me to wonder...

"How about you tell me what you've been up to over the last month?" I asked, trying to change the subject.

"Where'd you get the scar?" she deflected, looking down at my neck.

"A lion clawed me." I felt tough when I looked at it in the mirror, but saying the words out loud seemed strange, like another one of my poorly planned lies.

"Wicked! How deep are they? Did it crack your ribs?" She leaned in on her chair, pulling at the collar of my t-shirt. "Come on! Take it off, skinny! Let me see!"

"I will if you do," I laughed, pulling my shirt away from her grasp.

"You don't think I'll do it?" She started peeling the red flannel over her head, leaving only a sports bra as she leaned back in her chair. My jaw nearly came unhinged. Her arms folded over her athletic little frame. She was impressively toned for being malnourished, and a possible drunk.

I pulled my eyes away and gave in. I took my shirt off and showed off the cat's signature. The night air was still plenty cool for bare skin. My overly-white torso immediately compressed as the chill set in.

"Wow. That is insane! How'd you get it?" The excitement in her voice didn't fade at the mention of dying. Her fingers slowly ran along the top of my neckline and traced down my chest, to my abs. I flexed, of course.

For a homeless psychopath, she cleaned up well. Her wild hair smelled like lilac and cinnamon. The strain in her cheeks had disappeared, and with it, the strung-out appearance I'd attributed to starvation. Maybe she had been squatting here for a while.

She stopped as her finger came back to my neckline, pulling a chill up from my ribs. Her smile was crooked, like she'd lost a fight at some point. I remembered the night at the golf course. I was surprised how much I could recall, how alive I felt that night, not worrying about getting caught. I wanted to get that feeling back. I remembered when she jumped in my arms. I knew I wanted to kiss her then, but I wouldn't admit it.

I thought about Joss, and in place of sadness, I grew angry, betrayed even. How could she leave? Screw her.

I grabbed the moment. Piper's lips were warm and aggressive, like a challenge. Kissing her was a competition, to see who could enjoy it more. I leaned in, reaching to touch the small of her back and pulling her in closer, if that was possible. Her fingers scraped along my chest as we tore into a flood of hunger, forgetting to breathe.

"Nice try," she finally said, gulping air and shoving me back into my chair. "But, your scar isn't that tough." Laughing, she skipped back into the house, pulling her flannel back on as she went. Dumbfounded, I stewed in my chair, all worked up and no place to go.

I followed her into the kitchen. She had a whole plate of fried eggs, and some toasted ravioli. She sat a soda down next to the lamp as she glided into the living room, sitting cross-legged in front of the coffee table.

She shoveled in food like a starving mule. It was impressive. No wonder she looked better. She was consuming enough food for hibernation.

"Good god, are you even chewing?" A white-eyed glare shot across the table, warning me to shut my mouth. It seemed like a good idea, shutting my mouth, so I obliged and reached for her drink. Without breaking concentration on her plate, a tiny hand slapped mine away.

"Get your own."

"You've got to be kidding me. You just stole that from the pantry. It's not even yours."

"Possession is nine-tenths of the law."

"Yeah, quoting legalities—always a good idea while breaking and entering."

She rolled her eyes and crunched down on a ravioli, wiping her mouth with her sleeve.

Interrupting that moment was the first noise I'd heard on the street since we sat down. Across the way, a black SUV had pulled into the driveway of an old, rickety, grey house. I moved to the window, careful not to be seen through the shades. It was a two story Colonial, with maroon trim falling off. The shudders were caked with layers of grime, and the porch looked like it had more termites than nails.

Three goons lumbered from the driveway to the side of the house, carrying cardboard boxes in their arms. They didn't look like they belonged in the quaint little neighborhood, but after setting the boxes down in the freezer along the back stairwell, they trudged to the front porch and knocked on the door.

"Speaking of ravioli," Piper said, taking a sip of her drink. "Jericho eats a lot of it."

"What?" I asked. "What about Jericho?"

"He eats a lot of toasted ravioli. Check the boxes. They always keep that freezer stocked."

I turned back to the old house. The door opened slowly, creaking on its hinges. A wiry guy with bug-eyes and a do-rag stood defensively to the side. Stepping out on the front porch was Jericho. I quickly scooted to the doorway, straining to get a better picture. Two hands grabbed at my elbows, pulling me back from view.

"Calm down there, tiger," she said. "Don't want to get shot, do you?"

"Don't you know who that is?" Disbelief rang through my voice. I couldn't believe she'd found him. "Don't you remember? He stabbed that usher and threatened to kill you. You of all people--"

The golf course flashed through my head again I watched the curve of her sinister little brows. At the time, I didn't realize that it was all to get back at Boudreaux for holding her in jail. As I stared at the house across the street, Piper's taste for revenge grew clear.

"You've been lying," I said. "You chose this house because it was right across from Jericho. What are you planning on doing?"

"As I told you before, I'm just staying here while they're away. I couldn't care less about that guy."

"So, you're telling me that it's a big coincidence that you're staying across the street from a guy that threatened to kill you? I'm not an idiot, Piper."

"What do you think I'm going to do, stomp across the street and start blasting drug dealers? I don't have superpowers," she said, grinning at my hand.

"I don't either." Even if I did, I wasn't going to admit it to her. She'd want me to go do something crazy.

"Tell that to the bruise on my back," she hissed.

"That's still there?"

She nodded.

Jericho stepped back inside, shutting the door behind him. It was a gut instinct, but I walked across the room and grabbed the phone from the hook. Piper slammed it back down.

"What do you think you're doing?"

"I'm calling Boudreaux." Admittedly, I should've seen it coming. She tagged me along the side of the head with the receiver. I felt a trickle of blood above my ear as I braced myself for another shot.

"What's wrong with you?"

"Think about it," I said, wiping the blood dry. "With one phone call, I can take care of Boudreaux and Jericho."

"Yeah, because the system always works like it's supposed to. I'm sure you can trust the good detective." She flashed a wicked little grin. "Just like you trusted Billie..."

I looked into her eyes. "How'd you know she was up to something?"

She smiled and raised an eyebrow.

"Can you at least tell me what she's doing?" I asked.

"I don't know what she's up to. I just knew that you couldn't trust her. She's a liar."

"Whatever. I'm calling Boudreaux. I'm going to put an end to this whole thing."

"If you must... don't take me down with you." A cheap cell phone landed in my lap. Looking a little closer showed that it was one of those pay-as-you-go ones. Smart. She could ditch the cell phone any time she wanted. I thought I'd been pretty resourceful, but I still had a lot to learn.

I dialed 911 and held it up to my ear. She wasn't interested in listening. She'd already made her way back to the kitchen, yawning as she went. This time I did stare at her ass.

"Emergency hotline," a voice answered.

"I need to speak with Detective Boudreaux."

"Sir, is this an emergency?"

"Yes."

"What can I help you with?"

"Like I said, it's an emergency and I need to talk to Detective Boudreaux."

"Sir, why don't you call the main station number if you needed to talk Detective Boudreaux?"

"Because I didn't know that number, damn it."

"One moment, sir."

I held the phone from my face, wondering how helpful she'd be in an actual emergency situation.

"Boudreaux here," someone growled into the receiver.

"It's Seven."

"Interesting. And to what do I owe this honor?"

"I know where Jericho is."

"Well, great, I'll finally be able to close the case."

"I, well, I thought you'd want to know."

"Yep, thanks for that."

"Thanks for-" He wasn't making any sense. "Aren't you trying to find him?"

"I am, and trust me, I will. However, I'm thoroughly convinced that I can't trust a damn thing you say. You and your girlfriends have done nothing but lie since the moment I saw you. On top of that, you almost got me killed."

"You locked us up like we were criminals after Mardi Gras. Then you held a gun to my head and threatened to send us to prison."

"What do you not understand about this? You are criminals! Do you have some illusion that you're above the law? Have you forgotten that you nearly killed a man? Did you overlook the fact that Piper St. Clair assaulted a police officer? Oh, and the other one, Josslyn Gordon-she broke you out of police custody."

"You're taking those events out of context."

"Am I? Or have you created this alternate reality in your head where I'm the bad guy?"

Piper watched my reactions carefully. An I-told-you-so was eagerly waiting for me when I hung up the phone. "Do you want to know where Jericho is or not?"

"I want to know where your father is." I could hear the grind of his teeth through the receiver.

"So, you'd rather leave a drug dealer out on the streets until it's easier for you to make a case?"

"I can't keep explaining how this works, kid."

"I know exactly how this works. I lived through how it works."

"Then you understand that I need probable cause. I can't just go smashing my way into some house. I need something to go on."

"So he gets to do whatever he wants while you walk on egg shells not to break someone's rules?"

"Yes, that's exactly how it works. Those rules, or laws, are the difference. If I go around doing as I please, I'm no better than him. So, help me out. Help me find your father and I'll be able to lock up Jericho."

"Probable cause..."

"Yes, I need probable cause."

I hung up the phone, too furious to look at Piper's grin. The lamp was the only thing I could focus on for some reason, so I threw it into the bookshelf. Glass shards exploded all over the room and Piper snickered in delight.

I should've known better than to reach out to a cop, but I wanted him to be different. He wasn't. He was worthless. He had to know that if he ever wanted to catch Jericho, he was going to have to get his hands dirty.

It was a pipe dream to think it would be that easy, but at least I knew where he stood. I was on my own.

Without thinking, my feet led me out the front door and down to the sidewalk. Piper didn't try to stop me, but I heard her footsteps on the front porch. I glanced at the grey house, memorizing the yard, the porch, the stairwell to the basement. The lights weren't on upstairs, but they were throughout the rest of the house. The mailbox tilted badly to the street. Halloway was scratched off from the side.

Chapter 11
ARCHES

I wished I could slash Boudreaux's tires again. That was all I could think about as I walked in the bank. That, and the fact that Rusty hadn't been fed in a while. At least I finally had something to give him, thanks to Piper.

The building felt empty, and it bugged me that I noticed. I'd been on my own most of my life. Why would it matter now?

Loud music interrupted the silence. Picasso's was hopping, still cruising from the happy hour rush. I walked outside, leering across the street at the happy people enjoying their caffeinated high. I hadn't been back since that barista threw me out.

Before I could duck back inside my pathetic cave, Gabe's car screeched to a stop in front of the bank. He never drove that fast. I was surprised he actually could. Maybe he finally felt guilty for telling me to go to hell. I leaned over, looking in the passenger window.

"Well, look who decided to apologize. What in the world are you doing driving that fast?" Billie's concerned face stared back at me from the driver's seat. "Oh, it's you," I said through gnashed teeth, turning around and heading back inside. The car door slammed and her quick, athletic steps followed behind.

"Hey, hold up. I know you're angry with me, but stop."

"Angry?" I spun around and stood toe to toe with her. "I don't really think angry covers it. You lied to me. You lied to Gabe. Do you know, or even care how worried he was?" I slammed the door behind me but I knew she'd follow me in.

"You're not welcome here. Unless you've come to explain what you were doing at the zoo."

"Like I've told you before, you don't own this place, so you can't stop me from coming in."

My patience ran out, if I even had any to begin with. "Do I need to prove that I can?" My fingers flexed involuntarily. Energy was flowing from them. It shook as I forced it closed, like I was holding back a surge of electricity in my fist.

"I'm not scared of you," she said quietly. Liar.

"Why were you at the zoo?" I yelled, not caring if they could hear me at Picasso's.

She looked down at her phone, like the text she just got was more important than owning up.

"Why were you at the zoo?" I yelled again, louder than before.

She jumped at the crack of my voice. A look of shock crossed her face and she whipped her phone at me. "I was there because of you! For you, ya stupid prick!"

"This ought to be good," I said. "How were you there for me?"

"Do you want to know the real reason?"

"It's about time you started telling the truth."

"After the night at the theatre, I got scared. I could see what was going to happen. Jericho would eventually find you, and Gabe would be there too. I couldn't live with that. I couldn't let anything happen to you guys. I didn't have a choice.

"What did you do?" I demanded.

"You weren't supposed to find out."

"What did you do?" I yelled.

"I went to Jericho. I offered to help him find your dad as long as he didn't hurt you or Gabe," she said through tears.

I stepped back and tried to get words out. I didn't know what they'd be though. What should I say? Who was I looking at?

"I was only trying to help," she cried. "But I've messed everything up. I know I have. Gabe won't even talk to me."

I always gave Billie so much credit for being tough. She was. Smart, on the other hand, she was not.

"What kind of idiot does that? What the hell were you thinking?" I asked, laughing out of disbelief.

"I wanted to protect-"

"I don't need your protection! You're not my mother!"

She wiped her eyes and looked up. "No, you probably don't. But Gabe does."

"Really? How protected do you think he is now - now that Jericho knows who he is, how he's connected to me, and probably where he lives?"

My hand was so tight it hurt. I was using every muscle I could find to keep from wrapping it around her neck. Blood stuck to my fingernails where they dug into my palm.

"You think you're so damn smart. You didn't even find it necessary to talk to us before you went off half-cocked," I said.

"You wouldn't have listened to me even if I had," she said.

"Exactly! I would've known it was a dumb idea!"

"No, you're so dead set on getting even with your dad that you don't care who gets hurt in the process," she said.

"That's not true!" I felt light headed. My throat started to burn. If I didn't do something to calm down I might pass out from the pain in my hand.

"Really? It didn't stop you from dragging Gabe into this wild goose chase. Any time you need a ride, there's good ol' Gabe, like the best friend that he is."

That cut deep. I could say what I wanted, but it was the truth. I knew I'd been putting him in harm's way. I took a deep breath and closed my eyes.

Could she be lying about the whole thing? Would she actually go to Jericho? Was this just another ploy to gain my trust? I wished Piper was there. She'd be able to tell.

"He knew what he was getting into," I said.

"You didn't even know what you were getting into. How was he supposed to know? Even if he did, it wouldn't have stopped him. He'd do anything for you! You know that! So, don't act like you're so much better. I may have been stupid, but at least I was trying to protect him."

She hit me in the chest, but I didn't respond. I was numb everywhere, not just my hand.

"Where's he at?"

She looked at my hand, still shaking. "Check the phone."

I looked down as I picked up the phone with my other hand, beginning to understand why she'd been reading her texts. "Gabe's drinking?"

"Has been for a while." She glared at me. "He kind of flipped out today. You really need to see him."

A twinge of guilt tugged at my chest. "Where's he at?"

"Last I saw, at Laclede's Landing. He refused to leave, so I got desperate. You can be mad at me all you want, but he needs you. Come with me."

I looked down at the phone again, then back at her. Every instinct screamed at me to throw her out, but if Gabe was in trouble, I needed to be there.

"Fine, but we're making a stop on the way," I said, flipping the phone back to her.

"Where?"

"Just picking up some help."

* * *

"We're going where?" Piper asked, leery to leave the comfort of her hijacked house.

"Gabe needs some company."

"Tell him to get a dog."

"Come on," I said, pulling her up from the chair.

"I'm not Gabe's friend."

"You are tonight. Come on."

Piper stood at the door, with her hand on her hip, glancing over her shoulder at the car with Billie in the driver's seat. "What is this? A double date?"

"Don't get your hopes up," I said, grinning as I drug her out to the car.

We slid into the backseat and both girls hissed into the rear-view mirror. "Honey, can we get a new chauffeur, this one's a little too dykey for me," Piper said.

"That's a great look you got going. Did you cut it with pruning shears?" Billie said, looking at Piper's hair.

"Enough. Billie, you were the one who came to me for help. Both of you need to get over yourselves."

"Fine, but I don't understand how she's going to help," Billie said.

"I have to agree with jock strap."

"Shut up, both of you. Billie, drive!"

I'm not sure why, but they listened to what I said. We rode in silence the rest of the way. It was odd. I could feel the silent attacks flying through the air, but silence reigned. At one point, I hummed the national anthem, seeing which girl would get annoyed first. Apparently, the answer was neither. They were too consumed in their own battle to notice my feeble attempts.

Billie parked in the deck across the street from the Landing. When she got out, she headed in the opposite direction of the bars. Piper and I stood in confusion, watching her walk away.

"Where are you going?" I asked.

"He sent me another text. He left the bar." She kept walking.

"But the only thing over there is--" I looked up.

"What?" Piper asked.

"Gabe can be a bit of a drama queen sometimes," I explained.

"What the hell did you drag me into?" she asked.

The St. Louis Arch sat in the middle of an open park along the Mississippi River. We walked through grassy knolls while Billie kept getting texts. He wasn't sitting underneath the trees. We tried the waterfront, but it was empty too. We finally found him sitting up against one of the arch legs. Gabe's face was a mix of happy desperation. His right hand held a bottle of scotch and his left hand held his cell phone.

"Well, look who it is! I've been looking all over for you!" he said, slurring like a boxer after ten rounds.

"At what point did you think I would be at the arch?" she asked.

"Who's that?" he said, pointing at me.

"Very funny. What've you been up to, Gabe?" I looked to his side, where two more unopened bottles sat. The one in his hand reflected brown shades of streetlight. His shirt was drenched with sweat and a smell I couldn't place.

"Seven! I'm sorry about earlier. I would never turn you into Boudreaux."

"Don't worry about it," I said, shaking my head at Piper. She looked like she was about to take his head off.

"You know dad, priests are supposed to be the wise, consoling ones, not the other way around."

He looked like he'd been crying too. I'd never seen him this way. I could only think of one thing to do.

"All right, are you ready?" I asked.

"Ready for what?" he replied.

"When was your last confession?"

Piper scoffed as he smiled and sat up.

"Two months."

"Okay, tell me what you've done."

"Well, I think Billie should be the one to tell you. Honey, show him your finger," he said.

"Which one? I have one in particular that I'd like to share," she snapped back.

"Yeah, that's the one," he said.

I was confused. "You want her to flip me off?"

"He's talking about her ring finger," Piper said as she walked by, grabbing one of the unopened bottles.

Billie looked up at the sky as I finally figured out what they were talking about. Billie's finger had a sparkling rock, set on a simple, gold band. I wouldn't have believed it if her face wasn't red with embarrassment.

"You proposed?" I kind of shouted it. "Wait, he called you honey? I thought you said Gabe wouldn't talk to you!" I looked at Billie, then back at Gabe. "You proposed?"

"He asked me in a handwritten note with the ring sitting on top," Billie said.

I couldn't do anything but laugh. "Really, dad?"

"Oh, that reminds me; Honey, can you cover your ears for a sec?" He waited briefly and then continued. "I think we should do Vegas for the bachelor party."

"Yeah, good call. That's exactly where I'd take you for a bachelor party," I said, rolling my eyes.

"Huh. That's kind of funny. I hadn't thought about it like that. I suppose you wouldn't want to go there?"

"Let's talk about that a little later. Will someone sober please tell me what's going on here?"

"He also got accepted into Seminary, and told his dad he'd go," Billie said quietly, almost under her breath.

"Oh..." I said. "Oh... What kind of an idiot proposes and commits to Seminary in the same day?"

"Imagine that! I got in! What a relief. Oh, I bet they don't let you drink in Seminary," he said, holding up the bottle and looking through it with one eye.

Piper laughed, squatting down by him. She grabbed it and took a long swig. "Trust me, I've known a few priests. Smug old bastards. Drinking comes with the robes."

I looked down, holding back every urge to ask.

"You make me nervous," he replied to Piper. "But, I like you."

"Be careful. Your fiancé doesn't."

"Why not?" He nearly fell over. "You seem perfectly lovely."

"It's easy. She's a bitch," Billie replied.

"Oh, I see." He looked back at me.

"Why'd you propose?" I asked, getting back on track.

"Because I love her," he smiled crookedly. "I love you dear," he sloppily said, looking at Billie.

"Okay, but why'd you propose?"

"Isn't that what you're supposed to do?"

Piper leaned into his shoulder. "Priests aren't supposed to propose, Romeo."

"That reminds me, Seven, I have another confession sir."

Holding back a chuckle, I said, "Go ahead."

"I have broken a commandment. I have dishonored my father and mother."

"How did you do that?"

"Well, Dad wasn't very happy after I told him I was engaged."

"They threw him out," Billie said.

"They did what?" I asked. "Are we talking about the same people?"

I couldn't picture it. They've always been completely supportive of Gabe. I know his dad wanted him to be a priest but to throw him out...

"Dad said that I'm eighteen, and if I'm able to make a choice like that, I'm able to live on my own." He took another drink. "Dude, can I live with you?"

I nearly fell over. "Well, I can see why he'd be mad, or at least confused."

"So, the real question is: Why don't you want to pass out wafers? Besides the obvious," Piper asked.

I sat back and watched, mildly amused. After all, I brought her for a reason.

"I have a calling," he replied.

She looked up at the sky. "That's an empty, pathetic statement. You say that because you know people won't argue with it."

"It's true. It's a feeling I get when I'm in His presence."

"Yeah, I get a feeling too, but it ain't good," she said.

"That sounds like your own issue."

"You're right. What does that matter though? What if you do have a calling?" It looked like she was about to gag as the words came out. "Does that mean you have to act on it?"

He smiled. "Of course. That's how it works."

"No, I don't buy that. What do you think? Some supernatural being is going to hunt you down for choosing your own path?"

"I believe we'll be punished for straying from our path," Gabe said.

She giggled. "Well, I think you'll find the wave of retribution to be rather calm waters."

"You shouldn't mock someone's beliefs," Billie said.

"So, is this an intervention or something? Why are you ganging up on me?"

Piper took the bottle back and sat down on the concrete across from him, resting her feet across his shins. "We're not ganging up on you. Hell, I could care less. This is for my own personal," she took another drink, "amusement."

"What do you have against God?" Gabe asked.

"Don't look at me with those 'save the pagan' eyes. I don't have anything against God. I just don't think you should hide behind shim," she said.

"Shim?"

"When you got the calling, was it a he or she on the phone?" she asked.

"Touché," Gabe replied, taking the bottle back with a smile - the most unlikely friends I could picture.

"Why do you want someone else to make the decision for you?" I asked, grabbing a seat next to Piper.

"What do you mean?" he asked.

Billie gave in and found a spot next to Gabe on the cold concrete.

"Well, you're letting your dad tell you what to do with your life," I said.

"And you put a crackerjack prize on her finger so she would tell you not to enter the seminary," Piper added.

"Why aren't you saying anything?" Gabe asked Billie.

"Well, I actually agree with them, even her," Billie replied.

"Really?" he asked.

"Yeah. I mean, we're only eighteen, and I would marry you now. But, on the other hand, I don't want to do this just so you have an excuse. After all, we have the rest of our lives to figure it out."

"Yeah," Piper grabbed the bottle again. "Don't marry the wench. Don't go to seminary. It sounds like a great plan to me."

"What about my father?" he asked.

"Well, he already threw you out. Sounds like the problem is solved," Piper said.

"Now you've gone too far," Billie jumped in. "Just because your parents didn't love you doesn't mean you can tell him to run away!" She flushed beet red and clenched her fists as she stood up.

Piper leaned back, lying out on the grass, grinning back.

"She's not the only runaway here," I said, glaring up at her.

She stepped back, looking a little embarrassed. "You know I didn't mean you, Seven. He's got a good family. He shouldn't have to deal with what we've gone through."

"Why were you at the zoo?" I asked, trying to catch her off guard in front of the group.

Suddenly shaken, she turned and looked at me with tears in her eyes. She hid her hands in her jacket and stepped back again. "Why would you-"

"How'd you get away from the guy with the purple sash?" It was a shot in the dark, but I went for it.

Piper glanced back to me, looking a little confused.

"I didn't have to believe your stupid coming-back-to-life story, but I'm your friend. I thought I was," she said through tears.

Blood rushed to my cheeks. I hadn't realized Gabe had told her. Nicely played.

I could feel Piper's eyes all over me. "Coming-back-to-life?" she asked.

More embarrassment flowed in, forcing my head to drop. It felt like years since I'd told Gabe what happened. More than anything, I wish I'd kept it to myself. Lies flipped through my brain. Medication felt like the only excuse that could cover my temporary insanity, but then I'd have to explain. Piper was too smart to buy it.

"Seven says he died saving a couple of girls that knew his dad, Christine Dru and her daughter, Bree, from being run over by a car. He then went to purgatory, punched death, stole the key, and returned to earth. Now he has to find his dad, and the baby book that can incriminate him, before the Grim Reaper, who looks like his old friend from Vegas, drags him back to the afterlife," Gabe said, slurring every third word.

I had to give him credit. For a drunk, that was a pretty good summary.

"Really?" Piper turned to me with intrigue lurking in her snowy eyes. "So earlier, you weren't making that up?" She grabbed my right hand and held it in the air momentarily before she jerked her fingers free, already turning a light shade of blue.

"Dude, am I that drunk or did she just turn part-smurf?" Gabe asked.

Billie stared in shock, stumbled backwards, and took off in a sprint. I could hear loud sobs in between her athletic strides.

"Hey, come back!" Gabe took off after her. I watched in amusement as he tripped over his feet trying to catch up. It was like a bad episode of national geographic, where the giraffe chased the cheetah.

"That's a very interesting story," Piper whispered in my ear.

"Please, don't start."

"She'll get over it. All she really wants is for him to chase after her."

"She's still my friend. I can't just leave them. Come on," I said, pulling Piper to her feet. She groaned, but followed along.

We circled around the pond, chasing their tall shadows as the sun dipped below the horizon. As darkness fell, it became even harder to navigate through the park.

Two figures popped up from the corner of my eye. I grabbed Piper and dove behind a bench, still watching Gabe's shadow disappear over the hill.

"What are you doing?" Piper asked, slapping me on the shoulder.

"Shh!" I pulled her down to the grass and army crawled behind a bush.

"Seriously, what is going on?"

"Look down the path," I whispered.

Two men, hefty and out of breath, jogged by. They had on dark blue uniforms and carried flashlights, swinging them around as they jiggled down the path.

"I know I heard a girl scream," the first one said over his shoulder.

"Joey, hold up. We're supposed to call the police for this sort of thing," the slower one yelled back.

"I'm not waiting around for those guys if some girl's in trouble. Quit whining and keep up!"

Piper snickered after they were out of earshot. "You were worried about them? How slow are you?"

"It's not them that I'm worried about. In case you've forgotten, we pissed off every cop in the greater St. Louis area. If they recognize our faces, we'll both go to jail."

For a brief moment, I caught a solemn look in her eye. "I can't believe we're risking jail to chase after father tequila and his boyfriend," she said.

At a much quicker pace, we tore through the trees until we found the path. I could hear another commotion of voices up ahead. I held my hand out and accidentally touched Piper's arm with my cold hand. She jerked back and hissed.

"Damn it," she whispered. "It's just some kids."

She was right. Four teenagers with skateboards were playing around where the concrete path curved downhill.

"Sorry, that one's on me," I said, taking her hand with my left and walking slowly with our heads down.

"You know, we could just let those two work it out," she whispered, brushing her lips against my ear.

"You're trouble," I said, picking up the pace again, silently cursing Gabe as I went.

When we finally caught sight of the parking lot, it wasn't the scene we were expecting. A familiar black SUV screeched to a stop in front of Billie, forcing her to jump back. I didn't quite understand it at first, but I involuntarily let go of Piper's hand and sprinted toward the deck.

Two figures jumped out from the back seat. I immediately recognized them from Jericho's driveway. They weren't carrying ravioli boxes this time.

I was nearly to the concrete when they scooped up Billie, a white cloth wrapped around her mouth, overwhelming her struggle. The bigger of the two took her unconscious body around the side of the vehicle while the other one held a gun at Gabe's head, freezing him in place.

I ran to the right, circling around and ducking behind a yellow Volkswagen. Gabe held his ground while the gunman took one step back. "Stay back, son!" He fired two shots into the pavement, sending sparks everywhere.

I tore across the lot, mildly indifferent to his awareness. It wouldn't have been the first time I died trying to save someone.

Luckily, Gabe was able to hold his attention. I leapt through the air, hoping I could tackle him before he got off a shot. The gunman wasn't the one I needed to worry about though. Before I got close enough to knock him out, the SUV door flung open again and another familiar face popped out.

A bird tattoo marked his neck. His scraggily beard had grown out even more, but it still had the same grey streaks. It was the stocky thug from Dad's apartment. He came down with an overhand blow, crushing the top of my head and drilling me into the ground.

"Not this time, you little prick!" All the bracing in the world couldn't save me from the beating. His full weight came down over top of me, pushing my face into the concrete. Like sledgehammers, his knuckles came from both sides, pummeling my rib cage. I was spitting blood before I had time to breathe.

An explosion of glass shattered in my ear. My shoulders pulled in tight as I curled into a ball. Brown liquid came down all around me, filling my nose with the aroma of whiskey. He groaned and stumbled back, allowing me to breathe again. Piper's little feet stood in broken glass near my face.

"Randy! Get in already!" someone shouted from the SUV.

"If you ever want to see her again, bring your daddy to Jericho," Bird Tattoo said in a smug voice.

I heard two steps and the slam of a door. The engine thundered to life and exhaust washed over my face. The fumes torched my throat, seeping down into my lungs and mixing with the blood in my mouth.

As the vehicle sped off, Gabe's sloppy sobs were the only sound left in the night air.

Chapter 12
BEST LAID PLANS

At a certain point, the taste of your own blood becomes all too familiar. I wiped the sticky substance from my mouth as I stumbled to my knees and watched the taillights turn onto the highway.

"No!" Gabe screamed.

He may have been wrecked, but reality just smacked him sober. Panic rolled over his face, wiping clean the confusion, and raising the curtain for anger. He stomped over and picked me up by the armpits. He was stronger than I gave him credit for.

"We have to get her back! I don't care what we have to do. I don't care if we have to find your dad. I don't care if we have to kill them."

He dropped me to the ground and clawed his fingers through his hair. "This isn't happening."

"It's gonna be okay."

"Don't lie to him," Piper said. "She's probably going to die."

"She's not going to die!" My angry roar silenced the lot, but it couldn't suppress the burn in my chest. Gabe's panic spread like an infection, filling my head with images of an unconscious brunette in the back of that SUV. I didn't think Jericho would kill her until he got what he wanted, but what would he do to her in the meantime? How far would he take it?

I could see the same questions running through Gabe's head too. How long would it be until her finger was in an envelope, or something worse?

The guilt was killing me. This had nothing to do with Billie, or Gabe for that matter. Jericho was after me, or actually, my dad.

"We have to do something." His voice was suddenly calm, with a fabricated resolve that frightened me. I couldn't let him do something stupid, something that would get him killed.

"You're going to sober up. Get in the car," I demanded. I needed some time to think.

"Billie has the keys," Gabe said in an empty tone.

I looked at Piper, who rolled her eyes to the sky and cackled. Without so much as a nudge, she kicked through the driver side window and climbed in, ignoring the alarm.

"Does she know what she's doing?" Gabe asked.

The car jolted to life, killing the siren. "Lucky try," I said with a shrug. "Get in."

Reluctantly, he ducked into the back seat. I slid in the front, pushing Piper to the passenger seat.

"What gives?" she asked.

"Let's not add drunk driving to the list," I said.

The term driving was actually an insult to how I flew through traffic. I wished I could enjoy it, but I was too busy trying to come up with a plan.

"Why are you setting him up for disappointment? You know she's as good as dead. There's only one play here: tuck tail and run," Piper whispered.

"I'm not setting him up. I'm going to save her."

"Oh really?" She asked, clearly annoyed. "How do you even know that she needs saved?"

I scoffed but I already knew where she was going.

"Doesn't it seem funny that Jericho kidnapped Billie of all people? Why not Gabe? Why not blondie?"

I avoided the icy glare and kept my eyes on the road. Joss was the last thing I wanted to talk about. "I know what you're saying, but I can't afford to take that chance. I can't let her get hurt, not for me."

"You know that Jericho's going to kill her, kill you, or get everyone arrested. All roads end in jail or death."

I didn't answer. I knew she'd try to twist things in my head. I couldn't understand why though. I really believed she wasn't that selfish. She might not trust, or even like Billie, but she couldn't want her dead.

Regardless if she cared, we made it to the bank in record time. Gabe's car barely held together as we sped down the bumpy brick road. His shocks were probably destroyed but there wasn't even a whimper from the back seat.

I jumped out of the driver's seat and told Piper to park it around back. Moving Gabe would've been too much work. It wasn't going to be a long stop anyway. An idea was forming, but I needed a few things first.

Stepping into the lobby was like stepping into déjà vu. I didn't have many things, but they were all thrown about like an animal had escaped from the zoo. Hopefully the other lion didn't do it. I really didn't want to relive that nightmare.

"Hey!"

Nearly jumping out of my skin, I recovered to find Joss slipping up the stairs. A frightened look was etched across her face. Without thinking, she threw her arms around me, nearly knocking me over.

"I saw the mess and I thought," she paused, "I thought Jericho found you."

For a moment, I lost myself in her embrace. I pulled her in closer and leaned my cheek into her hair. It caught me by surprise how natural it felt. It was like we could go back in time and forget about all this crazy stuff. I couldn't though. Billie was counting on me. Against every instinct in my body, I broke the hug short and looked curiously into her eyes. "What are you doing here? What were you doing downstairs?"

Her chin shriveled up as she leaned back. "When I saw the mess, I went looking for you. Why?"

"I don't want Rusty to get out," I said flatly.

"I didn't see him. Are you sure he's down there?"

"He's probably hiding." I let go of her and moved to the counter.

No matter how much I wanted to, I couldn't think about Joss, not now. Keeping my head down, I focused on the drawer that I needed to open. It had a hidden latch to the side. I clicked it into place and heard the spring release, shooting it into my palm. Sitting on top of the only photo of my parents I had, was the thing I came back for; Boudreaux's keys. I stuffed them in my pocket and slammed the drawer shut.

"What are you doing?" she asked, moving closer.

"I need to go take care of something."

"Take care of what? Why are you so frazzled?"

It was the only time I remembered being irritated by her questions.

"Oh I don't know, maybe it's because you've been missing in action for the past three weeks. Maybe, it's because you didn't care enough to say goodbye. Maybe it's because you wouldn't even take my calls. Or, maybe it's because Billie is being tortured and it's my fault."

Her face flushed white. "Billie's being tortured? What's going on?"

"Look, I don't know where you've been, but I get it. I understand. Drug dealers and crooked cops aren't your thing. Save yourself the trouble; keep your distance."

"Seven, listen to me for a second. After the night at the zoo, I was overwhelmed. I was scared, and I didn't want to go to jail. So, I ran."

"I told you, I get it. Now, excuse me while I go help my friend."

"I'm trying to tell you that I made a mistake! I miss you."

I stopped a foot from the front door, taking a deep breath as my hand extended to the handle. "I forgive you, but that doesn't change anything. You need to stay away, for your own sake. Jericho did find me. We were at the park under the Arch. He grabbed Billie and he's going to torture her until I give him my dad."

She cycled through the information. "But, you don't know where your dad is. That's why you came here in the first place, to find him, right?"

I nodded, waiting for her reaction.

"What are you going to do?"

"I'm going to get her back."

"How?"

"I'm working on that, but I know where Jericho has her. He's staying in a house a few blocks from here."

Joss' eyes continued to dart back and forth.

"I can't let anything happen to her. If I don't do something, Gabe will. He'll get himself killed."

"As opposed to what you're going to do? Why does anyone have to die?"

"Someone has to stop him. Do you have any ideas?"

She grabbed me by the arms and squeezed hard, pushing me back against the banister. "Yes, you do what everyone else in the world would do. You call the police. You don't pass go. You don't collect $200. You go straight to the cops and explain what's happening."

I rolled my eyes, sick to my stomach as I thought about that scenario. I already called Boudreaux about the house. That was the last thing I wanted to do. He'd probably say she had to be missing for twenty-four hours before he could do anything, or something stupid like that.

"That's not an option. I'm not that guy, Joss. I can't sit around and hope someone takes care of it for me. They're my friends."

"What about your father? Can you find him?"

My eyes narrowed and my hands, both of them, wrapped around her shoulders. Her skin shuddered against my dead fingers and her eyes sunk. I tried to control my emotions but her heart steadied anyway. Whatever it was, I felt like I was learning to control it. "Why are you suddenly so interested in my father? What have you been doing here while I'm gone? Did you tear this place up?"

I released my cold hand from her shoulder. She gulped in a deep breath, eyes wide with disbelief. "Of course not! Are you accusing--"

"Fool me once, shame on me." I dug in tighter with my good hand. "I don't have time to figure out what game you're playing. Have fun with the place. Tear it up all you want. It's not mine anyway."

As I released my grip, she slumped against the wall, obviously in pain. I didn't care. Billie might be an idiot, but Joss had been there all along as well. She lied to me about DCFS. Twice she helped me escape from the cops, the one place Jericho couldn't go. Was she helping Jericho too? No way. I was being paranoid. It wasn't possible.

I shoved hard against the thick wood, slamming the door open and stepping onto the sidewalk. Piper's skinny frame jumped back.

"Whoa tiger! Where do you think you're going?"

I quickly looked back through the dusty window. She glanced over my shoulder to see who I'd been talking to. I closed my eyes in anticipation, but the explosion never came.

"Barbie?" she asked.

"Yeah," I grumbled.

"So, that's it then," she said, almost like a question. She was beautiful - blunt to a fault. And she deserved better than me.

I knew the truth. I wasn't over Joss, not even close. I couldn't trust her, not anymore, but she still had some kind of hold over me.

On the other hand, Piper was evil, but not to me. She didn't lie. She just told me things that I didn't want to hear. While Joss was always missing, Piper seemed to show up when I needed her most. For so many reasons, Piper was perfect.

Her only fault: she wasn't Joss.

"I don't know what it is," I said. "I'm just trying to save Billie."

"Yeah," she said, squinting.

"Where's Gabe?" I asked.

"He's in the car. I wasn't going to drag him out of there."

"Okay," I said, heading to the car.

"Nope," she said, holding me back. "Not so fast. Where are you going?"

"Don't try to stop me."

"Okay, I won't. What am I not stopping you from doing?"

"I'm going to get Billie back."

"You were serious about that? Fine." She nonchalantly turned in the opposite direction, gingerly heading for the street.

"That's it?" I asked, somewhat hurt by her lack of concern.

"Yeah, isn't that what you wanted? Not to stop you?"

"That's what I said, but--"

"But what? You want me to cry and tell you to come back?" She stepped back to me. "You want me to beg and plead so you'll stay? Put on a big messy show about why I can't live without you? If you want that, go back inside the bank. I'm sure she'll be happy to." Her v-shaped grin snuck across her face. "Please tell me you didn't think I'd be so pathetic."

"No, you're right. I guess I couldn't imagine you doing that."

She turned around and started walking again. I wondered if that was the last time I'd see her. That realization sent an unexpected shiver through me, deep into my core. I was paralyzed in the moment. Piper was a lot of things, but I never expected my heart to rip as I watched her walk away.

But it did.

My head swam in different directions. The emotions that had been silently brewing for weeks suddenly came bubbling to surface as I stood on that sidewalk.

I wasn't ignorant enough to act like she didn't mean something to me. I just didn't know what. Was she my muse? My siren? Or something more?

Had I only begun to understand who she was? Or was she simply an angry girl, trying to get back at the world?

"You know what I'd do?" She said, quickly turning around in the middle of the street, interrupting my emotional hurricane. Her pointer finger twirled in her dark, messy hair. "I'd burn it down."

"Burn it down? The house?" I asked.

"The whole damn thing."

"Oh, it's that simple for you? Just set it on fire and walk away? Kill everyone, including Billie?"

Her stone cold eyes didn't blink. A faint smile escaped as she lowered her head and looked back up from under her bangs. "It's always an option."

There it was.

That must've been her plan all along. That's how she was going to get her payback, by burning Jericho alive. But what that crazy little pixie didn't realize is that she gave me the idea I'd been searching for.

"What if I did both?"

"Both what?" She asked.

"I'll see you around, Piper," I said, walking away.

I had to move quickly or I might lose the nerve. The Metrolink was just a few blocks away. I pulled Gabe out of the car and guided him quietly through the streets. As he continued to sober up, our steps became strides, and houses became blocks.

The train stops blurred together, eating precious time. I kept hearing screams, seeing Billie's pain-ridden face all around me. She was on posters, advertisements, even the homeless woman in the back row of seats, staring at me like I was nuts.

Eventually, Gabe came back to life. "What is it with you and the train? My car was right back there."

"I'm not sure it would come back from where we're headed."

His eyes closed and his head shook. "What's the plan?" he asked, breathing heavily.

"You're not going to like it."

"I don't care what it takes to get her back. I'm in."

"Okay, that's good, because there's a good chance that this could end badly."

"What do we need to do?"

"First, we need to get some bait."

He scrunched his face in confusion.

"Just go with it," I said.

I didn't need to look at the map when we stepped off the train. I'd been there before. The police station was a grey box with rectangular holes stamped in along Clark Avenue, right in between the Treasurer's office, and a stone's throw from the hockey arena.

Standing across the street, I wondered if I actually had the balls to pull it off. There were probably five cameras focused on us at any moment, so I kept my head low, ensuring they couldn't catch my face.

Gabe kept a lookout as we waited for the game to end. We paced back and forth, listening for the horn. I knew it would come soon. The arena always grew quiet before the conclusion.

Finally, after nearly thirty minutes, it happened. The horn sounded and masses of blue and yellow fans spilled into the street. The rush of people created the storm we needed. I darted for them, moving in, through, and ducking beneath the crowd.

"Seven!" Gabe yelled. "What do I do now?"

"Pick a fight."

"Really?" he asked.

"And make sure everyone can see it."

Suddenly, Gabe was the friend I'd always wanted. There wasn't any scripture, or commandment to contemplate. He had to save Billie, and nothing was going to stop him. He stood up straight, expanded his frame, and threw a nasty haymaker, sucker punching some redneck with a blue jacket. Mr. Goatee fell to the ground, stunned, but furious. He threw his buddies to the side and parted the sea to reach Gabe.

Surprisingly, Gabe wasn't waiting for an invitation and leapt at him, taking down as many people in the process as he could. Unfortunately, one of those people was a sixty-year-old woman, but sometimes you had to crack a few eggs.

A group of guys came storming from the arena sidewalk, wearing blue staff shirts. A couple of them had radios. To the left, I saw the doors to the station open up. Some boys in blue walked out, making their way towards the commotion.

"Gabe, it's time to go!"

I couldn't wait around any longer. There wouldn't be a better diversion than the post-hockey scrum right in front of me. "Gabe, the cops!" I yelled, hoping Gabe heard my voice above the fight.

I scooted to the far right of the sidewalk, ducking behind anyone I could find. Eventually, I circled around the back and jumped over the barricade. I was pleasantly surprised, yet disappointed by the lack of surveillance. It smelled of arrogance. I guess they had a right to be. Who breaks in to a cop-shop?

Getting into the lot may not have been that difficult, but cameras were on every pole. I couldn't create a diversion for them, so I dropped to all fours and army crawled behind an oversized bush along the fence. I went as far as I could through the landscaping until I reached the back of a maintenance truck.

I hadn't thought through the plan very thoroughly. I couldn't think of a way around the cameras. No matter what I tried, I knew I was going to have to come out in the open. I didn't even know which car was the one I needed.

"Seven!" It was a whisper, but loud enough to be heard across the lot. "Seven!"

"What the hell, you moron!" I shouted back, wanting to strangle him. He strolled in between the cars, oblivious to his surroundings. A cop in a white pressed shirt got out of his car and looked around. He and Gabe exchanged glances as I kept down, trying to avoid his idiocy. Gabe kept sloppily walking through the lot, trying to avoid the stare-down.

He was headed right for me, so I moved to the left, behind a K-9 cruiser. If he got caught, I couldn't go down with him. Someone had to help Billie. Whether it was by luck or by design, the badge with slicked hair must've thought he was a drunk, spilling out from the game. He took one more look, but started for the back entrance to the station.

Gabe was already bruised up. His face was different shades of purple and crimson, but he was smiling like he'd just won the title.

"Dude! Why are you running away?"

"I'm not running away! You're tromping through a private lot behind the St. Louis police department! It's going to be hard to help Billie with you in the pen."

"Sometimes it helps to have a little faith."

"Don't start that shit with me now, dad."

"It's going to be fine. I'm not sure how, but I have a feeling everything is going to work out."

I wanted to argue with him. I wanted to set the expectation that he may not walk out of this unscathed, but I couldn't. Even if he was delusional, it was still better than him going half-cocked to Jericho and getting himself killed.

"What are we doing here?" he asked.

"How can you be so damn sure that it'll turn out all right if you don't even know what I'm up to?"

"I don't know... That's why I'm asking."

"You've lost it, dude. You've completely lost it. We're trying to find a car," I said, holding out Boudreaux's keys."

"So, what are you waiting for?" he asked.

"What are you talking about?"

"The keys-what are you waiting for?" I sat with a blank face, trying to figure him out.

"Here," he said, looking at me like I rode the short bus. He grabbed the key chain and pressed the big red button. A shiny white cruiser started flashing across the lot.

"There! That's the car, yes?"

Feeling stupid for not having thought of it, I nodded. There I was, trying to be a hero, and a drunken priest showed me up. Brilliant.

"Yeah, that's the one. Come on." We walked calmly, but quickly, through the maze. There was no use hiding anymore. Gabe had already ruined that hope.

"Seven?"

"Yeah?"

"Why are we stealing Boudreaux's car? Better question... How are we going to steal a cop car?"

"We're not stealing it. We're just going to take it for a ride."

I held up the key and clicked the unlock button. "Get in," I said, motioning to the car. Like an idiot, he tried to get in the back seat.

"What are you doing? Sit in the front!" Smiling, he shuffled around to the other side and climbed in. It'd been a while since I rode in one. Officer Kendrick, back in Vegas, made me ride in the back as he escorted me back to DCFS. I didn't remember there being so many gadgets. Boudreaux had a full-blown laptop built into the dash. I didn't even want to touch that thing. It'd probably try to read my fingerprint or something.

"Do you know how to drive one of these things?" Gabe asked.

"It's a car, not a submarine. What do you think it's going to do, shoot rockets if I push a wrong button?"

"I don't know. Just don't get caught." He nodded like he'd just made a grand decision on how to proceed.

"Sounds like a plan, but it looks like that window is closing," I replied, motioning to the side door of the station. Two more uniforms piled out and started walking to the back corner. Their eyes were shifty, constantly looking around. We ducked low, but I wasn't sure if they had seen us.

The purr of the engine from one of the cars along the fence allowed me to breathe, but only momentarily. When I peeked from my lounged position, I saw the car heading our way. They were cutting down the middle on their way to the exit.

Frantic, I searched for an escape route, but I couldn't find any. If we got out of the car, they'd see us for sure. We couldn't start the engine either.

I looked at Gabe, his eyes shifted from the window back to me. A red and blue shark fin slipped around the corner and swam closer. It seemed to be moving in slow motion. They saw something, or they thought they did. We slunk as low as we could get, almost kissing the floorboard. I couldn't believe we weren't even going to make it out of the parking lot. I'd stolen plenty of cars, but I found it ironic that the one time I actually used keys was when I was going to get caught.

The red and blue lights finally reached Boudreaux's car. I could feel their eyes piercing the door, trying to see who was inside. My hand started throbbing. The pain slowly crept from my fingers, through my wrist, until it reached my shoulder. My whole arm was a dead limb, thronging with pressure.

As if Gabe's faith somehow gave a push from above, the other car lurched forward and sped off. A deep breath filled my chest and Gabe started laughing like we'd just won the lottery. The pain in my arm subsided, but it still felt asleep, tingling with pins and needles.

The coast seemed clear as I peeked over the steering wheel. They'd left the parking lot and turned onto Clark. We could use the side exit, which was clear.

"Go ahead and relax. From here, it's smooth sailing. All we have to do is drive the stolen squad car, avoid getting spotted, and rescue your girlfriend from one of the most dangerous guys in the country."

"Yeah." The wind left his sails in a hurry. "What are we going to do?"

I kept my eyes on the road, cruising down I-70 at record pace. I didn't even need the lights on. People got out of the way regardless.

"What are we going to do?" he asked again.

"I'm not completely sure yet."

"Then why did we just steal Boudreaux's car?" His voice grew about eight octaves. "This isn't about being cute or rebellious, Seven. This isn't a game. This is Billie. Don't tell me you're pulling some insane stunt that's just going to get her killed." He ran his fingers back through his hair, nearly pulling some out in the process. "Why did we steal this car?"

Crackling static suddenly blared from the radio attached to the dash. "Will the driver of squad car 524 please identify yourself?"

It was faint, and even more muffled than usual, but I could out pick the detective's voice from the background noise. "I'd really like to know who's stupid enough to steal my car."

Before I could reach for it, Gabe had it to his mouth. "Oh, was this your car? I always do this. Sorry, I'll turn around and drop this back off at the station," he said, shrugging at me.

"Who is this? Do you realize how much trouble you're in?"

I snatched the handset from Gabe and clicked the button. "Detective Boudreaux... Nice to hear your voice. Did I get your attention?"

Silence.

"So, you're the one who took my keys. I'm sure you're very proud of yourself. You know I'm going to lock you up for a very long time, son."

"You have to come get me first."

"You realize that we can track where the car is at any time by GPS?"

"Good, then I won't have to tell you where I'm headed. Get your old ass in a car and come get me."

Gabe's eyes nearly exploded from his skull.

"Oh, don't you worry, I'm on my way," he said.

I pulled onto Third Street, turned off the headlights, and click off the radio. "Jackass," I said with a wry smile.

As I tossed it back at the dash, I wiped my brow in frustration. I could talk a big game, but deep down, I was afraid at what I'd just set in motion.

The look on Gabe's face kept me focused. Every minute that ticked off the clock pulled him further from sanity.

"If someone had taken seminary away from you, would you be this upset?" I asked.

"Life's full of tests, Seven," he answered.

I smiled. "Who grades them?"

"Go to hell."

"Been there... kind of. Look, I just want you to think about it. Just remember how you feel right now, how it would feel to lose her."

He looked away, staring into the darkness.

Like the conversation, the street was dead. With the windows down, all we could hear were early spring crickets, singing into the night. The car idled into an open spot, just a few houses down from Jericho's.

When I opened the car door, my foot touched down softly on the concrete. At the same moment, a light on the front porch nearest to us flipped on, nearly scaring me back into the car.

"It's a motion light," Gabe whispered.

"Thanks, I got that."

"For the last time, what are we doing here? Where is here and why did you tell Boudreaux to come get us?"

"Because we need him."

"Okay, that kind of makes sense. But we just stole his car. How is that going to help?"

"That's where I come in." I scanned across the street, trying to find any sign of movement. "Billie is in that house," I said, pointing over his shoulder.

With a greater force than I was ready for, he turned and dragged me to the middle of the street. It took every ounce of strength I had, but I finally got in front of him.

"How do you know?" he yelled.

I glanced back at the house Piper was squatting in. "I saw him, earlier tonight."

He pushed me aside again, stomping closer to the house.

"Hey! Stop! What are you thinking?"

"I'm going to get her out," he said with a desperate look in his eye.

"How do you expect to do that? By knocking on the door and asking for your girlfriend back?"

"Then how are we going to get her? Tell me, oh wise one. How are a couple of kids going to rescue Billie from a drug dealer? Better yet, why don't we just give him what he wants? Let's find your dad."

"I have a better plan." I grinned slightly, feeling a sense of freedom I usually only felt with Piper.

"I don't like that look," he said, watching me closely.

I wasn't even sure when or how it all came together. It felt like someone was feeding me ideas.

"Around the side of the house, there's a deep freeze. Come on." I didn't wait for a response and moved in a crouch along the sidewalk. I knew he was confused, based on his sudden apprehension to follow, but he eventually gave in and caught up with me.

I couldn't make my feet quiet enough so I stepped onto the grass and tried to stay clear of the light from the windows. I could hear gruff voices inside and a few footsteps, but no sign of Billie.

"Seven, do you see her?"

"No, do you?"

"Are you sure Jericho's here? Maybe you got the wrong house."

"Don't lose your nerve on me now. Billie's counting on us." I met his eyes and held them for a moment, ensuring it fully sank in.

We didn't waste any more time on justifications, explanations, or words. We snuck to the old, rotting deep freeze and lifted the lid, which croaked out a loud creaking noise.

"Shit." He cringed.

"Just keep your head down," I said, digging into the ice.

"What are we looking for? All I see is toasted ravioli. Are you seriously stealing food right now?"

"Have a little faith, holy man. You don't want to eat these ravioli." I tore open a box, ripped the plastic and pulled out an oversized breaded ravioli. I held it to my nose and took a long whiff. Immediately, the familiar smell ripped apart my nostrils and set my insides on fire.

I was suddenly eight years old, in my mom's apartment. I was sitting on the tattered couch that rubbed the bottom of my legs raw. Mom, a woman that looked nothing like me, watched from the corner of the coffee table. The only things between us were a few toys, an empty soda can, parental irresponsibility, and the white powder, spread out over the counter. That smell was unmistakable. It was the source of her happiness, and my despair.

I broke the ravioli open and watched the cocaine fall into the freezer. Gabe leaned in with a look of disbelief. "He's using ravioli to move the drugs... How'd you know?"

"It's a long story. Piper sort of figured it out."

"Figures," he said.

"Anyway, grab a few boxes."

He froze in place and grabbed my wrist. "Why? How is this possibly going to help us get Billie back?"

"You were the one talking about faith. Have a little and trust me!"

Contemplation filled his face, but his fingers lightly released their grip on my skin. I could only imagine the voices in his head, tearing him in opposite directions. Slowly, he reached in and grabbed two of the older boxes near the top of the ice.

"I'm trusting you," he said solemnly. "But, if this doesn't work... If she gets hurt..."

"I know. You won't have to. I'll do it myself."

I also grabbed a couple of boxes and we crept around to the front yard. Crouching in the wet grass, I motioned for him to sit next to me and avoid the light.

"Empty one of the boxes and tear open the ravioli. Pour the coke in here." I demonstrated with my own, creating a small snow drift of drugs in the cardboard. He followed along, but kept one eye on the house at all times.

"You're sure this is going to work?"

I ignored the question. "Combine your pile in here when you're done," I said quietly.

He was muttering some prayer under his breath, which I found mildly entertaining. I'm sure God received some strange prayers, but this particular situation couldn't come up that often.

"What do I do now?" he asked, keeping his focus on the house.

Sirens suddenly blared from the highway. Even though I'd been expecting them, the sound still sent a chill down my spine. Hell, I'd invited them. I practically double-dared Boudreaux.

"Now, you get the hell out of here. Go hide across the street or something," I said, motioning to a garage.

"Seven, I'm not going to just sit around--"

"Do you hear those sirens? You said it yourself; Boudreaux's not going to hand out a warning. If you want to save Billie, you have to stay out of trouble."

"I'm not going let you take the fall for this," he said.

"It's my mess."

"No."

I reached out and grabbed his wrist with my cold hand. He immediately tried to jerk back but I squeezed tighter, feeling his pulse, yanking at his soul. It was a rush of adrenaline that I couldn't understand but after a few seconds his eyes began to glaze over. I released his arm and watched him stumble back to the sidewalk.

"What the hell was that?" he asked, trying to catch his breath.

"You already know. I didn't dream up dying. It happened, all of it. I don't know how this is all connected, but I know that I'm still here for a reason. I came back for a purpose. Maybe this is it. Maybe I came back to save Billie. Maybe I came back to show you how much you need her."

He bore down on me, confused, but focused.

"This is my mess," I said. "I need to clean it up, and you need to be there when Billie gets free. Don't worry about me."

"That's pretty self-sacrificing, Seven. You know, if you aren't careful, you might end up being a good person after all."

"Blow me."

He chuckled quietly and picked himself off the ground. The sirens were getting closer. They'd reach the house in a few minutes.

"Are you sure about this?"

"Go hide!"

He bit his lip before finally turning and running across the street, ducking quietly behind the garage.

I had to work quickly. It wouldn't look so good if they pulled up and caught me red-handed with a box of drugs. Moving silently back to the grass, I starting pouring the white powder out on the grass in steady, deliberately curved lines. My handwriting wasn't great to begin with, yet alone with a lawn as a canvas.

It took longer than I expected, but I eventually finished up and poured a line to the sidewalk, leaving the box there. When I reached the car across the street, it started up with a loud roar, which I was afraid would alert

Jericho and the boys. I breathed a sigh of relief when no one came running out. I pulled it across the street and up onto the curb, slowly. It came to a stop right next to the box in the front yard. A smile formed on my face as I thought about Boudreaux. If he ever caught me, he'd surely kill me. I wouldn't even blame him.

I jumped out of the car, less careful about noise. The first of the squad cars appeared at the end of the long street, still too far to see me. I pulled the keys from the ignition, and slipped a silver Zippo lighter from my pocket. My finger traced number seven etched into the back. Somehow, I didn't think this was what Joss had in mind when she gave it to me. I flipped it a couple of times before it sparked up, forming a tiny flame at the end.

I looked down the street at the police. I looked at the house, where a couple of guys had heard the sirens and peeked out the front windows. I looked back at Gabe, hidden from the scene.

My cold fingers flipped the lighter through the air. I watched in slow motion as it landed with a white puff in the powdery box. The coke ignited, sending a fiery line in each direction.

On one side, the flames crawled into the grass, exposing the message I left in the front lawn for Boudreaux. On the other side, the fire jumped onto the end of his uniform that I took from the back seat. It fit perfectly in the gas tank after I wrapped it up like a towel.

I was half way across the street when I heard the explosion. The blue and orange inferno lit up the night and provided the landmark I promised.

The squad cars skidded to a halt in front of the house. A couple of the officers started using portable extinguishers on the car before they noticed the red, glowing words etched into the grass. A skinny figure stood with his gun pointed at the ground, reading the words aloud.

"Probable Cause."

"Son of a bitch," he muttered.

"What in the world is that, detective?" An officer to his side asked.

"It's a smart-ass kid, thinking he's funny. Forget about the fire!" he yelled back at the group. "Jericho Splitzer's inside. Cover the house, and spread out!"

"How do you know that Splitzer's inside?"

"I just got an anonymous tip," he replied.

A few of Jericho's men came out onto the front porch, wondering what all the commotion was. Boudreaux and his boys were ready though. They had the front of the house surrounded, guns drawn.

Slowly but surely, most of the men gave up. It was fun to watch, but there was no sign of Billie, or Jericho. Boudreaux stood on the porch, ready to enter the house, when he spun to scan the surrounding block. He froze on the bush I was hiding behind, but I knew he couldn't see me. I was hidden too well.

After a couple of sneering looks, he moved into the house, shouting out orders as he went. A few uniforms followed behind him on the sweep.

As he made his way through the house, I heard lots of yelling, but one sound stood out. The back door flew open and Billie stumbled into the street, being pushed forward by a familiar, box-shaped guy with curly hair. My favorite goon, Mr. bird tattoo, was forcing her across the street, trying to make a break for it. He was heading directly for Gabe's hiding place.

I darted across the street and grabbed a spade from the ground next to the tiny garden. I wasn't going to make it, though. My nightmare from earlier was coming true. This was Gabe's chance to do something stupid. I pictured it in my head. I was going to watch my friend die.

I gave up on being quiet and pushed my legs harder than I thought was possible. Hurdling a trashcan and the backside of a car, I closed the gap quickly, but no matter how fast I was, it didn't seem to be enough. Images of a bullet in Gabe's chest roared through my head as I screamed in agony, jumping in front of the goon.

I didn't hear a shot go off, but I didn't hear Gabe either. Where was he?

"I can't seem to get rid of you, can I kid?" he said.

"Here, take me. Let the girl go."

"I have a better idea," he said, raising his gun. "Why don't you just die?"

He tossed Billie to the ground and grabbed me by the neck. His chubby fingers were scaly and powerful, cutting off my air while he watched me writhe in pain.

"Stay where you are!" he yelled at Billie. His gun was pointed squarely at her forehead. "This will only take a second." He squeezed tighter, holding my limp body up further. I could feel the heavy weight in my brain. My chest pulled tight as my heart struggled to continue.

Whether it was from being shot or choked to death, I wasn't sure. But I had completely lost my grip on my surroundings. It wasn't until my fingers twitched that I realized I was still holding the spade. The idiot didn't even look to see if I had a weapon.

I didn't have much fight left, but with all the force I could muster, I swung the wooden handle with one arm and slammed it into his ear. It didn't feel solid, and the handle flew out of my hand as I connected, but his head whipped to the side like a top. Air immediately broke through the dam and filled my lungs, burning my chest as I heaved in and out. He fell to the side, face first into the concrete.

Two small hands helped me up, standing me on my feet. "Are you okay?" Billie looked at me with tears welling up in her brown eyes.

I nodded, not completely understanding what I was saying yes too.

Still groggy, I looked up and caught something out of the corner of my eye. Gun raised and a little wobbly, the drug dealer stood back up and was about to fire at Billie. Behind him, a familiar pair of bright eyes came into view. I'd seen a beast like that before, barreling straight for us.

The car's headlights were blinding, but I knew what I had to do. With my last ounce of energy I threw my shield, my body at Billie, knocking her out of the way and bracing for death.

There was a loud crash, but I never felt the impact. When I looked up, expecting to see Yawkey Way, all I saw was a hero. Gabe jumped out of the car and stood over the top of Jericho's man, making sure he was out.

"Are you guys okay?" Gabe asked.

"We are because of you," I groaned. "When did you get your car?"

"I figured we'd need a getaway car," he said, pulling Billie up to her feet and wrapping his arms around her. "The bank's only a few blocks from here."

"Wait!" she screamed, catching us both off guard.

I stumbled to my feet, checking myself for injuries.

"What?" I asked. "Seriously, a thank you would do."

She quickly kissed Gabe and looked back at me with concern that didn't make sense. She was safe now. What was she worried about?

"I can't lie to you guys anymore." She took a deep breath and gripped Gabe's arm tight.

My feet moved closer as Gabe stepped back.

"What are you up to?" I asked, barely able to restrain my anger.

"I found the book."

An angry storm brewed inside me. I could feel the blood rush to my head and my eyes begin to blur. I fought back my instinct to grab her with my dead hand and test Piper's theory once and for all. I didn't want to hurt her but hatred consumed my thoughts. It would be justified. She nearly got us killed with her lies. She deserves it. Just reach out and grab her.

"I was going to give it to you, I was. Once Jericho had your dad, I was going to give you the book. That way, you couldn't do anything about it. You wouldn't get into any more trouble."

"You've been working against us all along... You made the noise in my dad's closet on purpose. You wanted us to be found!" I thought ahead. "You didn't fall down the stairs at the theatre either. You were trying to slow us down." A chilling realization hit me. "The bank! You were the one who's been breaking in and trashing the place. You were looking for-"

"I fell in your dad's closet because I stepped on the book and slipped. When I saw you almost choke that guy to death, I decided to hold onto it." She shook her head. "I really did fall down the stairs at the theatre. As for the bank, yes that's why I kept coming over to clean. I was seeing if you'd been hiding anything."

"How could you?" Gabe asked. "How could you lie to me like that?"

She slid a thin package from under the back of her shirt. It was covered in a brown paper, badly taped together. I knew what it was but I had to see it to believe it.

A book with a picture of Mom, rocking me to sleep, was underneath the wrapping. The look on her face shocked me. It was the first picture I'd seen where she looked genuinely happy. I pulled it in close, trying to take in her smile. How could she throw that happiness away for drugs? I couldn't get a grip on my emotions. I was so angry at her, but I missed her so much.

The next page of the book didn't have anything to do with me. There weren't any pictures, just a list of names. Her handwriting was even shakier than I remember but it was still legible. I didn't recognize any of the people she wrote down, but each one had a short note to the right, explaining who they were. At the bottom of the list was a name that I was very familiar with: Jericho Splitzer.

It wasn't a list. It was a supply chain, a hierarchy.

I flipped through some more pages and saw some written accounts of deals she witnessed, but I didn't have time to read them. I could hardly believe I was holding it. On the last page, there was a picture loosely tucked into a flap. It was a picture of Senator Grey with Jericho Splitzer. That seemed odd. Why would Mom include that? As I looked closer, there was another face that I recognized in the background. A younger, much healthier Christine Dru stood in the background, holding a small, dark haired baby.

How were Grey, Splitzer, and Dru connected?

"I'm sorry," she sobbed. "That's why I've been so distant. I hated lying to you. I couldn't take it anymore. I wanted to tell you the truth, I did. But, I didn't trust you! I didn't want you to get Gabe killed."

"Why are you telling us this now?" I demanded.

"I overheard some things while I was in the house. I'm not sure how, but he knows you've been squatting at the bank. I never told him. That's why he's been staying down the road, in this house."

"He never came out of the house," I said. "Where is he now?"

"He's doing the same thing I'd been doing all those times at the bank. He's looking for the key." She stared deep into my eyes. "He knows about the vault."

Chapter 13
VIGILANTE

Most people don't run to funerals, especially their own, but that's exactly what I was doing. My strides were short and choppy and my lungs were on fire, but I had to make sure Joss was okay. I didn't even wait to find out how Billie knew about the vault, or if Gabe knew my secret. I didn't care that Jericho was going to kill me. None of that mattered anymore.

I'd spent a great portion of my first life alone. Drugs killed the only person I loved. Then, like a miracle I didn't deserve, two angels appeared. Each in their own way, they gave my second life purpose, a reason to exist. I wasn't going to let a drug dealer do the same to either of them.

Fear pushed me through the alley, eclipsing the mess of sirens in the distance. Eventually, the Missouri River and the echo of my sloppy footsteps were all I could hear. I grabbed a fence post and used it to turn left, heading uphill to Fourth Street. The fence rattled with the force of my weight.

Was that actually an echo?

I wasn't in an amphitheater. It was open air, with a couple buildings and running water nearby. Was I imagining things? I stopped at the end of the block and turned around. There was nothing but trees and shadows, all the way to the boathouse. It was just my imagination.

Turning back to the bank, my head swirled with images of earlier that night. Piper had left, but Joss was definitely inside when I took off. She wasn't a fighter. She wouldn't be able to handle Jericho for long. Picturing her in that scenario ripped my heart into pieces. How could I have accused her of being the rat? I'd probably shamed her into staying.

A panic set in as I imagined what would be inside. What if I couldn't save her?

What could I do? What was my plan? I couldn't just walk in and expect to save the day. I couldn't stop either. Every second that passed could be the difference between life and death. Maybe that was my answer. Maybe I couldn't save Joss, not without dying myself.

Was I ready for that? For the longest time, the only thing that held me to this life was in that vault. Was I ready to give that up?

When I finally reached the parking lot, I looked up at the fire escape. The steps would be too loud. I circled around to the front, trying to peek in the windows as I went.

When I reached the door, I noticed that the glass was broken in the bottom left corner, creating a hole big enough to fit an arm through. The door was cracked open and the lights were off. Piper had been right. This place was creepy.

The front room was like I'd left it, dark and torn to shreds, but the basement light was on. I cringed. Did Joss leave it on from earlier? That was hopeful thinking. I knew the truth. I'd been keeping secrets for too long, and they were coming back to haunt me.

I slowly crept down the metal staircase, my own personal plank, hoping for a miracle that she was still alive.

I didn't call for her. I wasn't sure I wanted to see what condition she was in. Two more steps to the landing. From there I could get an angle to the hallway. Finally, as my foot touched down on the creaky platform, I gave up. He would've been deaf not to hear that crunch beneath my shoe.

"Jericho!" I yelled, fighting back the urge to say, "Honey, I'm home."

"We're down here, Seven," he yelled back. I could hear the smirk in his voice, eager to finally get his hands on me.

My eyes closed and I took a long, deep breath. The weight of my grim reality bore down. Piper's voice rang in my ears. Burn it down and walk away. If I'd done that, would we all be safe? Would Jericho be in my basement? Would he have died in the fire?

Had I just traded our lives for Billie's?

"Don't keep us waiting, kid," he yelled again.

My mind was blank with options. The only thing I could do was face him and the music. I walked down the remaining stairs.

When I hit the floor, I had to step to the right of the concrete pole to see him. I already knew where he'd be. The bank vault was along the back wall, taking up most of the basement.

Jericho was leaning against the vault door, shaking his head and making a clicking noise with his mouth. Both of his arms were extended. One hand held a small revolver pointed at my face. The other held a silver berretta, pointed down, where Joss knelt, facing me.

"Who the hell are you, kid? Who lives in an abandoned bank?"

I didn't answer. I couldn't get past the look on Joss' face. Witnessing that might've been worse than death.

"Anyway, I've given up trying to crack this thing, and I can't seem to find the key, so I'm taking a new approach. Open it up or I do the blonde."

My hand thronged with spasms of pain, sending chills through my entire body as I caught a glimpse of Joss, itching to get free.

"Why don't you let her go and take me?" I asked.

He started laughing, until a pair of footsteps rattled down the stairs behind me. "Well, would you look at that? My little prisoner," Jericho snickered. "And you brought a friend." I looked over my shoulder to see Gabe and Billie, on the stairs, frozen in their tracks. "I'm so glad to see you. It means one less end to tie up."

I couldn't believe they followed me. "What the hell are you doing?" I whispered to Gabe as they walked down with their hands in the air.

"Trying to help you," he whispered back.

"Brilliant work," I said.

"Enough, enough," Jericho said. "Take your spots. We don't have all day." He eyed Billie as she knelt. "Oh, don't worry dear. I'll save you for last."

"This has nothing to do with any of them. Just let them go and you can deal with me. I'm the one you want anyway," I said.

"No, I think this is better. I've underestimated you so far and I'm not going to take any more chances. You're either going to open this vault, or I'm going to kill your friends."

Jericho flipped the safety and raised his gun a little higher. "Now, open the vault!"

I couldn't look at the faces kneeling in front of me anymore. I knew I only had one option. I walked to the vault and carefully entered the combination. Once I heard the normal pop, I stepped back, motioning him to the door.

He pushed it open all the way, revealing the secret I'd been hiding for nearly six months. Rusty Collins, my father, had been running from both Jericho and the cops when I finally caught up with him in a townie bar, just blocks from here. He was slunk back in a corner at the time, minding his own business. He was much skinnier than I remembered and his clothes smelled worse than mine. His hair was long and greasy, matching the sheen to his skin.

To this day, I was proud of my patience. I waited that entire night for him to finish drinking. He was paying with coins, counting them out as he went. Apparently, he'd been struggling worse than me. When he finally got up from his lonely stool, I followed him down Fifth Street. His sloppy steps were misleading. He was actually very quick when he wanted to be, but I was determined not to miss my opportunity.

At one point, he slowed down, probably to check over his shoulder. That was all the window I needed. I smashed a beer bottle over the top of his head and shoved him into an alley, knocking him unconscious.

Four blocks is a long way to drag someone, even if he was lighter than I remembered him. I grunted my way back to the bank, cussing him out along the way. Luckily, it was two in the morning on a Tuesday. Nobody noticed a thing.

The vault was the perfect home for him. I tied him to the bench that was bolted to the steel floor. When I shut the door, no one, not even me, could hear him scream.

He was belligerent at first, refusing to eat, yelling at me, threatening me; that was my favorite. Over time, he went from a weakened state, to a deathly one. His threats became more desperate, almost comical. Of late, he wasn't much more than a corpse that breathed. He gave up screaming long ago. It wasn't worth the energy he didn't have. The tears didn't do much for me either. Every time he cried, I pictured Mom's face. That was usually when I reared back and hit him.

When I was a kid, staying home alone in that cockroach infested apartment, he only came by when he needed to, when he had to. He didn't care about me. Hell, he barely recognized me as his son. Seven months after she overdosed, child services showed up at the door. I hadn't seen him for a while, so I knew then that he'd abandoned me.

That was my plan. After seven months, the life I knew ended. After seven months in the vault, his life would end too. That was the reason I came back. It wasn't to find my father. I already had him. It was to finish the job the system wouldn't do. I could be his judge, jury, and executioner. His reaper.

"Well, well, well... Rusty Collins. Isn't this funny? I've been chasing you around the country for nearly a year, and your scrawny son gets to you first," Jericho said. "What the hell did you do to piss him off so bad?"

Dad would've answered, but I left the gag in his mouth the other day when he wouldn't shut up.

Joss and Gabe gasped at the wiry figure tied to the bench. Billie didn't look surprised. "That's Rusty?" Gabe whispered.

"You," Jericho said, "Gabe is it?"

Gabe nodded slowly.

"You're the boy Billie's been protecting."

He nodded again.

"What did you say just then?"

"I... I always thought Rusty was a dog."

He smiled. "So Seven, you've been hiding him down here?"

"What's it matter? Just let my friends go and you can have us both," I said.

He held the small gun to Joss' temple, sending tears down her cheek.

"I want to know who else you told," he said.

"Nobody. He killed my mother and left me to die. I was only repaying him the favor."

He grabbed me by the neck and held me in front of the bars. Dad's stench was toxic that close to the vault. "What did he tell you?"

"He's so terrified of you that he won't even talk. In six months, he's barely said two words that didn't include some kind of threat."

He watched my eyes closely, trying to catch me in a lie.

"My dad didn't love me either, kid," Jericho said. "Get over it."

"I am. It's a long healing process."

"I'm not buying it. Kneel right there. Now, who knows he's here?"

"No one."

He fired a shot off at the floor next to my foot.

"Who did you tell?" he roared.

My fingers were exploding. I tried hold still, but they were scorching. I reached over to scratch my hand, but before I could, Gabe started laughing, slamming his right fist on the ground. He winked at me with determined eyes and began to stand up.

"You have to be the worst gangster in the history of crime," he snickered. "You got bested by someone who couldn't outrun a homeless kid? Seriously, you're freakin' pathetic."

"Fine. I guess I'll start with him," he said, stomping over to Gabe.

"No!" A rage ripped through my soul. I leapt up at him, springing off the cement floor and reaching out with my dead hand. I knew the bullet was going to hit me, but maybe I could get my fingers on him first.

The explosion rang out, echoing through the basement. I waited for it to rip through my ribs, my lungs, maybe my heart, but it didn't. When I opened my eyes, I had him by the throat, knocking him to the ground. I expected to feel cold. I braced for it, but all I could feel was his heart, pumping wildly, adrenaline kicking in, then it slowed. I didn't even have to focus on it. My anger was doing that for me. Steadily, methodically, it crawled.

At first, I thought I was pushing some kind of force on him, inflicting my will. I was wrong, though. I wasn't pushing anything. I was pulling, draining him of life, with a simple touch; a touch that dug into his trachea. My fingers grew white with pressure to match his fading skin. My teeth clenched as I realized how hard I was pulling. I was enjoying it. I was killing him.

The once brazen, lumberjack face, turned grey and almost leathery. The smile drooped and something flashed in my head. I wasn't staring at Jericho, I was staring at Darren.

I gasped and jumped back, releasing his neck. I wasn't... I couldn't...

Two soft hands pulled me up, embracing me from behind. Joss' hold was warm and forgiving. "Let him go," she whispered.

Jericho's color slowly came back as he gulped for air. Another shot rang out. This time, Jericho jolted in pain. A red stain soaked his jeans.

I flipped around and looked back to the stairs. Detective Boudreaux stood at the bottom, scanning the room.

"Jericho Splitzer, you have the right to remain silent." He walked over to him quickly and picked up the guns, tucking them into his belt.

"Where the hell did you come from?" Jericho gasped.

"After Seven stole my car and showed me where you were hiding out," he glared at me, "I followed him here. Little did I know that you'd be stupid enough to stick around."

"I came here to finish a job," he grumbled.

"I see. So you did," Boudreaux replied, looking in the vault. "It appears Mr. Murphy-Collins is revealing all sorts of goodies tonight."

"How long have you been standing there?" Joss asked.

"Long enough."

Before he could continue, his radio started blaring. He reached down and held the radio near his ear.

"Repeat that, Teddy."

"I said they're coming. Do you have Jericho?" The voice on the radio answered.

"I do. They're here already? How did they know?"

"You know the answer to that question. The Senator's got ears everywhere," said the voice.

My mind shot back to the picture in the back of my baby book. Senator Grey knew Jericho. What was their connection?

"How many?"

"Ten, I think," the voice replied.

"You've got to be kidding me. This is going too far. We're fully capable of taking care of this," Boudreaux said.

There was no answer. Boudreaux threw the radio against the wall, shattering it to pieces. His face was beet red and the big vein in his neck pulsed violently. He fidgeted as he stared at us, thoughts running through his head.

"What's the story, Detective?" I asked, still catching my breath.

Boudreaux walked over to me and squatted. His cigarette smoke surrounded me. His eyes were red with stress.

"Did you get the girl out of the house?"

I nodded. "She's right over there," I looked at Billie.

"Oh, so it is."

"She was trying to keep me from getting hurt," I said.

"I see. Well, I should lock you up for all this." He paused. "Hell, I should shoot you for this," he said, motioning to Rusty. He exhaled and rubbed his fingers through his hair. "On any other night, I would. Consider this your get-out-of-jail-free card."

"What did you just say?" I asked.

"I said you can go!" Boudreaux yelled.

"Why would you... Why is the Senator coming here?" My curiosity got the best of me.

"Didn't you hear what I just said? You're free to go. Now get out of here before I change my mind," he growled.

"What are you scared of?" I asked, refusing to let it go.

"Seven," Joss said. "What are you doing? Let's get out of here."

"Son, while you've been playing cops and robbers, the world has been changing. I'm not calling the shots anymore. Those purple sashes you were so curious about; they work for the Senator," he said, clenching his jaw tight.

"What does he want with Jericho?"

"How the hell am I supposed to know? If you want to find out for yourself, stick around. Ask the friendly men with purple sashes what the most powerful man in the country wants with a drug dealer. See where it gets you."

I didn't understand, but the sudden panic in his eye told me it was time to go. He looked past my shoulder, shaking his head. I swore I saw a hint of a grin cross his lips.

I took one last look at Rusty. He may not die in a month, but at least he was going to serve a purpose. Hopefully Boudreaux would get what he needed from him. Hopefully, he could put Jericho away for good.

I didn't want to, but I knew what I had to do. I pulled the baby book from the back of my pants and slipped the picture of Mom from the back. After I tucked the picture into my pocket, I tossed it to Boudreaux.

He looked at me curiously. "What is this?"

I sighed, still resenting that I was giving away the last thing I had of my Mom's. "It's what you're going to need to put them both away for good. My mother never trusted Rusty."

I silently made my way up the stairs, hobbling as I reached the fire escape in the back.

Chapter 14
UNISON

I rattled down the wet fire escape into a drizzly night, eager to be out of the bank. My mind was euphoric with a strange sense of relief or even disbelief, somehow lost in the events that had just occurred. Handing my dad over to the police wasn't the justice I'd planned, but I kind of liked the irony. After years of running, he would finally be locked up, in a real cell.

And Jericho? That bastard would have a long time to ponder how a seventeen-year-old kid bested him. I wasn't quite sure I understood that myself.

I probably just made Boudreaux's career. It had to be the biggest bust in the department's history. His name would be on the front page of the paper. I imagined him standing at a podium, brimming with pride while he stood for reporters' questions.

I didn't understand why he let us go, or why this Senator Grey guy was calling the shots, but I'm glad he did. I glanced over my shoulder at Joss, recalling her scowl at the Senator in the coffee shop, then again at the parade. I wondered what she wasn't telling me.

Either way, I had a sinking feeling it wouldn't be the last time we crossed paths with the good Senator.

Before I could finish that thought, I noticed Gabe's arm wrap tight around Billie's jittery shoulders. A light drizzle slicked his hair, somehow highlighting a new confidence that flushed over him. He pulled her in close and whispered softly in her ear. The tiny bumps along her neck struck me. She felt safe, at home. I wondered if I should feel the same. After all, my father was finally headed to jail.

A gentle brush of skin slid into place, interlocking my fingers. Joss' other arm wrapped around my elbow.

I realized then that I'd been chasing a sham. I admired Joss' outlook. I wanted things to be as she treated them, simple. But to do that, I had to be on my own. Things like family and friends created trouble, brought pain.

I had been alone for a long time, but I was kidding myself if I believed that now. My life wasn't simple. It was complicated, and the very people I couldn't live without felt like thick cords, propping me up, but yanking me apart.

I knew what I had to do. My dad was taken care of, but I was still doomed. Jackson wasn't going to give up. So, there was only one way I could keep my friends safe. I didn't want to admit it, but if I cared about any of them-Joss, Piper, Gabe, and even Billie, I had to leave. I had to go at it alone.

"Seven," Gabe said with a strain.

I looked up to see him throttle back, throwing Billie against the back of the building. My instincts moved quicker than my eyes. I didn't know why, but I did the same with Joss, stepping in front and lowering my stance to shield her from whatever Gabe saw.

I finally caught a glimpse of what ignited the scare. On the corner, leaning against the light post, oblivious to the mist, was a dark figure. The water glistened on his eyebrows, dark as they were. He straightened up, sticking his hands in his pockets and striding toward us.

"Is that Jackson?" Gabe asked.

I didn't waste time on an answer. "Run!"

The stubborn bastard didn't even flinch.

"What are you doing?" I yelled. "Get out of here! This isn't--"

"This isn't just about you anymore. We're not leaving," Gabe said.

"Why don't we all run?" asked Joss.

"It's too late. We'd never make it," I whispered. "But it's me that he wants. You can guys can make a break for it."

"Not a chance," Billie said, between jittery teeth. "We didn't go through all this just to ditch you now."

I was overwhelmed by their loyalty, but they needed to go. I couldn't let them get hurt for me, even Billie and all her stupidity.

Loud clicks echoed off the blacktop as Jackson strolled closer. With each step, he grew larger, more surreal. I could finally make out the rest of his face, snarled into a cocky grin. His short blond hair looked dark in the streetlight. Stubble ran over his chin.

"Kansas City Bar-B-Que isn't all it's cracked up to be," he said, resting his hand on an Audi.

My arm was stiff, ensuring Joss couldn't move forward, even if she wanted to. Fear coursed through me, but I held my ground. "Let them go. This is between us."

He laughed. "Tell that to your friend Darren. If he could talk, I'm guessing he'd disagree."

Joss pinched my tricep, forcing me to meet her eyes. They bore through me, warning me not to take his bait.

"He didn't have anything to do with this. He was innocent!"

"Don't lecture me on innocence! He'd still be alive if you wouldn't have been so selfish! There's a natural order to this whole thing. When you die, you're not supposed to come back. If you would've played by the rules, none of this would be happening."

"I wasn't ready to die," I said.

"No one ever is. But don't get me wrong, I'm not mad. I actually feel like I should thank you." He leaned into the hood of the car. The metal whined under the pressure.

"What are you talking about?" I stepped forward, pulling away from multiple hands trying to hold me back.

"How's your hand?" Jackson asked.

A current of electricity shot up my arm, followed by a dull burn. I thought through some lies, not wanting to reveal a weakness.

"Let me guess, you've killed someone, haven't you?" he asked.

"What? No."

Like a million lights going off at once, images came flooding back: the surge of energy when I hit the goon at Mardi Gras, then again in Rusty's apartment, Jericho's grey face as I drained the life from him, the constant chill running through my fingers. Every time I got angry, my hand throbbed in pain, itching beyond control.

He raised an eyebrow. "No? Don't worry, you will. Before long, you won't be able to control yourself. The chill will set in, and there's only one way to stop it: murder."

"What are you talking about?" I asked.

"How have you not put this together yet? You know what happens when Death touches someone?"

"They die," Joss said.

"Two points for you, honey," he replied. "Now, what about the other way? What happens when some fool willingly touches Death?"

I traded glances with Gabe. Joss shrugged.

"It took me until just recently to figure that out, but when you punched me--cheap shot by the way--some kind of exchange happened. When I woke up in the coffee shop, I felt different. Sure, I was mad at first, but then I started noticing things. The sun felt good on my skin. I hadn't felt the sun in years. I started feeling hungry too, and food tasted good. I wasn't in such a hurry to return to the afterlife anymore."

"You--" I started.

"I'm slowly coming to life," he said.

"Good for you. Then you don't need to worry about me anymore. Glad I could help."

"Not so fast, buddy," he smirked. "I said it was an exchange. If you transferred some life to me..."

"Seven's dying?" Gabe asked, almost under his breath.

"Kind of," Jackson said.

What was he smiling about? If I wasn't dying then what was happening to me? As his words circled in my head, I came to a thought that I wanted to dismiss. When I touched someone with my hand, it hurt them. It did more than that. It sucked the life from them. They turned cold and grey. I knew what he was hinting at, but I didn't want to believe it. What he wasn't saying, wasn't possible.

"You're saying I'm becoming a reaper?" I asked, terrified to hear the answer.

He smiled.

"If that's true, why have you been chasing after me? Why aren't you on a beach somewhere?"

"He's trying to make sure it's permanent," Joss murmured. "Aren't you?" she asked, looking up at Jackson.

"It's a good thing you've got smart friends," he replied.

"You have to find Christine Dru and her daughter," Gabe said. "Don't you? Everything started when Seven saved them from the car. You have to put things back in order, don't you?"

I was putting the pieces together in my head. "If you kill them, and there's no reaper to take them to the afterlife, then you're stuck here?"

"There you go! Good for you guys, putting together the pieces. You left out one thing though. What do you think is going to happen to our hero?"

A collective silence fell on the group.

"I'll help you out with that one. After the girls are gone, I'm going to make sure the boys upstairs don't have a reason to come after me," he said, pointing to the sky. "I'm going to give them their reaper."

"Me," I said gravely.

"I'm glad you brought your dad to justice, and took care of that Jericho guy, but the real fun's just begun," Jackson said, turning his back on me.

He took five long strides before my mind caught up. "Why are you telling me all this?" I shouted. "Why would you tell me your plan?"

He barely resembled my friend anymore, but I caught a small glimpse of him in that sinister grin. "Maybe I like a challenge. Actually, I'll take it even further. I'll tell you where she is. Christine's in Kansas City."

I pondered why he'd tell me that and whether I believed him.

"She took off after you saved her from that car." He waited for me to say something but I was too busy trying to make sense of everything.

"It's more fun this way," he said. "Like old times, don't you think? Betcha I find them first."

He walked a couple more steps, then stopped. "While we're on that subject, did you ever find out who tried to run her over?"

"No," I said, thinking how dumb it was that I'd never truly asked that question.

"Maybe it's just me, but that seems like it would be useful information."

And with that, he turned the corner, leaving us alone in the parking lot.

I stood in a haze, staring at my fingers.

"Stop it," Gabe said. His voice was wrapped in a calm command.

I looked at him, befuddled. "What?"

"Stop being like me. That fool thinks he can find them first? You're not alone. We just took on one of the baddest dudes in the country, and escaped from the cops in the process. We're going to find Christine, and we're going to send that son of a bitch back to hell!"

I could barely recognize my friend. He was like a whole new person. Billie jumped on his back, hugging him tight. "That's what I'm talking about!" she yelled.

They made for Gabe's car, swinging open the rusty door and starting up the sputtering engine. It was hard not to laugh at their enthusiasm. They had no idea what they were getting into. Hell, neither did I. How could I let them get involved?

"He's right," Joss said, grabbing my left hand. "We're in this together."

I knew they were right. I couldn't do it alone, and I couldn't stop them from helping. I needed them. Complicated, simple, it didn't matter. This was my life, and I was suddenly the one in need of saving.

Across the street, I caught another figure out of the corner of my eye. She was tucked in along the backside of the red brick store, concealed in the shadows. I couldn't miss her eyes though. I never could.

I squeezed Joss' hand and gave her a pleading look. I just needed a minute. She shook her head without any words being exchanged.

It was a long walk for only thirty feet. Piper was scowling, but not at me, not at anyone in particular. "How much did you hear?" I asked.

"As much as I needed to," she said. "Off to find Christine and Bree, huh?"

"It really is my only shot."

"I know that." She wouldn't look at me.

"What if you came with us," I asked, blurting the words out before I thought it through. Part of me couldn't let her go.

She let out a faint laugh. "Yeah, I don't see that happening," she said, looking in Joss' direction.

"I'm sorry."

I wanted to say more. I wanted to tell her that she meant a lot to me, probably more than I could admit. I wanted to tell her thanks for always being there for me, and she was. In a very strange, often reckless way, I could count on her.

But she wouldn't want to hear any of that. It wouldn't make it any easier.

"I really wish you would come. Aside from being my friend," I fought off a cringe, "I'm pretty sure you're the only one who knows how to catch Christine Dru."

"It takes a thief to know a thief?" she asked.

"Something like that."

"I'll be there when you need me, but not right now."

It was the most serious thing I'd ever heard her say.

Piper hissed and leaned in close, still smelling of lilac. "But, if I could introduce you today, I would say, this is Judas."

She lightly kissed my cheek and turned to the alley.

"When she flakes out, again..." she trailed off as she disappeared around the dumpster.

I smiled, hoping that she was finally wrong about something.

With that, the little red figure on my right shoulder had pointed me to the car. The little white figure on my left was doing the same. Both were, for this unique and solitary moment, in unison.

"Are you coming?" Gabe shouted out the window.

I climbed in the backseat, glancing around at the odd ensemble. I realized then how wrong I'd been. All this time, I thought I'd been searching for revenge. That wasn't it at all. As I looked at each of them, and another out the window, one thing became stupidly clear. I'd been searching for family, the one thing I'd never had, and the very thing that surrounded me all along. We weren't traditional, or simple. We were a mess of lies and love, sacrifice and treachery. But at the end of the day, I wasn't alone, and they were going to help me on this crazy crusade, even if it killed us all.

My first life's last thought was a question: Is this car really going to kill me?

As for my second life, hell, I guess I'd have to find out.

The End.

ACKNOWLEDGMENTS

My wife – Theresa. You are my hero. Throughout all of my crazy self-doubt, your love and encouragement knows no bounds.

The brain trust – Luke, Mikayla, Sakata. Thanks for your never-ending patience and honesty.

My family. Thank you for always supporting me. I couldn't do it without you.

My editor – Cassandra. Thank you for challenging me and making this book as good as it can be.

The artist – Kristi. You have an amazing talent. Thank you for creating such a kickass cover!

The Picasso's gang – Chris, Jon, Dan, Jen and Michelle. Thanks for brewing the best coffee in St. Louis!

Florence and the Machine – Thanks for powering me through this book. You rock!

CREDITS

Jacket cover art and design © 2011 by Kristi Collora

ABOUT THE AUTHOR

Flint Ory graduated with an MBA from Washington University in St. Louis, Missouri. He wrote Saving Seven in a little coffeehouse called Picasso's along the Missouri river where he consistently drank them out of pumpkin lattes. Across the street sat an old bank that has since turned into a restaurant.

You can visit him online at www.flintory.com.

Made in the USA
Monee, IL
20 February 2025

12671965R00125